I0679344

VIRAL

Starship Hope Book Three

T.S. VALMOND

The Starship Hope: Viral

T.S. Valmond

PRINT ISBN: 9 7 8 1 7 7 7 5 4 4 7 1 3

EBOOK ISBN: 9 7 8 1 7 7 7 5 4 4 7 0 6

Cover Design by: Goerz Designs

For Mom
a lifelong seeker of truth

THE MANIFEST

The Crew

Captain Dana Pinet

Commander Wade Chance - ex-boyfriend to Dana and fiancé to Maggie

Lieutenant Commander Adrian Valente - Security Officer

Lieutenant Nancy Westlake - Pilot

Commander Eric Rogan - Chief Engineer

Commander Esme Rogan - Chief Engineer (pregnant)

Ensign Cliff Harden - Communications officer and language specialist

ARI Three - (Artificial Robotic Intelligence) the android also known as Ari

Dr. Randall Jabar - Medical doctor and surgeon (twin)

Rido Jabar - Healer and therapist (twin)

The Passengers

Eartha MacLaren Singh - (stowaway adopted by the Rogans with mysterious origins)

Maggie Brooker - Reporter and fiancé to Commander Chance

Luke Geyer - former CAH member and genius friend to Eartha

Franklin Jennison - Oldest passenger and amateur historian

Peter Barnes - former SO and escaped prisoner

The Fashin Teku Aliens

Aswin Zeppel - Captain of the The Des Freighter (blond-haired)

Tovar Vaziri- Second in command (red-haired)

Oli Serei - Security Officer (black-haired)

CHAPTER 1

Captain's Personal Log: 4327.10.5

Those stinking, lying Begarans. They have our embryos, and I want them back.

They pointed us toward the Fashin Teku ship that stole from us, but only some of our cargo, and three of the Teku survived after the truth serum the Begarans gave them. Dr. Jabar cleared them for duty, helping refit the ship as we race back to the Begaran home-world. The crew's been working tirelessly. They were on twenty-four-hour shift rotations to make repairs after the explosion of the Des freighter knocked out propulsion, thermal regulators, life-support, and damaged the hull on decks eleven and twelve.

It's been two days, and the crew is dragging. Most days, everyone's work requires scrutiny, including mine. I know that, but we're moving again, at last. Without the Teku, it would have taken us over a week to get to the Begarans. At least with their help, we can cut that time in half. I don't trust them *anymore than I could pick one up and throw them, but at this point, my people don't have a choice.*

This morning I woke up in a pool of sweat. Not because of them, but because of Peter Barnes. I'd been running away from him again in my dream. Sometimes he's coming after me, other times it's like it was on Zelenia, where everyone gathered together behind him to accuse me. Between the nightmares and the repairs, the sleepless nights are showing under my eyes and in the headaches, though there's not much I can do about it. The ship has continued off-kilter since his escape, and worst of all, he knows my secret. It's not what he knows, but what he'll try to do with it that keeps me awake.

Rido's healing treatments have been helping, but to be honest, I find myself struggling with how I feel about him. He's a great guy, with a wonderful bedside manner, but beyond the basic attraction, I'm not sure I can go deep with someone like him. We don't have the same beliefs or ideals, and though I'm fascinated by him, there's something missing. It's not easy, like it was with Wade. I know I shouldn't compare, but I can't help it. Wade makes me think and laugh without even trying. Of course, he's going to marry Maggie any minute, and I need to come to terms with it. I had my chance with him, and I blew it. I'll put on a smile for the event, even if it kills me.

Today I'm going to take a nanodot.

DANA REACHED INTO HER SIDE TABLE AND PULLED OUT THE tin of nanodots. There were only five left, a reminder that Barnes had already taken three. Her hand trembled, the small tin rattling. She put it down on the table and stared inside. Each white anti-anxiety dot was nothing more than a means of control. For the Zelenian Space Fleet, it was against regulation for any captain to be using them, let alone depending on them, as she'd been. A captain dependent on anything artificially manufactured was in trouble.

She'd saved them after her psych treatments. After Kristoff's explosive betrayal, a former friend and member of the Coalition Against the Hierarchy, she'd been a wreck. It had taken her months to come to terms with losing those who'd gathered to throw her surprise party at the Breezy Blue. After, Dana had kept the remaining nanodots hidden in a treasure box her father had made her as a little girl, regulating them for emergencies only. Before the incident, she'd worn an unreadable mask when she was anxious. Now, there were times she couldn't disguise the anxiety. Dana reasoned it was just taking her longer than expected to get back to her old self.

No one needed to know about the dots. She wasn't out of control or anything. She just wasn't ready to lose the comfort knowing they were there gave her.

But now Barnes knew about them.

The question wasn't *if* Barnes would say anything, it was *when*. The longer he went free, the greater the anxiety grew within her, disrupting her dreams. He'd taken three of the nanodots as if to taunt her. He knew she couldn't go to the doctor and request more. Did he think he could use them to barter for his life? Would he threaten to expose her lie in order to get what he wanted?

Dana scoffed at the idea. She could quit whenever she wanted, she just needed a little more time. She wasn't going to let Barnes back her into a corner. Should the truth about her anxiety get out she'd deal with it, but for now, she'd have to wait for him to make his move.

She popped the white nanodot to the back of her throat and took a sip of water, swallowing both down.

CHAPTER 2

Even with the anti-anxiety drug coursing through her, Dana sat on the bridge, tapping her fingers on the arm of her chair. After four hours, they still weren't going fast enough. She waited for the latest report on their engines with the patience of a two-year-old. Who knew what the Begarans could do with their stolen embryos by the time they finally reached full speed again?

The chair on her left where Wade should be sat empty. Her First Officer was out overseeing their progress in the engine room where the Fashin Teku were hard at work getting their tech integrated with the ship's propulsion systems.

In Dana's opinion, it was the least they could do after stealing something so precious from them. The technology behind their upgrades was complex, but as far as she understood it, their advanced drive system, when coupled with their targeting coordinates, could propel them by bending space.

Ensign Cliff Harden cleared his throat from his standing station on her left. "Is everything all right, Captain?" he asked, glancing from her tapping fingers back to her face.

She waved him off. "I'm fine. I just want to know where we are on the upgrades. Any other reports coming in?"

He rolled his eyes. "No, but I'll check again."

Dana's eyes flew to his face. "Was that a *tone*, Ensign?"

"No, ma–Captain. No tone intended."

When Wade returned from engineering, Dana leaped out of her seat. He looked like he was fuming. She leaned in, whispering, "Are you all right?"

"I'm fine," he said, his voice several decibels louder than hers had been, causing the bridge crew to turn in their direction.

Dana raised an eyebrow at him, and he shook his head. It was all right if he didn't want to talk about it, but he didn't need to shout. She tried not to let it bother her, though it grated on her nerves that he'd behave this way in front of the others.

Their interactions had been off since she'd refused to officiate his wedding ceremony. Dana wanted to put it behind them as soon as possible. Rido, the Healer, had agreed to perform the ceremony in her place—*thank the Merciful.*

Neither the bride nor groom had said much to her since. Dana couldn't even be sure she'd be welcome at the wedding anymore. She didn't particularly want to attend the wedding of her ex, but she'd been willing to put that aside. Marrying them, however, was an entirely different matter. To Dana, it seemed more than a little inappropriate.

"Commander, report," Dana ordered, adjusting her tone and volume to match his terse one.

Wade blinked, as if he didn't understand her. Dana frowned.

"Commander? Are you sure you're all right?"

Wade shook his head, muttering to himself. Then he lifted his hands and let them drop, slapping hard against his sides. "I did my best, Captain. They're about as worthless as fleas on a dog."

It was Dana's turn to blink. He hadn't been down there that long. Perhaps there were some compatibility issues they hadn't considered. She needed every advantage she could get against the Begarans.

"Aren't the Fashin Teku helping you?" she asked. "If they're not pulling their weight, they can get off a lot sooner than the space station." Dana wasn't about to tolerate anything from them. They'd done enough damage.

"That would be way too good for them," Wade muttered, sitting down beside her and then standing up again in agitation.

"That's all you had to say. Have security escort them to the brig. I'll deal with them myself later."

"Ensign, have security escort our Fashin Teku guests to the brig," Wade said.

"Yes, sir," Cliff said as he relayed the message. A

moment later, he looked back up, confusion on his face. "Um, I'm sorry, sir... they won't do it."

Dana stood from her seat to face him. "What do you mean they won't do it?"

Cliff cleared his throat. "Well, um, they sent an audio message. Would you like me to play it for you?"

"Out with it, Ensign," Wade snapped.

Cliff looked nervous. "Are you sure you want me to play it aloud?"

Dana placed her hands on her hips. "Ensign, either play the message, or relay it, if that's not asking too much."

Cliff shrugged and pressed the buttons on the panel that would allow the entire bridge to hear the message:

"Tell the Commander we're busy at the moment, and if he'd like to get off of his backside, he can take care of the lousy pirates himself."

Dana's mouth fell open a beat before she could recover. "Who was that, Ensign?"

"I'm not sure, Captain. There's no identification code. It's from a panel on level four."

"Send security to—"

Wade cut her off by reaching over the panel, grabbing Cliff by the front of his shirt, and lifting him off the floor.

"Commander!" Dana reached out and pulled on the back of Wade's uniform. "Let him go! What's wrong with you? The message didn't come from *him,* it came from our security."

Wade was breathless. He couldn't seem to focus on her voice.

Dana clutched him by the back of the shirt, and with the help of Valente, pulled him off of Cliff. "I think you need to take a breather."

Wade blinked as if she'd slapped him. His eyes were a pinkish color. "What?"

"Valente," she continued, "escort the Commander to his quarters."

Dana nodded. "Wade, don't come back until you've cooled off."

Wade continued to stare at her seething, but she turned her attention to Valente. "When you return, I want a report on where we are with Barnes."

Valente gave her a look that showed how much he didn't like the idea of being sent off alone with Wade, but Dana shrugged. If anyone could deal with Wade, it was Valente.

Wade pulled his shoulders back and stormed off the bridge with Valente rushing behind him to keep up.

"What's gotten into everyone?" Dana asked, speaking to no one in particular. Wade had completely lost control. She'd never seen him so angry. "Are you all right, Cliff?"

He'd been rubbing at his chest but stopped when she turned her attention toward him. "I'm fine, Captain."

"See if you can track down one of the other members of the security team. Get them to round up the Fashin Teku and anyone else who might need time in the brig. It seems there may be a problem onboard."

"Yes, Captain."

Dana turned to her pilot. "What's our estimated time of arrival?"

"We're still over thirty-six hours out, Captain," Nancy said.

She nodded. "Inform me if there's any change or developments. I'll be in my office."

CHAPTER 3

Dana sat at her desk, staring at the file on Barnes. Valente had returned looking flustered and his report had contained little she didn't already know. He was still hiding on the ship someplace and someone might be helping him.

The three Fashin Teku arrived moments later. Ashwin and Tovar were out of breath, their eyes wild. Oli stood at attention with his hands behind his back and his legs spread as if preparing to fight.

"Captain," Ashwin stepped closer, examining her face and eyes until she was uncomfortable, "we need to speak with you, it is most urgent."

She pulled back in her chair. "Are you going to tell me what you're here for, or is this unexplained examination going to continue?"

"Many sorries, Captain. I was looking for the red eyes," he said, still huffing as if he were trying to catch his breath.

"Did you run here?" Dana asked.

He nodded. "This problem is most serious. The truth will disease your crew. You saw my ship in space before it was exploded. You must be in isolation, or risk losing everyone the same as we."

The three Fashin Teku were wringing their hands, looking from one to the other, their shaggy eyebrows drawn together.

Dana stood up, pinching the bridge of her nose. "What are the signs of infection again?"

"The red eyes, fast love, and fast tempers."

Dana stared at them, trying to make sense of their words. Despite the TMIs, there was still a gap between their languages, making it hard for them to speak in complete sentences. She nodded and moved to head out back onto the bridge.

"The engineers are already fighting," Ashwin added, following after her. "On the way here, we encountered several more in the corridors in either passionate embraces or fighting with fists."

Ashwin was still speaking when he bumped into Dana's back. She had come to a dead stop.

Lieutenant Nancy Westlake, her pilot, and Ensign Cliff Harden were engaged in some kind of amorous embrace. Two other relief crew members were fighting behind them. Dana thought she recognized them from the ship's security detail.

"I've always loved you," Cliff said, grabbing a fistful of Nancy's blonde hair.

"What's going on out here?" Dana demanded, pulling the two apart.

"Sorry, Captain, we have some things we need to say to each other in private," Nancy said, pulling Cliff by the front of the shirt and exiting the bridge.

"It's too late. It's already here," she heard Tovar say to Ashwin.

Dana walked over to the comms console and sent a message to the medical bay. Dr. Randall Jabar's face appeared on the main viewer. He looked haggard, with more than a day's worth of beard growth on his jaw. His brown eyes were red-rimmed, as if he'd been crying.

"Doctor, what's going on here? I thought you cleared my people of the infection?"

"Look, I'm not a miracle worker," he snapped. "I'm using the garbage systems we've got, and this is what you get when you're on a mediocre ship with mediocre supplies and less than subpar leadership. Perhaps it would have been a better idea to keep those pirates off the ship instead of selling us all out for a few shiny new parts."

"Careful, Doctor," Dana said, her tone a veiled warning.

He ran a hand over his short black hair and stared into the monitor. Pink tinted his eyes like she'd never seen before. "Sorry, Captain. I... I didn't mean that."

"Find a way to get this thing under control," Dana told him. "Slow it down, anything."

He nodded. "We'll do what we can, but don't expect much. Our sensors didn't detect it, and I'm not sure we could have contained it even if we had." His screen went dark.

"Thanks," Dana said to the blank screen.

Ashwin grabbed her by the arm. "Captain, your ship is like our ship. Not much time now."

"I need you to get to the med bay," she told him. "There's a reason you haven't been infected, and we'll need all the information we can get on why. How long did it take for your crew to show symptoms?"

"A day, but when we saw the problems..." Ashwin glanced over his shoulder, as if looking for someone. "It was too late."

Dana did the calculations. They were still at least a day away from the Begarans. At this rate, they'd all be infected by the time they reached Begaran space.

At least she wasn't showing any symptoms yet. That was something.

Tovar held up a hand for them to wait. "Captain, it is not safe to be going all around. Things will get aggressive."

"What exactly did those aliens give you?" Dana asked.

Ashwin and Tovar looked at each other.

"It's a type of truth dust," Ashwin explained. "They sprinkled it over the cargo we took. It will force you to speak the truth even if you don't want to."

"The same cargo you brought over to us?"

He shrugged. "We only today thought of the cargo." Ashwin raised his hands in the air. "We made no plans to give you the sickness. Please believe me."

Oli grunted and sniffed the air.

"Great." Dana scrubbed her palms over her face. "You're saying that everyone on this ship is going to be speaking only the truth to one another?"

"Yes. Extremely..." Ashwin paused over the word before deciding on, "uncomfortable."

"And aggressive," Tovar insisted.

"I see how that could happen," Dana muttered. She tried to think. If everyone was telling each other the truth, it might not be so bad. But then she thought of Wade, of how he'd gone from zero to a hundred. Then Cliff and Nancy, both of them almost undressed to the waist when she'd returned.

No, *uncomfortable* didn't cover it. They were in trouble.

Almost as she thought the words, the ship bucked to one side.

"What was that?"

Then, realizing she was the only one left on the bridge, she moved to the diagnostic panel to see what they'd hit. Without Nancy at the helm, she was going to have to get them to the Begarans on her own. She sat down and took over.

"You three had better find a place to hide. If people realize what you've done, they're going to come for you, and I'm going to be too busy keeping us from crashing into something else."

"The Nexus may save you," Ashwin said, his eyes pleading with her.

Dana shook her head. "No. We're going to the source. If

they can make it, they can cure it. The Begarans have everything we need. They're our only chance."

"They won't help us, Captain. The xenophobic people have a grudge."

"We have to try."

He sighed. "If you insist."

"I do." Then she remembered his previous offer. "What about those Begaran shield codes?"

Ashwin gave Tovar a look, and she nodded.

"Ah, yes, the codes." Ashwin shook his head. "No, Captain."

"No?"

He shrugged. "Suppose we give codes. Keeping us alive will not happen."

Dana growled, biting down on a swell of anger. He was right. Two seconds more, and she might throw him out the airlock herself.

"Captain, stay here, and keep others out," Tovar said. "Go, no matter what."

"At arrival, we will give codes. Many thank yous," Ashwin added in retreat.

"We will help you though," Tovar said, looking to Ashwin and Oli, who both seemed eager to move on to the next subject. "We can help engines work faster."

Dana glanced over her shoulder at them. It was risky sending them off on their own. However, they'd already proven themselves to be more than adequate in preserving their own lives. Perhaps that would work in her favor this time.

"Fine. Go down to the engine room first and see what you can do. I'll grant you access to work down there, but then you need to get to the med-bay. If you run into trouble, I'm afraid you're on your own."

The three Fashin Teku scuttled off the bridge, leaving Dana alone. She stood, taking in the empty room in a slow circle. The dread of their situation settling in her stomach like a stone. Dana needed to prepare for the worst. She'd be on the bridge for some time, and she didn't want everyone to have free rein on the ship.

"Computer, initiate a ship-wide dampening field."

"A dampening field will render all weapons inert," said the masculine COMP's neutral tone. *"Do you still want to proceed?"*

"Yes. That's exactly what I want."

Dana sat in Nancy's chair again and adjusted their course. Somehow, the dampening field didn't seem like it would be enough.

CHAPTER 4

A mother's love a cherished child is born to;
When it's lost, her words of wisdom bind you.
- Zelenian poet: Jean-Yves Louis

WADE

Wade stomped off to his quarters. Boiling angry and sweating, he thought of having a shower and settling down to watch a film with Maggie. She'd be able to get him out of the funk he was feeling. She had a way of talking to him that always calmed him down. He couldn't wait to call Maggie his wife. She was everything he'd always wanted; a smoking-hot reporter with brains and a heaping of good taste.

She wouldn't be expecting him, and a smile spread across his face as he thought of surprising her. They would have their wedding soon, and even though Dana had refused to perform the ceremony, it was still going to happen. She'd had the nerve to send him with an escort. Valente was no match for him, and their exchange of blows had been quick before the other man skulked off. Wade didn't need any help getting to his quarters, and he was going to enjoy his day off. That would teach Dana to relieve him of duty.

When he rushed inside and found Maggie crying on the couch, all of his plans hit the toilet. She leaped up from her seat like it was on fire. With tears in her eyes, she stumbled to put a hand over the image still playing in front of her. Wade knew what she was trying to hide—her message from home, the last video she'd received from a family member or friend. Though the man's image looked familiar, Wade knew he wasn't family.

"I was just—" Maggie said, but he cut her off before she finished her thought.

"No," Wade said, holding up a hand. "No more lies. Who is that?"

Wade pulled at the neck of his uniform, the heat creeping up from his chest choking him. He needed to burn off the energy building inside him. It was like he could run for miles. It didn't make sense, but he wanted to rip everything he saw apart.

He fought to keep it in check. This was Maggie. He loved her.

Didn't he?

Maggie crossed the room, tears still staining her cheeks, and touched his lip.

"Your lip. It's bleeding."

Wade pulled away from her. "Don't. You're trying to change the subject."

"It's no one," she said, waving a hand at the viewer. "Were you in a fight?"

Wade didn't let up. "Who is he?"

Maggie's mouth fell open. She looked like a gaping fish with overly-bright ruby lipstick on her lips. How come he'd never noticed that before?

The rage built inside of him. Wade knew he shouldn't fight with her now, not feeling like this, but he couldn't walk away. Not when another man's face had been on her vid message.

"What are you talking about?" Maggie said. "What's gotten into you?"

"Why does everyone keep asking me that?" Wade snapped. "Maybe it's *you*. I'm tired of tiptoeing around your vid and wondering what's the matter and watching you shut down. Just admit he's someone you used to date."

Maggie's eyes fell to the floor and she turned away from him. He grabbed her by the arm and turned her back toward him. He couldn't control the sudden need to kiss her, and his mouth slammed down hard against hers. When they parted, they were both short of breath.

"What's on that message?"

At first, she looked confused, then she sputtered out

half an answer before she stopped trying and fell silent. Her eyes dropped to her feet again.

Wade dropped her arm. "That's what I thought."

It was his turn to storm away. He turned on the shower and dropped his clothes, letting the door of the bath shut behind him. Cold water struck him in the face, and the heat from his skin created a light steam that billowed out away from him. For the first time in hours, he was cool again. His mind seemed to clear as the fever he'd been feeling earlier subsided. But as soon as he turned off the water, the energy built up within him again, the moisture evaporating off of his skin before he could dry himself off.

Even with the rising heat within him, Wade slipped into his running suit and shoes. Perhaps he could run off the energy building inside him on the track. He didn't trust himself to spar with Dana, but maybe someone else would be there.

Maggie was sitting on the chair by the viewer when he started for the door. She had a bewildered expression on her face, tears falling down her pale cheeks, but he was in no mood to coddle her.

Then he caught sight of the image of a man close to tears on the vid in front of her. She was watching the message *again*? Hadn't she seen it enough times?

The vid was still playing, the words he heard making Wade stop in his tracks:

"I love you Maggie, and I'm happy you're safe."

His stomach dropped, and he wanted to reach through the 3D image and grab the man by the neck. The image froze on the man's love-sick face before it disappeared at the end of the message.

It all made sense. Why she hadn't wanted to move in together before. She'd claimed she'd been keeping her apartment for work. The man on the vid was someone from work—her cameraman, Bill. She'd called him her 'work husband', but now the nickname took on a whole other meaning.

"You were seeing him. While you were dating me." It wasn't a question. It was an accusation.

Maggie crumpled in her seat. "I wanted to tell you. So many times, I wanted to confess the whole thing, but I was afraid of what you'd think of me. If I'd known how things would turn out . . ." She shook her head. "I should have said something sooner."

Wade took in several quick breaths as he tried to block out the image of the two of them sneaking off together every time they were apart.

"Bill and I . . . we were . . ." her voice trailed off as she moved her hands in a circular motion in front of her.

Wade moved to stand toe to toe with her, close enough that she couldn't escape his gaze. "Say it. Tell me the truth, and be sure to look me in the eye when you do."

Maggie stood up, squaring her shoulders, but couldn't quite bring her eyes up to meet his. "I was with Bill when you came along. I tried to end it, but he wouldn't take no for an answer." She shook her head. "When the *Hope* mission came up, I leaped at the opportunity. I knew it would be good for my career, and . . . and it was the easiest way to break things off with him."

"How long?" Wade's question was a growl.

"What?" Maggie sniffled.

"How long were you with him *and* me?" Wade asked between clenched teeth.

"From the day I met you until the day the *Hope* launched," Maggie admitted, then collapsed back onto the couch in tears.

Wade paced in front of her like a caged animal. "I can't believe this!" He picked up a decorative vase she'd collected from the Southern Continent. It was a hodge-podge of colors and swirls. He'd hated it from the first instant he'd seen it. She'd placed it at the door on the entryway table where he used to put his belt and weapon. She loved the thing, and right now he wanted to hurt her.

He threw it to the ground, and enjoyed watching it break into several large pieces and hundreds of smaller pieces that dusted the floor.

Maggie covered her scream with both hands, then bolted toward him, grasping at his arms. "Please, forgive me!"

"Forgive you?" He whipped his arm away from her. "Are you crazy? I can't even look at you. To think I put my own feelings aside for someone else to be with you."

Her bottom lip quivered, but the anger was visible in her sculpted eyebrows as they arched down. "What feelings?"

"You don't have the right to ask me about my feelings

anymore," he retorted. "We're no longer together or engaged. Pack up your garbage and get out. I don't want you here when I come back."

With that, Wade stormed out of the cabin. He tried to take in a deep breath as he stepped out into the corridor, but it didn't seem to reach his lungs. Wade ran, dodging couples either embracing or fighting. He wanted to scream, he wanted to fight, he wanted to be with the person who understood and knew him best.

He ran until he reached Dana's door.

Wade pounded on her cabin door for a full minute before he realized his mistake. Knowing her, she would still be on the bridge. That's where he'd look for her. He had to tell her what he was feeling right now. He wouldn't wait this time. He wouldn't let her push him away––not again.

THE BRIDGE WAS IN FULL LOCKDOWN WHEN HE ARRIVED. THE computer announced him by name, but the door remained closed. Dana called out to him from the other side, but he couldn't make out what she was saying through the haze.

"Dana, I need to speak with you! Computer, security override on the verbal order of Commander Wade Chance."

The computer replied in a clear, succinct tone.

"Security override of Commander Wade Chance, not authorized. That security clearance has been revoked."

"On whose orders?" Wade demanded.

"On the order of Captain Dana Pinet."

"What's going on? Why won't you let me in?" he asked, resting his head on the door.

Dana's hesitation was clear as she spoke from the other side of the door. "I'm pretty sure you're infected. What do you want?"

There was something wrong with the cadence of her speech, but he couldn't grasp what it was. Wade slapped both hands hard against the door.

"Dana, I'm fine. I need to ask you something."

When she didn't answer, he continued.

"Did you ever wonder what would have happened to us if you'd never pushed me away?"

"What?"

She was right against the door. He heard her breathless question as clear as if she were right beside him.

He pressed his ear to the door as he spoke. "I mean if you had let me in and hadn't insisted we take a break. Would we have gotten back together? Because I think we would have. When I think about it now, I'm sure we would have."

Dana didn't speak for a full minute.

"Did you hear me?" Wade asked.

"Are you saying...?"

"Yes," he insisted. "I'm saying we never should have broken up. My mother was right all along."

"What do you mean?" Dana called out from the other side of the door.

"My mother, in the vid she sent from home." Wade pressed his face against the cool metal of the door. "It's the reason I didn't want Maggie to see it. She said *you* were the one for me. You always were. I was a fool to let you go, and since the Majestic is giving me the chance to be with you again, I ought to take it."

Wade waited a minute before he heard Dana give the verbal commands to the computer on the other side of the door. Then the door slid open, and he took his first full breath in minutes.

He reached out and put his hands on Dana's shoulders. She seemed so small, so fragile. He wanted to scoop her up in his arms.

Dana was shaking her head. She looked tired, like she'd been crying. Was it too much to believe she'd been thinking of him? If she told him so, he'd believe it.

"Your eyes . . . they're pink," Dana said. "You're sick. You don't know what you're saying."

"I meant every word."

"What about Maggie? You're engaged." Her words as soft as a whisper as she pushed against his chest. The effect was soft and light, as if she gave up pushing the moment her hand touched him.

"We're not engaged. There's no more Maggie."

Dana smiled, but then her brow furrowed in concentration. He could see her testing the idea in her mind, reasoning it out. When she shook her head again, he leaned down, lifted her chin, and waited for her to take a breath. When she sucked in a deep breath, he placed his lips on hers and tasted.

Why did he think it wouldn't be the same? Kissing her was just like he remembered. Her scent this close was making him crazy. He wanted his hands on her, everywhere at once.

Dana gasped and let out a whispered, "Oh." When he captured her mouth again, it was like coming home. He gathered her up, lifting her small frame until her legs came up around his waist. He set her back down on the console behind her, but the beeping was making him crazy.

Then Dana slid out of his embrace and onto the opposite side of the table. "No, we can't."

Her eyes were wild as she looked around the room, like she was searching for a place to hide. At some point, she'd collapsed to the floor and crawled away from him. He didn't mind a little cat and mouse.

He got down on the floor behind her and reached for her foot. Once he'd grabbed hold of her, sliding her back toward him, he breathed her in again.

"We belong together," he whispered against her cheek.

"You're infected," she breathed. "I'm infected. I can feel it. Anger and desire rising in my chest at the same time . . . We're sick. The virus that the aliens brought on board is making us crazy. This isn't real."

Dana put a fist to her chest, and it was like she'd hit him in the chest, too. She continued to scan the room, pulling away from him and dashing from the bridge into her office. She held up a hand when he followed her inside.

"If you really care for me, you'll keep away."

He ignored her outstretched hand, letting it rest on his chest as he drew closer. He loved the feel of it, as if the energy he felt was passing between them.

"I have an idea," she said, still holding him at bay. "Before we do something we'll regret, we should lock down all the cabins. It's for the best." She pulled her hand back and scratched her head. "Why didn't I think of that before? The fewer people roaming the ship, the better. I didn't want to lock people out in the corridors, but it's too late now."

She gave the verbal command to the computer system, then ran a hand over her hair. Wade's eyes followed her hand, wondering what it would feel like to touch it himself. He raised his hand, reaching for her, but she pulled away.

He couldn't understand the words she said through the haze. She looked angry, but he knew she felt the same desire he did because she'd kissed him. After all this time, she'd been experiencing the same struggle.

His head was pounding, and he reached up to rub at his temples. Then he realized, no, it wasn't his head. It was the door.

A kick thudded against the bottom of Dana's office door, then the banging continued.

"Wade! I know you're in there with her! Open this door right now!"

CHAPTER 5

EARTHA

When another glass hit the dining room wall, Eartha flinched. She was already clutching her backpack in her arms, sitting in the corner of her bedroom, listening to the argument raging outside.

Esme and Eric Rogan were throwing things at each other now and screaming. Eartha wasn't sure what to do. With all the noise they were making, anyone passing by could hear them. Maybe someone had already called security. She didn't want to see either of her adoptive parents taken away, but they were a danger to each other.

They'd come back into their quarters from work arguing, and it hadn't stopped. Not even when she went out to convince them they should eat dinner. Now it was morning, and time for breakfast, but they were still at each other's throats.

She thought of how in sync the Rogans had been when she'd met them at her parent's anniversary party. They used to finish each other's sentences, share food from the same plate, laugh at each other's jokes. Eartha hadn't been with them two months, and now they were ready to kill each other.

Eartha fought the tears that blurred her vision. It was her fault they were fighting in the first place, and trying to stop them had only made it worse.

Esme was pregnant and just starting to show, and Eartha had made the mistake of saying something about the baby boy before they'd told her about it. It just slipped out sometimes. The voices were so real, Eartha sometimes forgot she was the only one who could hear them. It had started years ago, back on Zelenia, with her parents, but had only gotten worse as she grew older. When she'd shared her ability with Esme, it'd changed the way she looked at her. Ever since, she'd given Eartha strange looks and kept her distance, as if the voices were contagious.

Eric Rogan seemed to understand. He was comforting and protective, so much like her real father.

Well, not her biological father, but Michael Singh was the only father she'd known. After her medical exam on board the ship, they'd learned her genes were different from everyone else's; and she couldn't be the natural child of her mother and father, it seemed. It had taken two conversations with the doctor to convince her that what the captain had told her was true.

It made Eartha wonder what had happened to the child her first mother had carried and given birth to in the hospital. Why lie and say that the baby had been Eartha when it wasn't? Did their first baby die before they brought it home? Maybe she and another baby got switched after birth while in the same hospital.

None of that explained how much they all looked alike, but her father had confirmed it in the video message. He said she had real parents out there, maybe looking for her.

Twice adopted, and she didn't know who her biological family was. Only that they were different. Eartha often wondered what would make a mother abandon her own child. Esme seemed so attached to hers and was upset that Eric didn't show the same love for the baby boy that slept inside her.

Did her real parents hear the voices and see things the way she did? Had that been the reason they'd given her up on Zelenia? Had they known their baby wouldn't be safe with them? The thought settled in her mind and felt true in some way.

Eartha couldn't stay in their cabin and listen to them fight anymore.

She used the shelves in her narrow closet to climb up to the ventilation shaft. It was how she'd gotten around before, after her mother snuck her onboard and forced her to hide. The asteroid that killed everyone's family and friends had been her cue to finally come out of hiding and find the Rogans. However, Eartha had been crying so loudly that it was Mr. Rogan who'd found her. She'd been happy to stay with the Rogans, as instructed. Her mother said they would be glad to have her, but she'd only been half right.

The grate covering the conduit had screws, and five minutes later, still listening to her new adoptive parents yelling in the room next door, she'd gotten them out. Eartha threw her pack up into the shaft and climbed inside after it. She was careful to be quiet, though they'd never hear her over the screaming and crashing as more dishes shattered.

She didn't want to see them fighting. The sound of the event was enough, but she couldn't help her curiosity. As she passed the vent leading into the living room, she looked down. It was like a cyclone had sprung up in the living room, knocking over everything. The chairs and side tables had been turned over. Their family pictures from the mantle were lying face down on the glass-strewn floor. Even the flowers Eric had picked from the aeroponics suite to welcome Esme home were lying on the floor, the water they'd been sitting in a wet stain where it was soaking the gray carpet.

Esme and Eric chased each other from room to room as they argued. Esme was the one lifting and breaking plates as she threw them at Eric's head. It was violence like nothing Eartha had ever seen before between two people who loved each other. If she hadn't seen it herself, she wouldn't have believed it.

"You love her more than us!" Esme screamed; her voice hoarse from yelling. She reached for the large vase on the floor and lifted it above her head. Eric reached her in time and pulled it from her grasp, letting it fall unbroken to the carpeted floor. He held Esme's shoulders and shook her as he yelled into her face.

"That's not true! I love her *and* you. Why can't you understand that my feelings have no limit? I'm perfectly capable of loving her, you, and our baby."

"That's not true! I warned you this was a mistake, and you ignored it. There's something not right about her." Esme pulled away, standing her ground. "You have to choose. Is it going to be her, or us? I won't raise my child around her."

The words stung, and Eartha clutched her stomach to stop the ache. Esme let out a guttural sound and clutched her stomach at the same time, leaning against the back of the couch, the only piece of furniture still upright. Eartha covered her cry with one hand. Neither of the adults heard her resume her slow shuffle down the shaft in the conduit above them, their voices covering her movement.

"Stop this, Esme. You're going to hurt yourself. You know I love you. I'll do anything to prove it to you, but don't ask me to abandon Eartha. I couldn't do that. She's like my own child."

Eartha knew what she had to do. Eric's words made it harder. But Esme's words made it easy.

"She's *not* your child, don't you see that? You can't love her like you do our child. It's impossible. Ah!"

"You're having contractions. You need to lie down."

"It's too early. It's not time."

"I know. Just relax and breathe the way they taught us."

"Don't tell me what to do! You don't even care!"

Esme's voice echoed in the small space as Eartha moved from their apartment and continued through the conduits, their voices fading behind her. She crawled despite the tears streaming down her face and whimpered when she knew they wouldn't overhear her.

The Commons wasn't on the same level, so it took Eartha a while to reach the area where Ari worked. When she was sure no one was looking, she slipped out of the vent and dropped to the floor in the empty kitchen.

Something in there was burning, and she saw an unattended pot boiling over. She reached over and turned off the burner then stepped back, almost running into Ari.

"Eartha," Ari said as she turned to face him, "what are you doing here?"

Ari Three was her best friend. The android had been the one to keep her fed when she'd run out of food, and had kept her hidden when the Rogans first took her in. His blond hair was almost white, and he looked like someone who spent his days on the beach. His gray eyes, however, seemed to see through her, no doubt because he was always scanning her vitals, as if she might be ill. He held a tray of empty plates and glasses, as his job was to help keep the Commons dining area clean.

"I need to find a new place to live," Eartha told him, her vision blurring as her eyes filled. She whimpered, trying to force her tears back, though it only made things worse by giving her the hiccups.

A crash of a table flipping over on the far left of the Commons made her jump, and she realized two women were fighting here, too. Eartha hung her head, dropping her eyes to the floor. She didn't want to see any more fighting.

The brawl breaking out drew Ari's attention, and he pushed Eartha further toward the kitchen. He put down the tray and held up one finger. "Wait here."

He walked with purpose to the opposite side of the room and, without straining, picked up the two fighting women and put them outside the Commons' main doors. There were cheers and hoots, which he ignored, returning to the kitchen.

Eartha hadn't left her spot. Ari dragged her to a small booth in the corner opposite the area where the brawl had begun, away from the burning smells of the kitchen. A couple he hadn't noticed was making out in the booth, and he pulled Eartha away from them, shielding her eyes with his body. Then he turned and lifted the man by the back of the shirt and hauled him to his feet and away from the table. The woman with him refused to unlink her arms from around his neck, and rose to stand beside him.

"You must leave here now. Please go to your quarters to finish," Ari said.

The woman giggled as she adjusted her clothing, and the two lovers left, their arms still wrapped around each other. Eartha's cheeks flushed at the sight of them. She wondered for the hundredth time what it would be like to make out with someone.

"I apologize, Miss Eartha. It has been unruly in here today. Here, sit down. Let me get you something hot to drink. Would you like a chocolate?"

Eartha shook her head. She didn't feel like eating anything. She just wanted a place to strategize her next move away from all the fighting. Two men facing off in front of the food counter drew her attention. The intense energy in the room seemed to wash over her. Most days the Commons was a quiet place to visit with friends, but today it was almost too loud to hear yourself think. Eartha noted people tossing food and drinks aside as they stood to shove and yell at each other. What was going on with everyone?

When a glass hit the wall, she flinched. They were acting the same as Esme and Eric. She paid close attention to their words and their actions, and saw the same behavior from the people here.

"Ari, has it been like this all day?"

"Yes, and I am thinking there may be a problem onboard."

"Have you tried contacting the captain?"

"I tried the bridge earlier, but perhaps I should try again. Please wait here and hide if the fighting comes your way."

Eartha nodded and prepared to slide under the table if she saw anyone getting too close to her. However, just as she spotted another couple about to dive under a table, Ari returned, sitting directly in her sightline.

"I am not sure how long I can keep this place civilized. The captain said an alien virus has infected the crew. It is forcing people to speak the truth, and only the truth. You will see it in their red eyes."

"I don't know what color their eyes were, but the Rogans are fighting just like everyone here."

Ari nodded. "No doubt they are already infected. It appears to be moving through the ship rather quickly. It may be a contact virus, or it may be airborne. I cannot be sure until I check in with the med lab. The Captain seems to have locked down all the cabins and bays, but the Commons has an independent system. I am being reassigned to the medical bay to assist the doctor."

Eartha felt her eyes filling at the thought that a virus was making the Rogans fight. They were speaking their true feelings, but hurting each other with them at the same time. It made her feel worse knowing she was still the main reason they were angry at each other. "What do we do?"

"Do not cry, Miss Eartha." Ari used his human-like hand to wipe a stray tear from her cheek. "The captain has ordered me to lock down the commons and secure our rations before I go to the med-bay. I think it would be best if you came with me."

As he took her hand, a glass came flying in their direction. Ari caught it with one hand and placed it on a table. He then directed Eartha to stay seated at the table while he ushered everyone out of the Commons, clearing the room in fifteen minutes. He then used a code to lock down the doors to keep people out.

Eartha didn't want to leave. Now that it was quiet again, it seemed like the perfect place to hide from the Rogans and everyone else on the ship, but Ari took her hand and pulled her along after him.

"Wait," she protested, tugging lightly at his hand, "maybe I should stay here. It's safe now."

Ari shook his head. "I don't think the doors will keep people out for long. It is best that you stay with me, as I cannot be infected, and as long as you avoid contact with others, you should be safe."

He led them out into the corridor, avoiding people as if they were walking through a minefield. Clusters either fought or kissed. There was nothing in between. Eartha didn't understand what kind of virus could make you tell the truth and end up both fighting and kissing, but either way, she preferred not to catch it.

As they made their way through the scattered couples and trios, she clung to Ari and glanced at their eyes as they passed. It seemed they were all pink and infected, as Ari had warned.

They reached the med-bay with little resistance, but someone had locked the doors.

"How are we going to get inside?" Eartha asked, looking up for a ventilation shaft. There wasn't one, she reminded herself. She knew this area well, and they'd have to climb in from another corridor to get inside that way.

Ari looked down at her, and then back at the doors. "I

must pry it open, but once I do, it will be impossible to lock again."

Eartha nodded once, stepping back from the doors and to the side. Ari used his mechanical hand as a wedge between the two doors. The doors resisted at first, but then he used his other hand while bracing his toe on the opposite door and pulled. She heard the mechanism inside squeak, then snap.

Ari waved Eartha over, and she got a good look at the room. Inside, broken beakers and test tubes littered the floor. Ari pulled her inside and against the wall closest to the door. Bodies were scattered across the floor. Some of them were bleeding, some of them had clothing missing. They found Dr. Jabar's red eyes roaming the floor for moving bodies, yelling to himself about being overwhelmed. He placed an injector to the neck of a twitching body at his feet. Then his eyes clamped on to Eartha, and he moved toward her, the injector still in his hand.

Ari stepped between them and held out his hands. It stopped him short, and his hand with the injector dropped to his side.

"I am here to help you, Doctor Jabar. Is anyone here uninfected?"

"No. We're *all* infected with this virus. What was she thinking? Why does she have to be so noble? Let these pirates deal with their *own* problems. We shouldn't have to suffer for their mistakes. *They're* the thieves, for star's sake. She's going to get us all killed." He shook his head. "I should have seen it. I didn't see it in time. It's all my fault."

Dr. Jabar seemed to notice for the first time the door was open, waving a hand in its direction.

"The doors are open. Did you do that?"

"Yes, it was the only way to get inside to assist you."

"Assist me?"

"The captain ordered me to help you," Ari explained.

The doctor huffed and threw another beaker onto the floor, where it shattered. "We didn't even get the embryos back. If it wasn't for Captain Pinet, we wouldn't have had to chase them down. We never would have contracted this virus."

"Doctor, please focus," Ari said, trying to recapture the doctor's attention. "I need to learn how the virus spreads and if there is a way to stop it."

"No, the virus was on the cargo. I don't know how they kept it viable, but once it's contracted, a touch can spread it. The pirates touched the cargo, and then the pirates carried the virus right onto our ship. That much we know." He looked at Ari with a steely eye. "Though you're immune, you're probably carrying the virus yourself."

Ari glanced down at Eartha, and she followed his hands as he seemed to pull them closer to his sides. He turned back to the doctor. "Is there any place onboard that's safe from the virus?"

Dr. Jabar shook his head and laughed. There wasn't any humor in it. "The only safe place on the ship is in isolation locations like the brig." Dr. Jabar picked up a device from the nearest table and threw it at the wall.

Whatever it was, the broken pieces that fell off probably made it useless.

Eartha let out a startled squeak that drew the doctor's attention back to her. Dr. Jabar's head snapped up, and he moved toward her, leading with the injector again. He stalked around the broken glass like a monster hunting prey.

"Eartha, don't move," Ari said when he noticed her feet inching toward the door. "Doctor, please remain calm." His mechanical hand was at the doctor's chest. "She is unaffected. Note her eyes, they are clear."

Dr. Jabar stopped his intense tracking of her movements and seemed to take in Ari's words at last. Eartha saw his own eyes were bright pink, his movements jittery.

"Please relay in detail what has happened, and what the next steps are."

The doctor sneered back at him. "Don't you understand what I'm telling you, metal for brains? Those Fashin Teku brought it onboard with them. That's the only explanation. Now we're all infected, and they're still not showing any symptoms."

"Do they have some kind of immunity?" Ari asked.

"I couldn't find anything that suggested they were immune. My hypothesis is though they appear to be unaffected, it must take more time to manifest in them than it does in us. When they brought that cargo on board, it infected them along with our people. My guess is that they'll be showing symptoms before long, just like the rest of us."

"However, you are working on a solution," Ari theorized. "What do you need?"

"I need someone immune." Dr. Jabar stared at Eartha for a moment longer than she liked, forcing her to look away. "All I've got is the blood of those aliens. If I can figure out why the virus remained dormant in them for so long, it might save us all."

The people twitching on the floor weren't cured. Eartha didn't want to be next on the doctor's list, and backed away. Ari moved to the other table and got to work beside the doctor. There were vials of blood lined up in front of them.

"I wish you hadn't busted the door," Dr. Jabar muttered. "Putting them to sleep is the only thing that keeps them from hurting each other when they turn violent."

Eartha had a bad feeling in her stomach, and it reminded her she'd forgotten about someone.

"Ari, what about Luke?"

"He is safe," he assured her.

"How can you be sure?"

"He is in the brig below. It will cut him off from all others, and no doubt keep him and the others inside safe."

Eartha bit her lower lip. She didn't *feel* like he'd be safe. "We should check to make sure."

Ari shook his head. "It is too dangerous out there. I need to work on finding a cure. You could still become infected. Next to me is the safest place for you right now."

Eartha glanced at Doctor Jabar. He was busy working

on another formula, muttering to himself. Despite Ari's assurances, Eartha couldn't shake the feeling that Luke was in danger. She'd learned a long time ago that most adults didn't take her 'feelings' seriously until it was too late. Eartha wouldn't ignore them. People got hurt when she didn't do anything.

Luke was alone in a cell, but other passengers—*angry* passengers—knew where he was, and might try to hurt him and the others. She'd caught several people muttering about the Coalition terrorists. It didn't matter that Luke hadn't been an active member. They'd still come after him when they went after the others. Luke knew the head of the CAH, and that might be enough to get him killed. It didn't matter that their leader was just another kid.

Eartha could hear the sounds of a struggle out in the corridor. It wouldn't take long before people were inside the med-bay, breaking things. She had to hurry if she wanted to reach Luke in time. She scanned the lab and spotted a grate almost near the ceiling. If she pushed a hover bed close enough, she might make it.

The hover bed controls were on its side. Once she had it in place, she climbed on top and elevated the bed as high as it would go, giving her plenty of room to climb into the conduits. The only problem was she hadn't been quiet enough.

"Eartha, do not go into the ventilation shaft. You are not safe outside of this room," Ari said from the floor. It was the closest approximation to a scolding he'd ever given her.

"I'll be fine," she insisted. "I'm just going to make sure Luke's all right, and then I'll come right back." She glanced down at Ari. "He's my friend. You would do the same for me."

She didn't wait for his response as she replaced the grate behind her. Ari would have done the same for her, and she knew it.

The shaft was empty, as usual. The adults only climbed inside them when they were making repairs. If everyone on board was becoming infected with the virus, they wouldn't be climbing through the shafts looking for a kid.

She shuffled forward. Maybe Ari would even have a cure ready by the time she returned. Though, even as she thought it, something in her stomach clenched. No, the cure wouldn't be ready. She had to hurry.

CHAPTER 6

EARTHA

The conduits were buzzing with noise as Eartha started her descent to the brig. The med-bay was located two floors up, so she crawled the length of the ventilation tubing until she came to a vertical shaft. She poked her head out and listened for the sounds of anyone arguing. She didn't hear anything from within the shaft, and so climbed down.

The fighting was escalating between the men and women on the ship. Once in a while, she'd hear a *thump* as people were pushed into the bulkhead. She imagined broken items littering the carpeted halls. It was only within the conduits where she wouldn't have to crawl over shards of broken plastic or glass.

There were no ducts large enough for her to fit into

leading into the brig, as her mother had designed the room to have no crawlspace access. She'd told her that when she'd gone over the ship's map with her. Eartha had then learned for herself firsthand the first week she'd tried to sneak out to see Luke after his arrest.

By now, he should have been home. According to Eric and Esme, he and the other two Coalition members who hadn't been terrorizing the ship were technically free. The problem was that one guy had escaped, which had forced all the others back into their cells until he was found. Eric said keeping them locked up was for their own safety, though she couldn't understand how keeping Luke and the others caged down there away from their friends and family could be considered 'safe'.

Eartha positioned herself above a grate that would drop her down outside of the brig, using the sides to keep her up with her pack still strapped to her back. It was quiet on this level. The guard that usually stood outside of the brig doors was missing. She approached the doors to listen for activity inside, but they slid open without resistance. Inside, the guard who stood at the console was also missing, and inside the cells were the three Coalition members, worried frowns on their faces.

The doors closed behind her with a *whoosh*, and every eye in the room turned to her. Luke met her eyes and just stared while the other man and woman both spoke at once, firing statements at her when she didn't respond.

"Get us out of here!"

"Where is everyone?"

"We didn't do anything."

"Did you bring any food? No one has brought us any food since the guard left."

"What's going on out there?"

Eartha walked toward Luke's cell, ignoring the man and woman's pleas and focusing on his face. Luke was sitting on his cot, and stood up as she approached, giving her a better view of him. He seemed older. His upper lip and chin had long black hairs growing out of it. He was three years older than her, and though it had never come up before, it suddenly seemed like a lot. Luke was as tall as Eric. He'd pulled his shoulder-length brown hair back into a low ponytail, and his long fingers pressed against the duroglass.

"Eartha, what are you doing here?"

She reached up and put her hand on her side of the transparent barrier, matching her fingers with his. Luke stared at their hands a moment, then lifted his green eyes to hers. There was so much she'd wanted to say to him. When they'd hauled him out of the Commons in mag-cuffs, she'd defended him. She'd shouted that they were making a mistake, but Luke hadn't fought them.

Luke hadn't said a word when they'd taken him away. She'd memorized every twitch of his face when they played Honor Bound or Fortification of Heroes with Mr. Jennison, looking for anything that might give him away. She knew his face so well that the guilt she saw when he was being led away had been what silenced her.

Now here he was, looking at her with that same guilt

on his face, but he hadn't done anything to ruin the ship. He had, however, joined the Coalition of his own free will. Now there was only one question she wanted to know.

"Why did you do it?"

He looked down at the floor as his hand slid away from the duroglass. His palm print smudged the glass on his side. Eartha lifted her own hands away and let them fall to her hips, waiting for his answer.

"I don't know. I was different then. At the time, I liked being a part of something that felt real." His shoulders lifted slightly, then dropped. "I wish you could understand what it's like to not fit in anywhere."

One of his wavy brown tendrils had escaped the binder and fell into his face. He lifted a hand to tuck it out of the way behind his ear. Eartha's teeth clamped together, not trusting herself to hold back the tears. How could he say that? She had been orphaned *twice*. If anyone understood, it was her.

"I *do* understand."

His face fell as he realized what he'd said, and she saw him trying to correct his mistake with a shake of his head.

"No, of course you do. It's just that . . . I needed to belong to something bigger, more important than myself. When I figured out what the government was hiding from everyone, I wanted to share the truth with people. The Coalition gave me that opportunity."

Eartha nodded. It made sense. Luke was a genius. He could do the kind of math that even the ship's school-teacher didn't understand. Luke was special that way. But because of his past, he was stuck behind double-paned duroglass.

Eartha wondered if this would be the last time she'd see him. She focused on the idea, but there was no pain when she thought of Luke. It meant she would see him again. Perhaps when she did, they would be on the same side of the barrier. She glanced over her shoulder at the other two prisoners who were pacing their cells, but still didn't have pink or red eyes. What Ari had said was true. They were safer here than anywhere.

"I just wish you didn't have to be in here," she said, shifting from one foot to the other as she searched for another way into the cell, but there wasn't a vent large enough.

"I don't." Luke flashed her the most dimple filled smile she'd ever seen on his sullen face, and it made her knees go to jelly. "You could let me out of here."

At the sound of a potential prison break, the other two found their voices again.

"Kid, break us out of here," said one of the male prisoners.

Eartha shook her head. She couldn't let them out and risk them becoming infected like everyone else.

"Eartha, how did you get in here in the first place?" Luke asked. "Where's the guard?"

She spoke loud enough for the other two prisoners to hear. "Everyone is sick with an alien virus. Because you're in here, you can't get infected. If I let you out, the virus will change you."

"Change us how?" Luke asked.

Eartha thought about what she'd seen. "I'm not sure exactly. Everyone is either fighting or kissing." Eartha wondered if Luke would be the latter, or if he'd want to fight like the Rogans. "The alien ship exploded. Everyone saw it from the viewports. The same thing is happening here."

"What about a vaccine?" the man asked.

At the same time, the woman asked, "There's no cure?"

"No. Ari is working on it with Dr. Jabar, but the doctor is infected, too."

"We need to get out of here and help figure out a cure," the woman said.

Before Eartha could give it a second thought, the doors of the brig opened again and a cacophony of shouting from the corridor reached them as a dozen bodies poured inside. Eartha knew then that Ari had been right.

The man and woman repeated their cries as they banged on their enclosures again, but stopped when the crowd pressed against the glass screaming and cursing at them. James, the boy she'd had a crush on back on Zelenia, separated himself from the crowd and stepped toward the glass in front of Luke. His brown wavy hair was standing up in wild clumps on his head and his bright, blood-shot eyes glared at Luke.

"Jamie, what are you doing here?" Luke asked.

"He's infected," Eartha said, stepping back from both of them.

A lifetime ago, Eartha had sat in her best friend Becky's

bedroom and called his house. She'd been too nervous to say anything more than hello. James was the cutest boy in her class, and Becky had been determined to make sure Eartha had a boyfriend that summer. James, with his easy smile and athleticism, had made the shortlist. But by the time she'd stowed away on the *Hope*, she didn't have a crush on him anymore. She wasn't sure which of them was more surprised.

Eartha stood with her back against the cell's duroglass wall as the brig's door opened again and several more people crowded inside. The man who truly seemed to be leading the mob was holding a standing lamp, the head of it dented as if he'd already used it against something hard enough to bend the metal alloy.

"Oh, I'm sorry, am I interrupting a Coalition meeting?" a woman behind him asked as she made her way forward. In her hand was a large metal rod, and it looked like there was the stain of red on the end. "May I have a turn to speak? I wanted to talk to you about my daughter. You see, she was in that classroom you helped blow up back on Zelenia."

Eartha's mouth went dry with fear. She'd have to shove past the mob to get to the corridor and back to the ventilation shaft. There was no way to get around the crowd without getting infected.

"That wasn't me! I wasn't anywhere near the classroom!" one of the female prisoners shouted as she backed away from the barrier.

"Who cares if you were there? You supported the

people that hurt my little girl!" The rod bounced off the duroglass shield and back at her. The man with the lamp tried next. Again, there was no effect on the barrier, to Eartha's relief. Luke would be safe from infection, but as she stood there with the crowd pressing in, Eartha realized *she* wouldn't be.

"Eartha, you need to get out of here," Luke said, beating on the duroglass for the first time.

"You lied to me," James said, speaking to Luke. "You said you were my big brother forever and that you'd never hurt me. But you did. You hurt me when you signed up with the Coalition. You're nothing but a liar!" He threw his hands hard against the barrier, but it didn't budge. It should have hurt him, but he didn't react to the pain at all.

"I meant it, I swear," Luke said, signaling with his head to Eartha.

Eartha took a step toward the door as the rest of the mob seemed focused on the two adults. Only James had moved close enough to the barrier to talk to Luke.

"I'm sorry. I didn't know what I was doing back then, believe me," Luke shouted. Eartha turned and saw his eyes on hers. He'd been answering his brother and speaking to her at the same time.

"Why would I believe anything you say?" James shot back. "You upset mom and dad. Doesn't that matter to you?"

"Of course it does. When I get out of here, we'll talk about it as a family."

James sneered back at him. "I wouldn't get my hopes

up. You're not going anywhere anytime soon. Don't worry, I'll take good care of your *girlfriend*."

Before Eartha knew what was happening, James's hand whipped out and grabbed her, pulling her back against his chest her backpack crushed between them. He was a head taller than her, and she could feel his warm breath against her ear.

"How does it feel when someone *you* care about is hurting?"

Eartha let out a squeak as his arms tightened around her waist and throat. She saw her own panic mirrored in Luke's face. James was burning up. The heat was rolling off of him in waves. She squirmed against his hold, but he was unbelievably strong.

"She's not my girlfriend, she's just a kid!" Luke shouted from the other side. "You know she's the same age as you. Leave her alone."

There was a swift jab in her chest at his words. Just a kid? She knew it shouldn't have bothered her. They were just friends. But somehow comparing her to James made Eartha feel like maybe they weren't as close as she thought.

"The same age as the people the Coalition attacked," James said.

Eartha beat her fists against his arms, but it didn't faze him. Luke's face had gone red with anger. He was helpless to do anything, and James knew it.

"Let her go!" Luke's fist came down against the barrier.

James held fast to her, widening his stance so she couldn't stomp on his feet.

"Get off me!" Eartha shouted as she fought against his grip, but he didn't let go.

The others were busy using their pieces of furniture to bang against the duroglass walls where the other Coalition members remained locked inside.

James didn't seem to hear his brother's pleas as he kept his arm under Eartha's throat, glaring back at Luke. She kicked out to throw him off balance, but she'd never been in a fight with anyone before. The vids always made it look easy, but nothing seemed to work, and she was beginning to see stars.

CHAPTER 7

EARTHA

In an instant, Eartha went from being choked to down on her hands and knees, gasping. In the commotion, none of them had heard the brig doors slide open and then closed again.

Ari was holding James up in the air by the back of the shirt. "Are you all right, Miss Eartha?" he asked.

"I'm okay now," she gasped, her voice barely loud enough to hear over the others shouting in the room.

Ari injected something into James' neck then lowered him to the floor, where he collapsed. Eartha let out a gasp of surprise.

"What did you do to my brother?" Luke asked.

"I am testing a potential antidote. One of the side effects is the subject loses consciousness. I am not sure if it will be successful, but for now, he is all right." Ari was looking Eartha over with a curious expression. "We must leave here, Miss Eartha. It is not safe."

Eartha had to think for a moment. "We need to get Luke out of here. People will keep coming here and trying to hurt him and the others for being members of the Coalition." She pointed to the group that was still beating against the barrier.

"How long have you been in here?" Ari asked.

"Maybe fifteen minutes before James grabbed me. I lost track of time after that."

"That is strange . . . I have touched you, and now someone else has touched you, yet you are not exhibiting symptoms. Everyone else who has come into even mild contact with the virus showed symptoms a half hour after contact. I must continue to monitor your condition."

Luke looked at Eartha and nodded for her to leave. She wondered if he meant the thing he'd said about her being just a kid.

"I will need to run some more tests to be sure, but you may be helpful in finding a cure for the rest of the crew," Ari continued. "I need you to come with me."

"What about Luke?" Eartha asked.

Ari glanced over at the people beating their hands bloody against the barrier. He shrugged.

"I believe he will be safer here than with us."

"They'll get him!" Eartha said, digging in her heels. "They'll figure out how to open the other cells. We have to do something."

There were two men pressing random icons on the console, trying to do just that. Ari lifted the fleshy end off of his right-hand pointer finger, exposing the metal skeleton beneath, and touched it to the console. It electrified everyone touching it and rendered the console useless. The group halved itself in size as its members ran out of the brig and back into the corridor.

"They are sealed inside the cells until the crew can come and fix the panels. We should go."

Eartha refused to move. She stared back at Luke. He mouthed the word 'go', both hands pushing against the barrier as if he could nudge her along. She nodded once before turning back to Ari.

"Luke is safe," he insisted. "Come with me."

"He'll be safe," she repeated. When the words didn't come with any pain, she knew them to be true.

Ari had lost his patience and gave up reasoning with her, dragging Eartha out of the brig by the hand. They left Luke curled up on the bench, listening to the rest of the mob beating on the duroglass.

"We should make haste. Can you run?" Ari asked.

"Yes."

Eartha ran with Ari back to the medical labs. Ari cleared the path so well she could have run with her eyes closed most of the way. When they reached the lab, Ari used a special code to enter.

"You fixed the doors?" Eartha stared up at them in wonder.

Once inside, he entered the code to lock it again

"Not, I, but the Fashin Teku."

Eartha started at the sight of the three alien Fashin Teku behind her. Two had red-rimmed eyes while the third, the one with the black hair and black skin, fidgeted in place, his eyes closed, humming to himself. They must have come in while the Doctor and Ari were working. Eartha ducked behind Ari at the sight of them.

"Where is Dr. Jabar?" Ari asked, looking around the room.

"He left. He is too sick," the dark one said, keeping his eyes closed.

Not only had they fixed the door, but Eartha also noticed, the unconscious people who'd been on the floor had been moved. The med-bay was quiet, and she glanced around, taking in the row of empty beds until her eyes landed on the aliens again. She poked a head out still clutching Ari's sleeve.

"They're helping you?"

"Yes, the Fashin Teku are excellent engineers," Ari explained. "Not only did they upgrade our engines, but they helped me repair the door and clear out the room."

Ari lifted Eartha up on an examination table where she could sit without touching the floor. The Fashin Teku's heads didn't reach her perch, but if they were determined, their arms could.

"She's not sick," said the one with the golden hair growing from his head and face. She knew he was the one in charge from the interviews on Maggie Brooker's reports. The three aliens had pretended to be their friends until they'd stolen from them. The trio came in blond, orange-red, and black, each of them with hair growing to the floor from every part of their body except the middle of their faces, where their eyes, nose, and mouth sat. Eartha didn't like the look of them. Their beady eyes and faces of hair made it difficult to know which were male and which were female. The three of them staring at her with red-rimmed eyes made her itch.

"Yes," Ari answered as he continued with tubes of blood and a tablet of notes. "But she may have been recently infected. I will have to watch her to see how the virus is progressing."

"Many sorries," the blond one said with a bow of his head. "We did not want to ruin your ship."

"True, it appears that your people, though more resilient, are not immune."

"All sick now. Not many times left," said the red-haired Teku. "These two are want to be free and desires grow within me." When the red-haired Teku stroked the one with the blond hair, Eartha realized she must be the female.

"I bore of you, Tovar the second," Ashwin said, his eyes blazing red.

Tovar's face reddened as she spat on the floor at their feet. Then Eartha noticed they were all confined within a barrier force field she could only see when they touched it. She relaxed, realizing none of them could reach her even if they wanted.

"Ack!" Tovar spat. "You bore me, Ash. I can't wait until

Oli is free to beat you into sense. You brought sickness upon us, you meatball!"

The language only deteriorated from there, and Eartha looked to Ari, who was listening with his head tilted to one side.

"You must hurry, android," said the dark one Tovar had called Oli. He had brown skin darker than Eartha's father. The long, wavy black hair looked heavy as it shifted and moved with his body. Only the two braids at his temples kept the mane off his face. He had braided his beard into one braid, similar to the others. However, his eyes were gradually turning a pale pink. Maybe that's why she noticed the intricate design of his vest; similar, but different from the others.

"Oli, describe your symptoms for me," Ari prompted.

"You ask me a simple question, yet I prefer to rip the head from your body and watch the wires dangle."

Ari ignored the insult and returned to his work.

"Now, with the knowing of this, what will you do?" Oli asked.

"It appears there is a person on the ship who is immune, and it is her blood I will test next."

"Who's immune? Why didn't you say that before?" Eartha asked, looking at the Fashin Teku female with confusion. She obviously wasn't immune.

"The person I think is immune, Eartha, is you."

Eartha looked back at him with surprise. "Me?"

"You have shown no symptoms, despite being within close proximity to several of the infected."

"James only touched me twenty minutes ago."

"Not James. You were in contact with the Rogans," Ari explained. "Two of the first to show symptoms, as they were most likely infected directly from the shipment of containers." Ari stared down at the tablet again. "Yes . . . it seems you are immune, and I need to figure out how to create a vaccine from one source sample."

"What's a source sample?"

"I will need to take some blood from you."

"Blood?" Eartha inched away from him toward the other end of the table. "You didn't say anything about taking my blood before."

Ari caught her by the shoulder and eased her back into place, within easy reach of his assembled tools.

"I will take some of your blood and break it down into tiny fractions. I will extract the small parts that contain what we need to create a medicine to help the others. This will enable them to fight the virus the way your body does."

He lined up his things while Eartha sat there, nervously watching his movements. When the vials and needles were out on the doctor's table, Ari turned back to her. He tilted his head to one side, as if analyzing her for symptoms.

"Do you understand what I need to do?"

Eartha nodded. Everyone on the ship was sick, and they needed a cure before it was too late. If her blood could help them, this was the only way to find out how.

That didn't mean she had to *like* it, though.

"Give me your arm and look away. I will tell you when I have finished."

Eartha tried to remember that Ari was her friend, and he wouldn't hurt her on purpose. She nodded, turning her head to the opposite wall with her eyes shut tight.

"This should not hurt you at all." Ari lifted her sleeve, exposing her honey brown skin underneath. At the crease of her elbow, he sterilized the area with one tool, then used a needle and vials to extract her blood. Eartha felt the pinch and winced.

"See, now that did not hurt at all."

Eartha stole a peek at his face. "What would you know about hurt? You can't feel anything."

Ari smiled faintly. "That is true, but it is something I have heard Dr. Jabar say. This seemed like the appropriate time to use the phrase."

It didn't take more than a couple of minutes for him to fill the vials he'd laid out with her blood. When he'd finished, he placed a dab of liquid second-skin over the area, making the small puncture invisible. Eartha turned to watch Ari work beside her, using her blood and another blue mixture. When he finished mixing the two, he transferred it into another injector.

"I need to run some tests and create several samples to try."

Eartha frowned. "Does that mean the one you used on James didn't work?"

"That is correct."

"What if this one doesn't work either?"

"We should be close enough to the Begarans to ask for help. The ship is still moving, thanks to the Fashin Teku."

"What if they refuse to help us?"

Ari looked up from the samples with a thoughtful expression. "Then we may have to come up with another plan."

Eartha bit her lower lip. She couldn't think of anything that would save everyone. If only the other doctors weren't sick.

An incessant pounding started on the door to the lab.

"Why do they want to get in here?" Eartha asked, shrinking back from the door.

"They want us," Oli growled. The other two Fashin Teku were yelling insults and making growling noises as well. The force-field was the only thing keeping them from running to the door.

Eartha tugged on Ari's sleeve. "What are you going to do with them?"

Ari looked from the Fashin Teku to the door, then back to her samples. "It is not safe for them to be out among the others."

Eartha nodded her understanding and backed away from the wall. The Fashin Teku were growing angrier and more demanding. She wanted to be anywhere but here. Between the shouts of the people outside and the aliens inside, she worried they'd somehow get the doors open, and she and Ari didn't have any other place to go.

"I've completed the tests," Ari announced. "Your blood may be an antidote, but we still need to disperse it among the infected. Wait here while I contact the captain."

He turned away, moving to the panel nearest the door where the pounding was loudest. Eartha moved to the corner of the table nearest the wall and hugged her knees as she hummed the Fashin Teku calming song under her breath.

CHAPTER 8

Secrets secrets are no fun, secrets secrets hurt someone.

D ana watched as Maggie charged into her office wearing a mauve nightie and matching silk robe.

"Five minutes," Maggie said, strolling up to point a finger in Wade's face. "You couldn't last five minutes."

"I told you, it's over," Wade argued, moving to keep himself between her and Dana's desk.

"You took all of five minutes before running back to her!" She lifted a painted finger and pointed at Dana. "And you, Madam Captain, I knew you couldn't keep your hands off him. From the moment I met you. You've been just waiting for this day to come."

Maggie crossed the room in three strides, bringing

herself nose to nose with Wade. Only the width of his arm kept them apart.

"You're wrong," Dana said from behind Wade's back. "Not that I have to justify my actions to you, or anyone else."

Dana's hand trembled into a fist, and she could visualize hitting Maggie in her full face of make-up. She forced her hand to relax when she noticed the pink tinting Maggie's eyes.

"We're all sick," she said. "We have to get control ourselves." The urge to hurl herself over the table and into Wade's arms was almost as strong as her desire to beat Maggie to a pulp. She had to think before it was too late.

"What about me?" Wade asked, glaring at Maggie. "I guess I'm just supposed to roll over and accept that you were with another man while we were together?"

"Wait, what?" Dana said, looking between them.

"Should *I* tell her, or do you want to?" Wade asked, taking another dangerous step closer to Maggie. She rubbed at her chest, trying to control her breathing. They were all feeling it. The insatiable heat had forced the truth out of them.

"Maggie," Dana warned, "it's not safe for you here."

"You wanna bet?" she shot back, missing Dana's meaning. "I'll take you any time, any day. You may have him today, but I'll have him tomorrow."

Maggie leaned back to take a swing, but Wade grabbed her fist mid-air. Dana, anticipating the move, had both knees on the table and was sliding toward her when Wade held out his other arm, stopping her fist from landing. He shook his head as if trying to clear it.

Dana slid behind him, pushing him toward the table, then shoved Maggie hard to the floor, landing on her chest and raising her arm—And then she remembered what she was supposed to be doing—mainly, *not* decking the redhead.

Maggie was looking up at her from the floor, seething. Wade had his back to the table, shaking his head. Dana leaped up from Maggie's chest and backed herself up to the wall.

"Computer, initiate a trifold force-field, dividing the room at the table and two meters from the Captain's office door. Seal all entrances. Voice verification: Captain Dana Pinet Alpha Seven. Lock until combination voice recognition Dr. Randall Jabar, Gamma 1, confirms."

The force-field came down, keeping the three of them away from each other. Wade was stuck with the table nearest the windows. Maggie was at the door, and Dana was on the left, nearest the door to her office and the bridge.

After a moment, Wade recovered. "Wait, what did you do?"

"I'm saving your lives. One more minute and I was going to kill her. One more minute with you..." Dana's voice trailed off. "Well, let's just say I'm not that strong."

"You put one hand on him, and—" Maggie's fist made contact with the force-field and Dana heard a *crunch*. She must have broken a finger. The knowledge of it didn't bother her, and she couldn't figure out why.

"Stop, Maggie. We're done," Wade said. He slid onto the table, laying with his hands crossed over his chest. Other than the heavy breathing, he appeared to be drifting off to sleep.

Maggie's face dropped, tears springing to her red-rimmed eyes. She sank back to the floor, sobbing.

Dana watched as the defeated woman curled herself into a ball of grief. She'd never seen Maggie looking so disheveled and distraught in public. It was doubtful anyone had.

"I'm sorry . . . that was my fault," Wade said.

"That's right, it was your fault." Dana turned her back on him. "You're the one who brought her onboard. You're the one who flaunted her in front of my face, pretending to be happy and engaged. I mean, who does that? Tells their ex they're engaged and then invites them to perform the wedding ceremony."

"I wasn't pretending. I was happy. You should have been happy for me." Wade shook his head. "You don't get it, do you? I've always had feelings for you, but I thought you'd moved on. She was special. If it weren't for Bill, I would've married her."

"Who's Bill?"

"Her camera guy," Wade sighed. "And the man who was in love with her when she started dating me."

"Oh right . . . the one from the vid."

"Wait, how do you know about the vid?" Wade asked whirling on her.

Her hand flew to her mouth. She'd forgotten she wasn't supposed to have seen the vid, but Barnes had left it for her to find. Dana had confronted Maggie, warned her that keeping it from Wade would be a mistake. Looking at him now, Dana was glad she hadn't been the one to tell him. She'd never seen him so murderous.

"He was an incurable romantic," Maggie cried out through the tears and drawing Wade's attention back to her. "You can't blame me for loving him back. He was in my life long before you."

"Actually, I *do* blame you," Wade said.

"So, I guess you're pretty ticked off that he's already dead?" Dana asked.

"Exactly *how* can I be angry with a guy who's already dead?" Wade gripped the ends of his hair, and the effect was mesmerizing. Dana had the strongest impulse to reach for his shirt and pull him forward.

Her hand hit the force-field, and it dropped lifelessly to her side. It should have hurt more than it did. Instead, she shook off the sensation and plopped down on the floor. The temperature in the room had risen, and she was sweating through her uniform. She peeled off her jacket and threw it to the floor.

"COMP, lower room temperature by five degrees."

Three beeps reminded her she was behind a force-field with no access to the controls.

"Who can work in this heat, anyway?" Maggie

muttered, finished with her crying. She was back to angry as she paced her make-shift cell.

Dana ignored her as Wade continued to stare at her from his side of the force field like a hungry wolf.

"You and I shouldn't be behind force-fields," he said lowly. "We're not going to hurt each other. We're going to love each other."

"Don't be disgusting!" Maggie roared.

"No," Dana said firmly. "It stays until Dr. Jabar and I both give verbal clearance. I did it that way on purpose."

"Somehow, I don't see Dr. Jabar giving us the all-clear if he's got the virus, too." Wade laughed as if he'd made a joke.

Dana let out a frustrated sigh and undid her boots, slipping them off along with her socks. She was sweating even more and wasn't sure what to do about it when the wall panel signaled.

"This is Ari Three paging the captain on all channels, please respond."

"Oops, that's me," Dana said. The panel was within the force-field. She hadn't planned it that way, but thankfully she knew what to do. Placing her hand on the panel, she answered, "Yes?"

"Captain, we appear to be in distress," Ari said.

Dana giggled uncontrollably as she looked around the room at the three of them behind force-fields. Then straightened, fixing her features. "You could say that."

"I believe we may be in an emergency that would

require the only unaffected person onboard taking command of the ship. Would you agree?"

Dana nodded, a smirk on her face.

"Captain, try to focus. I need you to give me the command codes for the ship. I will transfer all emergency and non-emergency systems over to my control until we reach our destination and receive a cure for this disease."

"Hey, who do you think you are?" Wade called out from the other side of the room. "You're just a machine, you're not a person. We can't relinquish all the command codes over to you."

"Oh, shut up! Who asked you?" Maggie yelled. "*You're* not the captain."

"I beg your pardon, Captain," Ari pressed, "but in this situation, I am the only one who cannot be affected by this virus. Reason dictates I would be the most ideal choice in this circumstance. I can ensure our crew and passengers' safety until the Captain has gained control of her own emotions again."

Dana put a hand over her mouth to stop from laughing.

"The answer is no!" Wade called out. "Don't ask again, or you'll end up a pile of scrap metal."

She didn't like him speaking for her as if she couldn't make up her own mind. Though she was having a hard time focusing, she knew the android wasn't wrong.

"I can speak for myself." Dana turned her attention back to the panel. "Yes, Ari, I would love to give you all the command codes so you can ensure our safety to . . ." Her brain was all fuzzy again. She tried to remember their mission. "Where were we going again?"

"Captain, we are returning to the alien planet where the virus originated," Ari said.

Dana snapped her fingers together. "Yes, yes, you're right. I believe that would be best. However, I'm locked in a force-field. The COMP won't recognize my authority from within here. I need Dr. Jabar to give me clearance."

"That'll never happen," Wade muttered.

Dana giggled again, and this time Wade joined her, both breaking into hysterics. Ari disconnected, leaving Dana talking to the empty panel.

"Now what?" Wade asked.

Dana shrugged. "I don't know."

"If you would let me, I could love you."

Anger and lust warred within her, the two vying emotions controlling her thoughts, making it difficult to focus on what came next. Dana's blood boiled to choke him, and her skin burned for his touch.

"I can't trust you," she said. "I want to hit you as much as kiss you right now."

"That's just the virus talking," Wade said, waving his hand. "You want to kiss me, that's the truth."

"No, it's not. I mean, not any more than wanting to kick you." Dana pulled at her hair to stop her brain from scrambling again. She struggled to keep the words inside, the truth about how she felt about him.

"Vi-rus," Wade said, singing the word.

"No, it's not." Dana gripped a handful of her curls. Why was it so hard to think? "This is all happening so fast. I'm all mixed up inside. I want to hate you for bringing that woman onboard, but every time I see you, I can't help but wish we were together."

"Don't you hear me? We *can* be together."

"No, we can't. It's too late."

"That makes two of us who don't want you!" Maggie called out.

Dana kicked the force-field. Wade stared at her in stunned silence. When he looked her in the eye, she wanted to cry.

"You broke my heart," he said, his voice just above a whisper.

"I know."

"All I wanted was to be there for you, but you pushed me away."

"I did." Her eyes flashed to Maggie, who was crying again, but still angry. "But you recovered, didn't you?" She had no control over the volume or intensity of her words.

His temper flared up to meet hers like an ignited flame. "What's *that* supposed to mean?"

"It means you had no trouble moving on after me," Dana snapped. "You found a beautiful, famous redhead to keep your bed warm while I went home every night alone."

"You think I'm beautiful?" Maggie asked, turning to her.

"Yes. Don't you think so?"

"Well, of course I do, but it's different coming from another woman." Maggie smiled. "I think if it weren't for Wade, you and I would have been friends."

Dana shook her head, but the ringing in her ears made her stop.

"Yes, you would have liked me," she said in a sing-song voice, wiggling her finger at Dana, who sighed.

"Okay, fine. If it weren't for Wade, I would have liked you."

Maggie hiccuped and nodded. "Too bad we're both in love with the same man."

Dana's voice hitched as she choked back angry tears. "He moved on, but I couldn't."

"Whose fault is that?" Wade walked away from the force-field and slammed his hand down on the conference table. "You can't fault me for that. I loved you, and you threw me away."

His eyes were a brilliant red, and he looked close to tears. He moved from the table to pace along the viewport wall, his hands clenched into fists, looking for something more satisfying to smash them against.

"I may have pushed you away, but I never threw you away," Dana argued. "When you left, I was grieving. I didn't have the strength to love you then."

He stopped, looking over at her. "Can you love me now?"

Dana shook her head. "I don't know."

She was still too hot. She wanted her clothes off. Dana

slipped out of her uniform until she was standing in her underwear and a white tank-top. Wade did the same, and she hated herself for watching him, but her eyes refused to look away. Maggie had stripped out of her robe a long time ago. She, of course, had matching undergarments in mauve with lace in places that Dana thought would itch.

Wade lay on the table on his side of the force-field, and Dana settled onto the floor.

"Being on my own hasn't been all bad," Dana said.

"You and me together would be better," Wade muttered. "If you hadn't put up another wall between us, I would have shown you that."

Maggie sprawled out on the floor behind her force-field and spoke to the ceiling. "He would have. I mean, he convinced me I could do better than Bill. Wade's amazing."

Dana huffed. "I'm not going to be your rebound after Maggie. Find someone else to test out your real feelings."

"Aren't you at least going to give us a second chance?" he asked.

"You're still in love with Maggie!" Dana shouted.

"You are?" Maggie asked, turning her head to one side, desire in her eyes.

Wade ran a rough hand through his hair, ignoring her. "She betrayed me. I won't go crawling back to her."

"You said the same thing about me once," Dana said.

"So . . . is that a no?" Wade asked.

"She didn't say no," Maggie said, kicking a bare foot against the force-field wall she shared with Dana.

"It wasn't a yes, either," Dana said. An alarm interrupted their conversation. Dana blinked as she looked up at the comms system then frowned. "What is that?"

"It feels like our ship is falling out of the sky," Wade said. Then turned to glare at Dana. "What did you do?"

CHAPTER 9

EARTHA

Ari returned after speaking with the captain, and Eartha wanted to squeal in relief. Several of the people on the floor were waking up. The Fashin Teku were spinning within their force-fields, as if preparing to pounce on anyone who looked at them sideways.

"I have to take control of the ship," Ari told her. "If I do not, we cannot maintain course. I am also still working on an antidote. I admit, I may not be able to do both with efficiency."

Then he stopped. His head tilted to one side, as if he were processing information.

"The ship has come to a halt. Our stabilizers are misaligned," Ari said, more to himself than to Eartha, who didn't understand a word of what he was saying. "Computer, lock out all temperature controls and signal a red alert."

"What's wrong?" Eartha asked.

Ari held up a finger as the computer answered.

"You do not have the authority to lock out all temperature controls or signal a red alert."

"Who has the authority?"

"The ship's commander and chief of security can signal a red alert. The captain can lock out all temperature controls using the appropriate key code."

Ari's voice modulated until he sounded like Commander Chance, then he spoke the command.

"COMP, signal a red alert."

The lights pulsated red, and Ari picked the people who were waking up from the floor and walked them out of the med-bay. Once they were all out, he picked up an injector and lowered the force-fields so he could grab the female Fashin Teku. He shot something into her neck, then the dark one, Oli, went down. When Ari reached for Ashwin, the alien grabbed him by the arm.

"Wait! There's something I need to give you."

He whispered something that only Ari could hear. Ari nodded, then put the device to his neck, and Ashwin dropped to the floor next to the others. Eartha must have let out an audible gasp, because Ari turned toward her. His voice was soft and even when he spoke.

"It is all right. They are only asleep."

He lifted each of them and brought them into a section

of the med-bay lined with metal boxes. Ari pulled out three. They looked like small metal drawers. He placed one Fashin Teku in each, and then locked the doors. Eartha heard the hiss of something like air escaping.

"How will they breathe in there?" Eartha asked, pointing to the drawers.

"I have activated the cryostasis oxygen pump. It will not freeze them. However, they will sleep and breathe with ease inside. I locked the doors in case they try to get out. They should remain hidden. I do not believe anyone will look for them here."

Eartha shivered. She couldn't imagine waking up locked inside a metal box.

Ari gathered his samples and put them into a small tray where the tubes could stand up. From the sample of her blood, he created a vile of purple liquid, then held it up.

"We need another subject to test it on," Ari said, studying the doors. "I will be right back."

"Wait, don't leave me here!" Eartha said, glancing around the empty room and then to the three locked drawers.

"I need to find the Captain. I will return. There is no need for you to be afraid. Stay here where it's safe."

"*Here*? You've got to be kidding. There's no way I'm staying here. This place is wrecked." Eartha gestured to the room around them in shambles.

"Eartha, you will be fine here," he insisted shortly. "I need to go now before things get any worse. It is becoming more difficult to keep the entire ship running, particularly with so many of the crew trying to open restricted areas. I promise to return shortly."

Ari turned and left the room, stepping into the corridor, leaving Eartha in front of the drawer where the Fashin Teku slept. The loud thumping eased, and soon there was no sound at the door. Eartha's heart was pounding as she listened to the sound of Ari securing the door again and locking her inside. She wouldn't be able to leave the lab until he returned.

———

Eartha's eyes snapped open at a clanging against the door. *Must have fallen asleep*, she thought as she rubbed at her eyes. She'd been awake now for almost a full nineteen hours, so it was no surprise. Where was Ari? What was taking him so long?

The noise at the door grew louder, and soon she could hear the sound of metal on metal being wrenched apart.

They'd gotten through the doors.

The place under the table where she'd hid would come into clear view once whoever was out there made their way in. The clatter of running feet on broken glass made her cringe closer to the wall.

"Where is he?" a woman asked.

A man with a deeper voice answered. "He comes here sometimes . . . I don't know."

"Who asked you anyway?"

It might have been another woman, but Eartha wasn't sure until she heard the growl of the fight.

"You did!"

"Stop it! No!"

Eartha screamed to get their attention, but in their haze, they neither cared, nor paid any attention to her.

Then at that moment, she felt it. Someone was in the room with her. It was like when the Fashin Teku had been watching the ship, but different. This was someone she couldn't see, watching her and only her. The icy shiver of it made her cry in frustration. It scared her as much as the sight of the adults pummeling each other.

Sleep.

Sleep.

The word was like a demanding whisper in her ear. Ari had used something to put James to sleep so he couldn't hurt her. What if everyone in the room fell asleep? It would end the fighting. The passing thought was an idea, and then it was a desire. Eartha closed her eyes tight and screamed the word in her mind. She imagined them all asleep.

The quiet that passed over the room made her open her eyes. Everyone had fallen to the floor where they'd stood.

Eartha was shaking with nerves and exhaustion. It was as if she'd run a hundred-meter-sprint without stopping. Still gasping for breath, she crawled out of her hiding place and, after two attempts, stood up. The pack still on her back felt like was filled with rocks and she swayed in place. Taking in the room, she noted there had been six people in all, far more than she'd imagined. Now they lay at her feet at odd angles, some face-down in the glass. Eartha swayed when she tried to take a step forward. The energy that it had taken to scream made her dizzy, the fog left in her head making it hard to concentrate. Had she made them all fall down? That wasn't possible . . . it wasn't human.

She put her hands on her knees and slowed her breathing. After feeling steadier, she leaned down and put her hand in front of the face of the nearest person. A woman with olive skin and long, dark hair had fallen face up. Her breath was steady. So they were still alive, just sleeping, just as she'd imagined them. This was new.

Eartha's ability to see things that no one else could wasn't something she'd gotten used to; putting people to sleep seemed even more dangerous. If people knew she'd done it, she would be taken away from the Rogans, and who knew what the doctors on board would do to her. How long had the Fashin Teku been tested on and guarded? They still had guards watching them all the time.

Eartha squeezed her eyes closed and then opened them again. Everyone else in the room lay unconscious except for her. Eartha ran for the door. She needed to get away from the sleeping people. She didn't want to be there when they woke up.

In the corridor, more people were lying on the floor. She strained to listen for the sound of anything, anyone.

"Hello?" she called out.

No one answered.

Then she heard a loud crash in the distance.

Not everyone was asleep.

She stepped over the people in front of her, moving away from the sounds of struggle. If Ari had the antidote, then maybe he'd gone to the bridge to give it to someone there. The captain or one of the others might already be clear of the virus.

After she turned down the next hall, she stopped. Ari was there, standing in the middle of the corridor, the antidote still in his mechanical hand.

"Oh no . . ." she breathed. She quickly moved to his side, grabbing hold of his human-like hand. "Ari, we need to run!"

She tugged harder on his hand, but he didn't move. His head was down on his chest, the tube with the antidote still full in the fingers of his mechanical hand. He'd never made it. She thought of the people she'd had to step over before she got to Ari. Eartha couldn't understand how she'd made him sleep at the same time as the others. He was a machine. She shouldn't have been able to affect him.

"Come on, Ari, wake up! We don't have a lot of time." Eartha snapped her fingers in front of Ari's face. Despite his eyes being open, they were dead. He couldn't see or hear her. "What's wrong with you?"

"He's not going anywhere," a man's voice said from behind her.

Startled, Eartha whirled around and stared up at the man's face. His ruddy complexion and bright red hair seemed familiar. He wore passenger's clothing and on his face were patches of hair, as if he were trying to grow a beard. If she were on Zelenia, she'd have wondered if he was a vago; those who lived off of the land instead of in houses with families.

She checked his blue eyes for any signs of the virus, but they were clear. He wasn't acting violently or anything, and he wasn't carrying a weapon. He stared down at her face, looking at her eyes, too.

"I'm not sick," she said, as if to reassure him. Although it seemed strange that he would seem more afraid of her than she of him. "We need to wake Ari. He's got the cure for the virus and can make more."

"He's not going anywhere. Someone hit him over the head several times. See the wires?"

He pointed to the side of Ari's head furthest from them. Eartha then saw the wires that were falling out on the other side of his head. Someone had hit him with something, breaking open a panel, the blond hair attached to it sticking out at a weird angle.

So she hadn't put him to sleep along with the others. She was relieved, and at the same time sorry that someone had hurt him.

"He's the only one with the cure," Eartha said, her voice a whisper.

The man suddenly grabbed her by the pack and snatched her back into the corner. A mob of people entered the corridor, shouting and screaming. They were fighting among themselves and hadn't yet seen them standing there with Ari.

"Come on." The man kept ahold of one arm as he pulled her along after him. "We've got to go."

Eartha threw her weight the other way, stopping them. "Wait, not yet. We can't leave him."

"He weighs a ton. We can't shift him. Now come on."

"The cure!" Eartha protested. "He's got some in his hand."

The man shook his head. "It's not enough for the entire ship. We should go before someone sees us."

"No! I'm not leaving Ari."

Eartha wiggled out of his grasp and took off, leaving the strange man behind. She tried to grab the vial of liquid, but it wouldn't budge from Ari's tightly gripped fingers. She had to lift each finger one by one to loosen it. They were so tight, she had to use two hands.

The group of people coming their way stopped partway down the hall and started shoving each other.

"Hurry up, kid, or you're on your own," the man said between his teeth.

When she had the vial in her hand at last, she felt the back of her jacket lift. The man pulled her backward and out of sight just before the next group of infected people caught up to her. Distracted by Ari, they pushed him down and hit him with their weapons before continuing on their way.

The man held a finger up to his lips and pointed to a shaft

behind him. Eartha crawled in, and he followed, securing the door behind him. A sudden rush of memories from her first days onboard washed over her. She tucked the vial into her pocket, fearing it might slip out of her sweaty hands.

The noise of the angry crowd echoed back to them, but she kept crawling away from the hatch until she reached a fork. Not sure which direction they should go, she stopped, looking back at him.

"Which way?"

"Up."

Eartha tilted her head up and saw a hatch just above her. It had large yellow and black markings to show it wasn't safe. Her mother had told her to avoid them when she'd been hiding in the ventilation shafts.

As if reading her mind, he added, "I know where we're going. Don't worry."

She climbed the ladder, squeezed through the hole, and then waited for him to follow.

"Start climbing. I've got to close the hatch."

Once the hatch was secured again, the shouting disappeared. Several meters from where they started, the man directed Eartha to take another right down the shaft. She saw a large vestibule open up in front of her and stopped. Unwilling to go any further, she waited until the man inched around her and stepped out into the small room, dominated by a pulsing generator.

"Be careful and stick to the side," he said as he shimmied to the left.

Eartha was trembling and panting by the time she

caught up to him, avoiding looking down at the space below them that seemed to stretch for miles. She gulped down her fear a few times and once again shut her eyes tight. Her hands tightened on the grips when she opened them again, and she saw the man getting further and further ahead. She had to keep moving.

He climbed inside a small hatch above him and waited for her to catch up. He didn't yell at her for taking her time. Instead, he waited without comment for her to reach him, then grasped her trembling hand to help her inside before securing the hatch. Eartha took several minutes to catch her breath before she was able to take in the crawl space. It wasn't as spacious as hers had been, only large enough to kneel inside, though it seemed he was far more comfortable than she'd been.

He had organized his things into neat piles. He had a pack on the floor that might work for a pillow when it wasn't full. The pieces of a comm panel were laying to one side. She wondered if it worked. Maybe they could call the Captain. She was about to ask about it when she spotted the weapon. It was lying there with the other items, but she knew it must still work because it wasn't in pieces.

Eartha took up a position near the hatch as the man gathered his things together into the pack.

That's when it all made sense. The terrorist with the Coalition who'd set off the bombs onboard and killed someone, the one security hadn't been able to find . . . that's why underneath the beard and shaggy hair he seemed so familiar. He'd been hiding here.

"You're the man they're looking for."

He gave her a smirk and a shrug. "Not that it matters anymore, but yes. My name is Peter Barnes. You're the stowaway girl."

She ignored that. "You hurt all those people. You almost killed Esme."

"Look, I was following orders. I understand why no one wants to hear the truth, but they built this ship on a lie." He went back to his pack. "People should know that."

Eartha shook her head. Nothing he could say would make up for almost killing her new mother. Besides, she knew more than he could imagine.

"My mother helped build this ship so that you could be here today."

Peter waved a hand to dismiss her. "You're just a kid. I don't expect you to understand the politics."

Eartha's face got hot as she grew angrier. "A kid only a few years older than me gave you your orders. You mean you had a plan for the end of the world that was better than this one?"

Peter shook his head. "No, I mean I don't expect you to accept the truth. You're from a charmed life. Nothing of the government's corruption has ever touched you."

"So you'd kill us off to make a point? Sounds to me like if you blow up the ship, there won't be anyone around to tell you that you're right."

She must have said something that shocked him, because he gave her another strange look. "What's your name again, kid?"

"Eartha McLaren Singh."

"Oh, right, the designer's kid." He shrugged. "Well, as wise as you sound, you're just like the rest of them. You'd rather not know the truth. I don't have time to school you on all the things the Hierarchy's done wrong—their lack of preparation for another alien invasion being one of them. But just so you know, this isn't the only ship they built, and my people are on all of them." He finished arranging the things in his pack. "Let's get some rest and wait for the Captain to get things back in order."

He situated himself so he was lying almost flat, his arms crossed behind his head over a bag of clothes. She could smell old sweat on them. Eartha thought about what he'd meant when he'd said, 'alien invasion'. Who would want to invade Zelenia, a small planet with fewer humans than there ever were on Blue Earth?

His eyes were closed when she gave him the next bit of bad news.

"The captain can't help us. We're on our own."

He kept his eyes closed as he answered. "She's the only one who can keep the ship flying. If I know Pinet, she's probably on her way back to the planet with the aliens that did this."

"No, I mean the captain is infected. She can't do anything now. Ari was on his way to get the command codes from her so he could fly the ship. There's no one doing anything."

"Who's Ari?"

Eartha scowled at him. "The android we left behind in the corridor."

Peter's eyes flew open, and he sat up, staring at her as if she'd grown another head. "You mean the one with the wires coming out of his head? He's supposed to be running the ship?"

Eartha nodded. "Ari was on his way to test the antidote when he must have been attacked. He never tested it, and he never got the command codes."

Peter ran a hand through his hair. His fingers tapped out a rhythm only he could hear on his chin.

"What now?" Eartha asked.

She had to wait a full minute for the answer.

"We need to find out if the stuff works," Peter said, frowning to himself. "If it does, then we'll need someone who can fix the ARI. I'm not infected, but I don't think the captain would ever give me the command codes. If the serum works, it might not matter."

"What do we do first?"

"I don't know. If the serum doesn't work on the Captain, we'll be worse off and further away from getting help. If we knew where to find Dr. Walker, we could get him to help us fix the ARI, but he could be anywhere."

Peter sighed. Then it came to her. She knew someone who was skilled enough to fix Ari. If given the right materials he could build an android from scratch, and she knew exactly where to find him.

"Wait. My friend Luke, he's a genius. He can fix Ari."

Peter gave her a dubious look. "I thought you said everyone was infected."

"Luke's not infected. He's protected for the moment, but we should hurry." Eartha kneeled, preparing to crawl back out.

Peter shrugged, gathering up his pack. "Fine, let's go get this friend of yours. Is he locked in his quarters or something?"

"Or something," Eartha mumbled.

Peter frowned at her. "What level is he on?"

"The lowest one."

CHAPTER 10

EARTHA

"No way!" Peter waved both hands in front of his face as if he could erase her words. It didn't occur to her until that moment that Peter might be a coward.

"We have to. Without Ari, we can't get control of the ship. Luke is the only one who can fix him who's not infected. We just need to bring Ari to him."

As the words rushed out of her, she could tell this was the right thing to do. She knew, but Peter was a stranger. He didn't know what she and her friends were capable of together. She needed Peter to go along with her plan or they might be in more trouble than they were in now. Peter had saved her, but he didn't seem to want to help anyone else. If only she'd found Mr. Jennison. He'd have understood what they were doing right away.

Convincing Peter to do it was like trying to get Becky to stop wearing lip gloss. She tried everything from pouting to reasoning with him, but nothing worked.

Instead, he insisted on trying to find Ari's designer. They were walking down an empty corridor when he took a left at the junction. Eartha shook her head.

"This is all wrong. The doctor's lab is the other way." Eartha pointed back in the direction of the med-bay.

"I'm not going to the doctor's lab," Peter said. Then he reached back and pushed her behind him. "Just be quiet and stay out of sight."

"You're just wasting time," Eartha huffed, throwing her arms up over her chest and following after him.

"I told you to stay put. Don't you ever listen?" Peter said as he crept along the corridor, looking for more infected people.

"I'm not staying back there by myself. What if something happens to you?"

"I'm touched, you care about me." Peter winked. a smirk on his red-bearded face.

"No, you're probably not going to make it. I'll be standing around longer than I need to before I give up and have to go get Luke and Ari without you." Though, as she said the words, there was a sting in her side that told her it wasn't true.

"Wow, aren't you a ball of sunshine? No wonder your mother left you here." Peter laughed at his own joke.

Eartha's eyes went to slits, and she mumbled to herself, "That's not funny."

When they reached the Commons, Peter left her at the door as he went inside. Pointing a finger in her face, he gave her strict instructions.

"Do not come inside, no matter what. I'm pretty sure whatever is going on in here is something you shouldn't see."

"How will I know if you're coming back?"

"You won't, so wait as long as you like," he said with a shrug as he turned to enter the Commons. Someone must have forced the doors open as Ari expected, because there was just enough for one person to squeeze inside at a time.

Eartha saw glimpses of skin as a man and woman darted past the door. She averted her eyes to the floor, resting her back against the wall. She wasn't sure she wanted to see what was going on in there either.

A few moments later, Peter returned, shaking his head.

"Well?" Eartha asked, her arms crossed over her chest.

"I didn't find the doctor. I tried to get out of there as fast as I could, but someone touched me."

Eartha took a sharp step back. "You're infected."

"Yes, but I've got a little time left before I go truthsayer on you."

"What?"

"Nothing, it's an old expression. Just stay back from me. One of us needs to stay clear."

"I don't think I can get it."

"Really?" Peter asked looking her over thoughtfully,

then shrugged. "Well, it doesn't matter, I'd rather not risk it—"

His words were cut off when the ship rocked to one side, knocking them both against the walls.

Peter picked up a communicator and spoke into the device.

"Computer, what was that?"

"The ship has encountered an asteroid belt. A course correction is required to avoid complete shield failure."

Another hit followed, knocking them in the opposite direction.

"Now are you ready to get Ari?" Eartha snapped.

"Man, you've got a smart mouth, kid. Fine, let's get your mechanical buddy."

"We have to hurry!" Eartha had to yell over the blaring of the alerts as she ran ahead of him and back to where Ari had been.

"Wait, slow down!" Peter called out from behind her.

When the ship rocked again, she stumbled, and Peter reached out to catch her. She crawled away from him before he could touch her. He nodded, lifting his hands in the air.

"Slow down. There's no one driving this ship." He lifted the communicator to his face again. "Computer, what is the condition of our shields?"

"Shields are at seventy-five percent."

"Let's move." Peter darted off to the left and Eartha stopped.

"You're going the wrong way. Ari is this way."

Peter stopped and nodded.

She led the way back to where they'd left Ari. There was no one in the corridor this time and Ari was lying prone on the floor. She glanced around, listening for any activity, but the group of people that had been crowding the halls had moved on. As they drew closer, she got a better look at him. She gasped. Ari's mechanical wiring had been pulled out and cut. The side of his face was dented. She could see a split on his forehead where someone had hit him with something that had pierced his synthetic skin enough for it to peel away from the metal structure beneath.

"What did they do to you?" Eartha whispered under her breath as she tilted his head to one side, exposing more loose wires.

"You want to carry that thing to the brig? Now I know you're crazy."

Eartha huffed. Why was Peter he being so frustrating? Didn't he want to get control of the ship?

"It's the only way. We'll bring him to the brig, and Luke can tell us what to do. Unless you have a better idea."

"I have about ten better ideas, but they won't do you any good," Peter grumbled to himself.

Peter tried to lift Ari by the arm, but it disconnected from the rest of his frame. It must not have been secure anymore. Then Peter tried to come at him from the other side, lifting Ari from the middle. Peter strained until his face went red and he looked ready to pop. Ari was too heavy for him. Eartha tried to lift Ari's legs to help, but she only put them both off balance and Ari went down on top of Peter.

"Oof!" Peter fought to push Ari off of his chest. Eartha had to get on the floor and brace herself against the wall, using her feet to help turn Ari over. She had no idea he weighed so much.

"Look, this is ridiculous. I can't carry that heavy thing to the brig. There has to be another way." Peter kicked Ari's side and Eartha slid away from him, watching his behavior for signs of the virus. He held out his hand to her. "You could give me the sample, and that way we can see if it works."

Her voice sounded small as she spoke. "No, I'm not going to give it to you unless there's no one else."

"Look around, sweetheart. There isn't anyone else."

"Ari is still our best chance at a cure," she argued. "We need to keep this sample so he can replicate it. He can fix the ship, I'm sure of it, and the virus can't hurt him."

"I'm looking at evidence to the exact contrary." Peter's voice was too loud. He must have seen the worry on her face because he ran a hand over his beard and smiled. "I'm fine. Computer, what is our current shield condition?"

"Shields are at fifty percent."

Eartha stared down at her friend's feet, wondering what to do. Without Luke's help, they couldn't turn Ari back on. Without Ari, the ship was in danger of everything it passed in space. The ship rocked as if to confirm that itself. Then there was the cure. She didn't want to give their only sample to Peter, but if he started to turn, she wondered if giving it to him would be better than being alone.

Eartha heard angry voices coming from the other corridor. Peter looked up, and then down at Ari, a strange smile on his face.

He reached down with two hands and disconnected Ari's whole head from his body.

"What are you doing?" Eartha yelled.

"Keep your voice down," he hissed. "This is the only part of the thing we need to get working. Let's go."

Peter tucked Ari's head under his arm and dove back into the shaft, not waiting for Eartha to follow. She scrambled inside and secured the grate. The voices of the crowd carried throughout the ducts, making it hard to figure out where they were coming from. It didn't matter now, though. None of the infected had ventured into the ventilation shafts yet, and they were finally on their way to Luke.

Peter led the way and Eartha followed, trying to ignore the blank look on Ari's dented face as Peter dragged him along. When they reached the lower levels, she could hear crowds of people yelling outside the brig, banging on the doors and shouting. Eartha thought they seemed ready to hurt each other as much as whoever was coming through the door.

Peter stopped crawling two meters ahead of her.

"What's wrong?" she asked.

"We're here. But there's no way to get around the

crowd. They're out for blood. If they see me, they'll beat the sou out of me."

Eartha looked at Ari's disconnected head, and then back toward the sound of the mob outside.

Sleep.

The familiar voice called out to her again. She knew what to do but wasn't sure she had the strength to do it. The last time she'd been left so tired she'd had to crawl out of the med-lab. And this wasn't a secret she was ready to share with anyone, especially not Peter—a known Coalition terrorist who had escaped the brig.

"We're not going to make it through. Let's head back," Peter said, already turning down another shaft and preparing to leave her behind. When the ship rocked again, Eartha knew she had to act. She lifted the shaft's hatch and moved it to one side. The crowd below hadn't noticed her, too busy trying to figure out how to get through the brig's door. She'd have to drop in behind them. Preparing to climb down, Peter caught her by the sleeve, careful not to touch her skin.

"Wait, what are you doing?"

"It's okay. I'll get rid of them."

"No, you can't, you little idiot," he hissed. "You could get infected."

Eartha shook her head. "No, I don't think so. Ari was using my blood to make the antidote. Otherwise, I'd already be infected by now."

Peter's eyes grew wide, and he let go of her sleeve and

backed up a couple of inches. She didn't know if it was awe or fear in his eyes, but there wasn't time to figure it out.

She climbed down. The crowd was in front of her, jostling back and forth to get at the door of the brig. Eartha had to focus not to listen to their angry shouts. She stood behind them as they continued to yell and beat on the door, her mind shutting out the sounds around her as she turned her thoughts inward.

Sleep.

Yes, I know, she said to the voice in her mind.

Then before anyone noticed what she was doing, she closed her eyes. Eartha raised her left hand, reaching out in front of her as she focused on the mob and envisioned them all going to sleep.

At first, nothing happened. The shouting was a dull roar in her mind.

And then, silence.

Eartha fell to the floor, vaguely wondering if she'd just tried to put herself to sleep. It wasn't until Peter was crouched down beside her that she knew it had worked.

"What did you do to them?"

Eartha's head ached and her muscles felt like jelly. "I don't know. I just wanted them to sleep."

Peter didn't help her get up, but turned to the brig's door, moving people off to one side so there was a clear path to the panel.

"Well, it worked, because they're out. The question is, for how long?"

He dropped Ari's head and his pack to the floor. Then

he reached inside the bag and pulled out a tool he used to force the panel open.

"I don't know." Eartha had to form the words around the cotton in her mouth.

"Then I guess we'd better get moving again before they wake up." He looked sideways at her. "By the way, I wouldn't tell anyone what you can do. They've thrown people out of the airlock for less."

Eartha's skin buzzed in the aftermath of what she'd done. She lifted a hand to her head to ground herself again and clear the fog. *Tell anyone?* No, she hadn't told anyone about this. She didn't even know what *this* was.

"Don't worry about me," he added. "You don't tell anyone where I've been hiding, and I won't tell anyone about your sleeping trick."

Peter had the door open a moment later, and she glanced up to see Luke standing at the duroglass. She saw the worry on his face as she stood up on shaky legs, but there wasn't any time to explain. Peter was already lifting his pack and Ari's head.

"Come on, kid, double-time," he told her as he passed.

Eartha caught up to him and walked straight to where Luke was standing.

"What are you doing here?" he asked from the other side of the duroglass. "You just opened the door like it was nothing. There was a mob outside, where did they go?"

"I came back for you," Eartha said, then dropped her eyes to the floor when she realized how silly it sounded.

She was trying to think of a way to rephrase it when Luke continued.

"I thought— I mean, after James grabbed you . . . I thought you'd be sick."

Eartha lifted a shoulder. She couldn't explain it the way Ari had, so she didn't bother trying. She was glad James wasn't here again. He hadn't even been in the crowd outside.

At that moment, Peter strolled over and plopped Ari's head down between her feet and the duroglass before he moved to the guard's control console.

"Are you sure about this?" Peter asked. "Once I get this panel fixed and open the doors, there's no closing them again. Someone will eventually infect them."

Eartha nodded. "I'm sure. Do it."

The others in the room weren't so agreeable to the plan.

"No, they'll kill us!" the woman protested. "Don't leave us without any way to defend ourselves, Barnes."

"What are you doing with him?" Luke asked her, his anger seething behind the protective barrier.

"It's okay. He's helping me. We need your help with him." She nodded toward Ari's detached head, and with some horror, she noted he was facing her, and she had to look away before she got queasy again.

Eartha knew she could trust Luke with her life. Even though he was three years older, he'd been more of a friend to her than anyone else in school. Besides, he was a genius, and he never talked down to her or made her feel like she would never understand anything.

Though, he'd told his brother he still thought of her as a kid. But maybe he was just saying that to convince him to let her go.

The cell doors opened, setting the three criminals free. Luke knelt

in front of her while she turned, watching the others with Peter.

"Where do we go?" the woman asked, wringing her hands and staring at the door.

"If I were in your shoes—which, by the way, I am," Peter said, "I'd find a tidy place to hide or risk being killed. The virus infecting the ship is more than a truth serum. It's brutal. You won't survive out here if a mob finds you."

"Can you lock us back in?" the woman asked.

"It won't do any good. Like the door, once the panels are off, it wouldn't take a trained monkey long to figure them out again. Run and hide yourselves."

"I should hate you, but thank you," the man said, slapping Peter on the back then darting out the door.

The woman was slower, but she gradually slipped out, too.

"Maybe I should—" Eartha turned back to speak to Luke, but he was already working.

"No, I've got it. I just need some smaller tools. I could rewire his central processing unit and maybe get him talking."

"Peter," Eartha asked, "can Luke borrow your tools?"

Peter pulled out a small box and passed it to Luke, a smile spreading over his face when he saw what was inside.

"If we can get the head working, we might have a chance of saving the ship before we lose our shielding. Can you work any faster, kid?" Peter asked Luke.

Luke glared at him. "We wouldn't be in here if it wasn't for you."

"You can thank me later."

"Thank you?"

Peter shrugged. "Hey, if you were out already, you'd be infected with the virus and probably be dead by now."

Luke scowled, looking back down at Ari's head. "Eartha, come here and hold these wires to one side so I can work."

Eartha moved so she was able to hold the wires. As Luke worked, his head bent over Ari's, she was close enough to see the small, diamond-shaped birthmark at the base of his neck when his hair parted.

"Better hurry," Peter prompted him. "I don't know what you're doing, but we've still got to get to the bridge yet, and those angry folks outside could wake up any second."

"If you'd stop pestering me so I can think," Luke snapped. Then in a softer tone he spoke to Eartha. "No, not that one. Hold the end of the light green one and leave the dark green one. Okay, now take this dark blue one and attach it to the light blue one there while I work on the red and pink."

When the connection sparked, Eartha dropped her hands.

"Careful," he warned. "Now there should be some kind of reset. Feel around and see if you can find it."

Eartha felt strange touching Ari's head and face. Her hand grazed his eyes, and she jerked it back. Luke shifted so he could look at her face. He must have seen her fear, because he lowered his voice to a whisper.

"It's okay. The reset should be around the ears or the base of his head just under my arms." His smile was filled with warmth and understanding.

"Computer, shield strength?" Peter asked.

"Shields are at fifteen percent. Hull breach on decks six through eight imminent."

Eartha didn't find the button until she put her finger inside of Ari's right ear. Inside, there was something hard, and she pressed it. Nothing happened.

"I feel something," she said. "It's small and hard, but when I press it, nothing happens."

"Try a press and hold for two seconds before you let go."

Eartha did so. Ari's eyes flew open, and she yelped.

"Eartha. Luke. Peter Barnes," he greeted them calmy. "What am I doing on the floor, and where is the rest of my body?"

"You met with a bit of an accident," Peter explained. "We saved your head because we need your help to take over the ship."

Ari's eyes swiveled to look at him. "You are a known CAH criminal. I cannot be of any assistance to you."

"It's okay, Ari. He's helping us save the ship. You're the only one with the codes, and the ship is about to break apart because of the asteroids," Eartha said in a rush.

"I believe we will arrive at the planet of the Begarans soon. Take me to the bridge." He looked at Eartha. "Do you have the antidote I made?"

"Yes," Eartha said, holding it up.

"Good. Then I have an idea."

Peter started down the corridor, muttering, "Great, everyone is full of ideas."

"Wait, where are you going?" Eartha asked him.

Peter didn't turn around as he scanned the corridor. One of the bodies on the floor near his feet shifted, and he leaped back.

"Are you sure about him, Eartha?" Ari asked softly.

She shrugged. Peter was the last person anyone else on the ship would trust, but he'd taken care of her until now. "We don't have time to worry about it." She shifted her attention. "Peter, I need to get Ari to the bridge."

"Fine, take the boy with you," he told her. "I'm already infected. I'll hold these people off. Just hurry."

"You can come with us."

He shrugged. "No, the tin man is right. I'm a criminal. Now go."

"Don't let them kill you," Eartha said, and meant it.

"Sure, kid. I've got this. Just go!"

CHAPTER 11

EARTHA

Eartha and Luke, carrying Ari's head, were almost to the lift leading to the bridge when a man stumbled out of a corridor and bumped into Luke. Eartha felt something like a kick in her chest, realizing what it meant, and stared back at Luke's wide eyes. The infected man marched on without stopping, but the damage was already done. He had infected Luke, which meant he didn't have much time.

Once they were inside the lift, Luke stepped to one side as far from Eartha as he could manage in the small space. She wanted to say something to Luke to reassure him.

"Luke, it will be all right," she told him, and when she didn't get the gut-wrenching pain that came with a lie, she knew it was true, and smiled.

He frowned and turned away from her. "You don't know that. It doesn't matter. Let's just get this done so we can save everybody."

When they reached the bridge level, they found it locked. Someone had secured the bridge, which, according to Ari, was a good thing.

"They were prepared in case those infected made their way up here," Ari explained. "We will have to bypass the controls and the authorization."

Luke shrugged. "I don't have any tools. I left them with Barnes."

They'd come so far. If they didn't get on the bridge, they might lose the ship.

"I have an idea. Give me a moment," Ari started. "Computer, the bridge is currently sealed under what authority level?"

"The bridge is level one secured. Captain Dana Pinet authorization code required."

The ship rocked violently, and both Luke and Eartha fell to the floor, Ari's head rolling and ending up facedown.

"We need to adjust our course to reach our objective," Ari continued, his voice muffled. Luke lifted him again, and he spoke to the lift. "Deck nine."

They exited one floor down, where they spilled out into an empty corridor as the ship careened to the left.

"The ship is out of control! How are we going to get to the bridge?" Luke called out.

"I suggest we employ Eartha's method and see if we

can get to the captain," Ari supplied. "She has an excellent way of getting around the ship."

"I do?" Eartha asked.

"Yes, the ventilation shaft. It is small enough for all three of us now, and there is a ventilation unit between the bridge and the office of the captain."

Eartha frowned. "But I don't know how to get there."

"Do not worry, I know the way. Just point my head in the right direction, and I will guide you."

The three didn't waste any time in the shafts leading to the bridge. Eartha was quick, despite the constant tilting of the ship. They eventually slid into a grate facing the bridge.

"What do you see?" Ari asked.

"It's like we thought," Luke told him. "There's no one in there."

"That means that the Captain cannot be far. Turn left here and proceed to the next grate."

Eartha did as he asked until she could see the captain's office below her.

"There are three people in there," she said.

"Do you see the captain?" Ari asked.

Eartha tilted her head to one side, and then the other. "Yes. But there's some kind of barrier between them. They're fighting," she said. Eartha wasn't sure why she felt the need to say it, as the others could certainly hear them.

"Can you see if we are within the boundaries of the barriers?"

Eartha focused on the three corners of the room and

shook her head. "No, I think if we climb down, we'll be sort of in the middle."

"That will have to do. Go ahead and climb down."

"They're infected," Luke needlessly reminded them. "We don't want to get too close to them." He placed Ari's head down and prepared to help Eartha through the grate, then must have realized he was infected with the virus and pulled back. Eartha didn't have time to explain to him that he couldn't get her sick.

"That is the plan, but we must hurry," Ari insisted. "This asteroid field has damaged some of our critical systems. If we do not change our heading soon, the ship will be beyond repair."

Eartha was the first through the grate. Once her feet landed on the floor, she looked up and held out her arms for Ari's head.

The three adults in the room turned their attention on her, and she had to focus to tune them out or risk putting them to sleep. Barnes had warned her that things could be much worse for her if she told anyone else about her newly discovered talent.

Luke dropped Ari's head down to her. It fell through her hands and to the floor rolling until it was facing one of the barriers. The woman inside dressed in her underwear screamed. Eartha shuffled over to grab him as Luke jumped through the grate last. Once she had Ari's heavy head in her hands, he spoke to her.

"I need to face the captain."

Eartha grunted as she hauled him over to the barrier where Captain Pinet was pacing like a caged animal.

"This is an absolute disaster," she mumbled to herself.

"Captain," Ari said to her, "I'm going to get you out of there, but I need your authorization codes."

She shook her head. "Fool! Don't you think if all it took were my authorization codes, I'd be out of here already and killing that gutter trash over there?"

She tilted her head referring to the other woman. It was Maggie Brooker, the reporter, and she was in the daintiest underwear Eartha had ever seen. Though it showed more than it covered, it was still beautiful.

"Who are you calling gutter trash?" Maggie Brooker shot back, her chin lifted in the air, looking down her nose at the captain. "You wouldn't know fashion if it hit you over the head and took your man!"

The captain flew at the side of the barrier closest to her. Maggie Brooker did the same, but nothing came of it, as they were each stuck behind the glowing red barrier of the force-fields.

"Captain," Ari pressed on, "what is the level of authorization needed to open the barrier?"

"I used my authorization and the voice authorization of Dr. Jabar because I figured he'd have a cure by now." She scoffed. "I clearly overestimated his abilities."

"You have a habit of doing that," the Commander said with a snicker from behind them.

Eartha whirled around to see him lying on the table, half-dressed and smirking. It seemed he'd sweat through his clothes, as the two women had. Her eyes flew to Luke, and she saw beads of sweat forming on his brow as well. He was also infected, and he didn't have much time.

"Eartha, please focus," Ari said. He was still in her hands, and she'd forgotten, turning away from the Captain to look at Luke.

"Captain, please listen," Ari continued when he'd been turned her way again. "I am capable of synthesizing my voice to match that of Dr. Jabar's, but you still need to give your authorization code to clear the barrier."

"Finally," the Commander said. "I need to get out of here. There's a time to be alone, and there's a time to be with the person you love." He stared at the Captain like a cat ready to pounce.

Eartha caught the burning hatred on the face of his fiancé. Maybe they'd broken up already. She'd been right about him watching the captain. He still liked her. Then she glanced over at Luke again. Eartha wondered if when the virus infected him, he would profess his true feelings for her. She couldn't help but imagine it . . .

"Eartha, if you please?" Ari said, breaking into her thoughts.

She looked down and realized she'd lowered Ari's head. He was so heavy.

"Here, I'll take him for a bit," Luke offered, reaching over and holding Ari's head up toward the captain.

"Are you ready, Captain?" Ari asked.

"Of course I'm ready," Captain Pinet barked. "Don't

patronize me. I don't like people speaking down to me as if I only got this commission for my ovaries."

"Yes, ma'am."

"And don't call me ma'am, or you'll be in the recycler before you can say, 'Please don't put me in the recycler, ma'am.'"

"Yes, Captain."

"Computer, release the force-field that encloses the corner of the office," Captain Pinet demanded.

"Command authorization required," the COMP responded.

"Command authorization Charlie 2-0-9-4-0-3-4-5-9 Romeo Zulu Tango."

"Dr. Jabar voice authorization, required to confirm."

Ari spoke, doing a perfect imitation of the doctor's voice and tone. "This is Dr. Jabar."

"Voice authorization confirmed."

The field released the Captain, and she stood in front of them half-dressed, looking from left to right as if she wasn't sure who she wanted to fight first. The ship pitched back and forth as they hit something again.

"Why is the ship rocking so much?" The Captain glared at Eartha and Luke as if they were personally responsible for ruining the ship. "What the *sou* is going on?"

"Captain, we have a virus antidote for you to try." Ari spoke loud enough to get Eartha's attention.

She had been so caught up in their conversation that

she'd forgotten she had the vial in her pocket. "Here it is," she said, pulling it out.

"You want me to drink that?" Captain Pinet asked, shaking her head and backing away.

"An injection would be faster, if you have access to one," Ari replied.

"Dana!" the Commander called out from behind them. "Don't do this. Don't run from your feelings!"

"My feelings want to punch you in the face," the Captain said.

"You love me! Stop being stubborn and just admit it."

"She loves you. It's so obvious," Maggie Brooker said from her side of the room.

"What do you know of love when you're juggling *two* men?" the Captain spat at her.

Maggie Brooker gasped, taking a step back as if the captain had struck her.

"Captain, please focus," Ari cut in. "Where is the injector?"

"There's one on the bridge in the emergency kit behind the captain's chair on the panel along the floor."

The Captain led them through the doors to the bridge, and they followed her inside. Eartha's mouth fell open at the sight of the command deck. She'd seen pictures, but they didn't do the space justice. It was much larger than she'd imagined, and the captain's seat was in the middle of the room, the most gorgeous view of the stars laid out before it.

"Eartha," Ari said, "we need you to get the injector."

That's when she realized she'd been staring out the window. The Captain had sat down in the chair and was fanning herself as if she were on fire. Eartha went to the panel as instructed and pulled out the emergency kit while the captain stared out the window.

"Why are we in the middle of an asteroid field?"

"Everyone on the ship has contracted the virus, Captain," Ari explained calmly. "Please hold still while Eartha injects you with the serum."

"*Me*?" Eartha asked. The last thing she wanted to do was get too close to the Captain in this state. She looked ready to hit someone.

"Luke is holding my head, and I have no arms or legs. Besides that, you are immune. Please hurry."

Eartha's hands shook as she pressed the vial into the chamber of the injector, and then held it out for the captain.

She snatched it out of Eartha's hand and held it to her own neck. She flinched, but it was quick.

"Well, that wasn't so bad. But I don't think—"

The transformation was quicker than Eartha imagined. The Captain looked down at the injector in her hand. She looked ready to cry. Instead, she groaned, rubbing her eyes like she was waking up from a nap. Then the Captain's eyes focused on Eartha's face. The red had disappeared, and she shivered with cold, looking down at her own unclothed body. Then she glanced over and saw Luke holding Ari's head and her eyes widened in shock, then narrowed to slits.

"What the *sou* am I doing here in my underwear?"

CHAPTER 12

A month on our new home, and we've discovered a mysterious pink apple-like fruit that is sweet like candy to taste. Unfortunately, we've lost two of our crew before we realized its effects. The sweet nectar has an addictive quality which keeps you eating to excess. After you've sickened yourself on the fruit, the body is overly poisoned, which slows the breathing until death. Our scientists have found a cure. We've warned our people to avoid the fruit in its concentrated form. We call the pink apple a fruzsi.
-Captain Robert Lethbridge
Log Entry 4122.1.5

I
t was in that embarrassing moment between looking for her pants and avoiding Wade's lust-filled stare that it all came back to her—every single declaration, curse, and fight between the three of them. How

could she make command decisions standing in her underwear in front of a couple of kids and a robot head?

She'd dashed back into her office to retrieve her abandoned uniform. Dana had to ignore the vile words spewing from Maggie and the heart-wrenching proclamations of undying love from Wade as she snatched up her clothes. Without sparing either of them a word or a glance, she donned her clothing to a modest, if not professional, style, and returned to the bridge, where the others were waiting.

Still fastening her clothing, she moved to sit down at the helm. Priority one was getting their ship out of harm's way. She corrected their trajectory, steering them out of the asteroid field, and started in on figuring out how much damage they'd sustained.

"Computer, where are my shields?"

"The shields suffered a complete failure event at zero three hundred and fifteen RST."

"Okay, let's see if we can avoid hitting any space dust in the meantime." Dana held her head with one hand before getting up and moving to the command chair. "Divert any and all non-essential power to engines and shields."

"Please specify."

"Do I have to do everything?" she grumbled.

"Unable to respond. Please repeat your request."

"Oh, shut it!" She slammed a hand against the console and looked to the ARI. "I can't get this ship repaired without a crew. If you've got a cure, how come you haven't dispensed it to everyone?"

"I did not know if the vaccine would be successful," the

ARI explained. "I am still not satisfied it is a cure. It may wear off."

Dana rubbed a finger and thumb against her temples.

"Other than a blazing headache, I don't think there are any side effects. I need my infected crew to take whatever you've got for a cure as soon as possible."

"Yes, Captain. There is also the current problem of my head being detached from my body. I have no way to make anymore."

Dana looked from the ARI to the boy holding the ARI's head, staring at her in awe. She recognized him . . . Luke Geyer, the kid closest to the Coalition leader. The one who knew about the other three ark ships that may have made it off of Zelenia along with the *Hope*. He, and the others who had had no direct involvement in the sabotage of the ship, had been sent to the brig until they could track down Barnes. She also vaguely remembered sending the Fashin Teku there as well.

"How did you get out of the brig?" Dana asked him.

"Peter Barnes and I broke him out so he could save Ari," Eartha said, her voice matter-of-fact.

Dana leaped up from the helm to look down at them. "You've seen Barnes?"

Eartha nodded. "He and I were the only ones other than Ari who weren't infected. But that was until someone touched him. He's infected now, like everyone else." She gave the boy at her side, Luke, a pitying glance.

Dana noted the red starting to creep into his eyes and the way he fidgeted with the ARI in his hands. He was showing signs of infection already. He was young, so it would take him half the time to be as useless as the rest of the crew. But they had all seen Barnes, which meant he had found a place to hide. And as he'd managed not to get the virus before exposure, it put him hiding some place where he wasn't in contact with anyone else.

Dana was glad no one was hiding him. That would have complicated matters. But she'd have to deal with him later.

That left Eartha.

"And you're immune?" she asked.

The girl glanced at the ARI before she answered, "Yes, I guess."

The Ari spoke up, his disembodied head still rather unsettling. Rather than make eye-contact, Dana examined the ship's systems as it spoke. "A blood sample revealed she has a special antibody that, when isolated, serves to provide a potential for a vaccine when injected. However, I could only make up a few variations. This one was the most likely to succeed. I am happy to report that I was right. The bad news is that there are not any more vials of the vaccine, and you are the only test subject. We will not know for sure if it works until you have been exposed to the virus again."

"Yeah, I caught that," Dana grumbled. "Well, if you have the genius-kid with you, can you manage to get your body back and make more serum?"

"The likelihood of success is one in—"

Dana waved a hand in front of his face. "If there's no

other way to get the serum, this is our only option. Bring Goo-Goo eyes with you and get going."

Luke's head snapped away from her face and dropped to the floor. She saw a flash of anger there before it subsided. His cheeks and neck, however, bore a flush of red where his emotions couldn't hide.

"I suspect that would be best," the ARI answered, his eyes rolling upward.

The ARI directed the young man off the bridge, and as they left, Eartha called out after them, though Dana was sure it was more for the boy than for the android.

"See you later."

There was something in the boy's eyes when he turned back. If the ARI hadn't made a show of clearing his non-existent throat, he'd have stood there staring back at Dana.

By the Majestic!

She glanced back at Eartha and saw the disappointment and longing in her eyes. The girl had a major crush on the sixteen-year-old, but like most boys his age, he would be oblivious until she got a bit older. Eartha's baby face and wild hair might not turn heads yet, but Dana recognized the signs of natural beauty. The girl was going to grow up to be a stunner. The Rogans were going to have their hands full with her.

"That leaves you and me," Dana said, pointing to the helm. "I want you to sit here."

Eartha nodded before sliding into the chair. Dana pointed to the console.

"Keep your fingers on these two buttons. When we

need a course correction to the left, you push this one. When we need to go right, the other. Do you understand?" Dana crossed her arms and stared down at her, looking for signs of doubt or confusion.

The girl's eyebrows drew together. "I think so. But how do I know when I need to correct our course?"

"I'll tell you. For now, I need to figure out what we can do to begin repairs on the ship from here. Without the help of your parents, we're stuck doing everything from here, which means we're in a bit of trouble." Dana shrugged. "But I suspect now that I have the vaccine, there's a chance we'll at least live to see the planet we're trying to reach."

"The planet of aliens who stole the babies." It wasn't a question, and by the tight way she held her mouth, Dana could see it bothered this child as much as it bothered her.

"That's right." Dana checked the console readout. "Course correction to the right four degrees."

Eartha stared at the console a moment before she pushed the button and adjusted the heading.

"Exactly," Dana said. "Well done. You'll make a fine pilot."

"I've never flown anything before."

"Well, you're flying this ship right now."

"I am?" Eartha's face lit up with joy, her eyes almost disappearing above her round cheeks.

Dana remembered her first time flying with her father. She'd had to sit on his lap just to reach the controls. He hadn't been there for her first steps, as her mother had always been quick to point out, but he had been there for her first flight. To Dana, that meant so much more.

"Get used to it. You're going to have to pull your weight around here. You won't be in school forever, and eventually you need to find your place on board as a member of the crew."

The girl nodded resolutely. "I'll do whatever I can to help."

"I know. I got your proposal for the food dispensers. Very impressive," Dana said as she returned to the captain's chair. She needed to check the rest of the ship's systems.

"That wasn't all me. Luke helped me with the calculations and the design. He's so smart," Eartha said with a far-off look on her face.

Behind her back, Dana smiled. "Yes, I got that."

Was she ever that obvious when it came to boys? She thought back to barely an hour ago, when she'd been under the effects of the virus with Wade and Maggie. She'd made a proper fool of herself, and the shame of it still reached her as she entered their current situation into the ship's computer log.

"So, you and Barnes were working together to save everyone?" Dana asked.

Eartha turned in her chair to look at her, both of her toes unable to keep contact with the floor. "Yes. When I realized Ari was in trouble, I grabbed the vial he had, but Peter wouldn't believe me at first. He didn't think we needed Ari or Luke."

"What was he going to do?"

"I think he was just going to hide."

Dana wondered then if the girl had seen Barnes' hide-out. If she knew where he'd been hiding, he wouldn't be able to go back. He'd finally answer for his crimes onboard her ship.

"Where?"

Eartha's eyes met hers, and then she shrugged, looking away. "I don't know."

"You didn't see where he's been hiding all this time?" Dana pressed.

Eartha lifted one shoulder this time but didn't answer.

"I see."

Eartha wouldn't tell her about his hiding place. Perhaps it was out of some misplaced loyalty because he'd saved her. Dana wondered if the girl even understood what he'd done.

"Barnes is Coalition. You know that he's dangerous to our people and the ship."

Eartha was about to speak, but then her mouth clamped closed.

"He killed someone," Dana said, waiting for the words to sink in. "He destroyed our cryostasis pods and tried to cripple the ship."

"No." Eartha shook her head.

It surprised Dana to hear this girl coming to Barnes' defense, but denial wasn't something they could afford. She didn't trust Barnes, and it would be a mistake for him to convince people he wasn't a criminal. Her original thought that someone might hide him returned, and the dread was like a heavy cloak over her shoulders.

"Yes. He ruined our chance of finding a new planet. We wouldn't be here now if it weren't for him destroying those pods."

Eartha shook her head again, looking Dana in the eye. "He didn't destroy the cryo-pods. I know because I was there. I saw who did it."

Dana remembered Shu. "You mean you saw Ensign Shu destroying the pods? As I was saying, they were working together, so it's the same thing."

Eartha looked confused. "The man from Maggie Brooker's Broadcast? No, it wasn't him I saw."

Dana wondered if it was one of the others that had gone free, or perhaps it was Luke after all. She moved from the helm and knelt in front of the girl. Her answer might change the ruling for one of them, and she needed to know who.

"Who did you see destroying the pods?"

Eartha's face scrunched up in thought.

"Can you describe them?" Dana pressed.

"I was in the ventilation shaft. My mom told me to go to my pod if I didn't feel safe. When the bomb went off, I was scared. I crawled all the way to the cargo bay where my mom hid my pod behind some crates. Before I could climb down, I saw a man with dark hair wearing a blue and yellow uniform like yours pacing around the room. I was waiting for him to leave, but then the explosions started again, and I had to hurry back to where I was hiding to avoid the smoke."

Shu wouldn't have had time to get to the cargo bay from where he'd placed the other charges. If it hadn't been Barnes, then someone else had access to the area. The other three in the brig were civilians who, according to their testimonies and alibis, hadn't done anything to sabotage the ship.

But what if there were more?

"Did you see the face of the person in the uniform?" Dana was still thinking it might be Shu. From Eartha's vantage point she could have gotten the height wrong.

"No." Eartha's shoulders fell, and she sighed. "He looked sort of like Commander Chance."

Dana stood up abruptly, the pounding in her head and chest competing for dominance over her body. She shook her head. It couldn't be Wade. She'd seen Wade confront Barnes for almost killing those people. When she'd arrived, Wade had his weapon aimed at Barnes. No, she wouldn't believe it.

"But you didn't see his face, so it could be someone who looks like Commander Chance from the back."

Eartha's head tilted to one side, and she seemed relieved as she smiled. "Yes, exactly."

Dana could see that Eartha didn't want it to be Wade any more than she did, but she wasn't lying about what she'd seen. It would have to be enough. There was nothing she could do about it now, as unsettling as it was to know there was probably another CAH loyalist walking among them. If the others had any idea who it might be, they would have turned them in by now.

"Don't worry," Dana said, "we'll figure it out later. Right now, we've got other things to do."

Eartha swirled back around in her chair. Dana sat back in her own chair to monitor their course. They were headed in the correct direction, but she still had to divert more power to the shields, which meant she needed to reroute some power from non-essential systems. With a heavy dose of creative thinking, she boosted their shielding strength by diverting the climate control systems. All that was left were the engines, but for that, she needed at least one engineer.

She stood up and moved to the comms system, then signaled the med-bay. If the ARI was functioning, he'd be in the med-lab, and she could get an update. The comms were working, but no one answered.

"Do you think they made it?" Eartha asked.

"I'm sure they're fine. Why are you still worrying about it?" Dana snapped, her words coming out hasher than she'd meant them to. She glanced down at the climate controls. She had lowered the overall temperature of the ship, so why did it feel like she'd done the opposite?

"Luke is infected. He'll end up like his brother, fighting someone somewhere," Eartha said, her head slumped over the console.

"He's a smart kid. He can take care of himself. We have much bigger problems, and right now I need you to focus on what you're doing instead of daydreaming about some boy. Can you do that?"

Eartha whirled around to stare at her.

Dana frowned back at her. "What are you looking at?"

"Captain . . . you're sweating."

"I know," she scoffed. "What the *sou* is going on in here? I just turned down the temp controls and it's still blazing hot in here."

Dana reached for the top buttons of her coat and opened it again, letting in some air as she fanned the flap back and forth.

"Adjust course four degrees and stay on that heading, or else," Dana growled.

"Yes, Captain," Eartha said. When she finished course-correcting, she got up from the helm and moved to stand in front of her, her face falling. "Your eyes are red, Captain. The vaccine didn't work. You're still infected."

"Don't you think I know that?" Dana snapped, fanning the flap faster. "Return to your station. We're almost there."

"What are we going to do when we get there?" Eartha asked, her voice a high-pitched whine that Dana suddenly wanted to strangle out of her.

"I don't know. I need to think. The Fashin Teku gave us some old codes to get through their defense system, but I doubt they work, those lying, stealing—" The curses were flowing, but her thoughts were still a jumble. "The Begarans and their weapons. They'll shoot us out of the sky before we even have a chance."

"We need to be invisible, so they won't attack us," Eartha said.

"Yes, invisible. Too bad that's not something—" Dana interrupted herself with a sliver of thought. A memory. Something about their shield capabilities allowing them to reflect the space around them, making them virtually invisible.

"Computer, initiate reflective shielding."

"*Unable to comply.*"

"Why not?"

"*Shielding strength required is seventy-five percent. Current shielding is forty-five percent.*"

"Of course it is." Dana slammed a hand down on her thigh and stared into space. "If Wade were here, he'd know what to do. I should go and ask him."

Dana was on her feet before she knew it, and then Eartha, moving like lightning, was standing in front of her. The girl wasn't much shorter than her, and she held her arms out to stop her.

"What are you doing?" Dana demanded, incensed. "Go back to your post."

"Captain, you're infected with the virus. You can't go back into your office. The Commander and Maggie Brooker are in there."

"Maggie," Dana growled. She'd been meaning to give the woman a beating. How had that slipped her mind?

Now was as good a time as any. She whipped off her jacket, letting it fall to the floor. She was too hot to argue in that thing.

"Wait!" Eartha pleaded.

CHAPTER 13

The bridge doors signaled, but Dana ignored it. Whoever it was, they could wait. She had to see the look on Maggie's face when she popped her with a right hook.

"Captain, the door! It's Ari!"

"Ari?" Dana blinked, trying to remember why the name should matter.

"The android," Eartha insisted. "He's back with the cure."

"Fine." She waved a hand in front of her face. "Let's get the robot in here to fix a few things."

"It's *you* that needs to be fixed," Eartha said.

Dana's eyes went from her office door down to Eartha. There was worry etched on the girl's face, but she stood her ground.

"Computer, open the bridge door to the android," Dana ordered.

The doors opened, and Ari entered, head back on his body, restored to full working order.

"Captain, I see that the serum had the effect I was expecting. It only helped for about an hour. I think I've increased the time with this one."

He rushed at her with the injector in his hand and Dana stumbled to step back, but he grabbed her with a mechanical hand like a vice and put the injector to her neck.

"Sorry it took me so long. Eartha, it is good to see you are still unaffected," the ARI was saying as Dana's mind cleared. His head was at an odd angle, as if he were listening to something far off.

"I don't know what she was about to do," Eartha said.

Dana shivered and realized she'd taken off her jacket again. The symptoms were back again, faster than last time. "How long will this one last?"

"It should give you at least three hours this time."

"I guess I can't complain about two more hours. We're about to reach Begaran space. I was doing something a moment ago . . ." Dana scanned the room, trying to find her ideas as if they would be scattered on the floor.

"You were going to make us invisible with the shields," Eartha reminded her.

Dana snapped her fingers. "That's right." She moved back to the captain's chair. "Computer, increase shielding to seventy-five percent."

"*Unable to comply. There is not enough power available to divert to shielding.*"

"Sure there is, don't play hard to get," Dana said, crossing one leg over the other. "ARI Three, any ideas of where we can pull power from to divert to shielding that will allow us to creep up on the Begarans and potentially land on their planet?"

"Land?" Eartha echoed as she whirled around from the helm.

"Yes," Dana replied. "We're going to land our big fat infected ship right in their backyard unless they give us exactly what we want."

The ARI nodded. "I believe I understand. If you divert energy from all areas of the ship not currently occupied, you will gain another twenty percent. We can also gain some by lowering power in all other areas. We do not need all the lights on to do what we must."

Dana smiled. "I like the way you think."

Then she frowned, remembering it wouldn't be much help without the Begaran shield codes. Ashwin, the former Fashin Teku captain, hadn't trusted her with the codes in exchange for his life. She'd planned to hold up her end of the bargain, but in her infected state, she might have thrown him and the other two out the airlock without a thought. Dana hadn't been able to remember the aliens until now.

"How long would it take you to try the vaccine you just gave me on them?" she asked. "They should be in the brig."

"It would not take long at all to test the vaccine on them," the ARI replied. "However, they are in temporary cryostasis in the med-bay. I thought it best for their own protection that they be out of reach and out of sight. Regardless, it is doubtful this temporary remedy would have the same time differential." He waved his synthetic hand in an oddly human way. "In any case, you do not need the Fashin Teku. I have the codes to the Begaran defense shield."

Dana frowned, pulling her head back in surprise. "How did you get it?"

"Ashwin Zeppel entrusted it to me before I put him into cryostasis."

"Excellent," Dana said, still surprised but happy to get on without having to deal with the lying little fur balls. "Assuming they'll work, we'll be able to slip through undetected."

Dana diverted the power necessary to get the shielding to allow for reflective function. As she did, she wanted to pick up speed.

"Ari, can you get us moving any faster?"

"I doubt that will be possible, but I will see what I can do."

"Use Chief Rogan's station in the back."

The ARI moved to the console, and she waited. After several moments there was an increase in speed, but not by much. It would still take them over an hour to reach Begaran space. At least this would give them time to test the new serum. The last one wore off without contact with the infection. This one needed to be better.

CHAPTER 14

An hour later, they were in Begaran space, and they hadn't even armed the *Hope's* weapons. They had no idea Dana and her ship were breathing down their necks. She enjoyed sneaking up on them.

"We need to find a place to land," Dana said. "I'm looking for someplace quiet, but not too far from civilization."

"I see a location in the western hemisphere that matches your specifications," the ARI reported.

"Prepare to put the ship down. Eartha, I need you to give up your seat to the ARI."

Eartha moved to sit in the commander's chair, constantly checking Dana's face for signs of the infection.

"I'm fine," Dana said, smiling down at her. The cold of the ship had seeped into her bones, but she held her jaw stiff to keep her teeth from chattering.

"We will not be entirely invisible once we set down on

the planet," Ari said. "We should prepare to meet resistance."

"I'm prepared. Just do it," Dana said, squaring her shoulders. She moved to the comms system to make a ship wide announcement. She was doubtful there was anyone listening, but she made it anyway. "All hands, prepare for planet atmosphere entry. I repeat, all hands, prepare yourselves for a surface landing."

"Captain, we are losing our port-side engines, and that is where our shielding is weakest," Ari reported. "We may be reflective, but the smoke trailing us will not be invisible."

"I understand." Dana turned to Eartha and moved to strap her in. The harness had been built for an adult, but it would do for a rough landing if it came to it.

The ship rocked as it entered the planet's atmosphere.

"We have an incoming ship bearing down on our position," Ari warned her. "They have spotted us."

"How many?" Dana asked.

"Three manned fighter class ships with full shielding activated." He looked down at the console. "I cannot read how many weapons they carry."

"Acknowledged. Proceed."

The ship touched down with a slight bounce as the landing gear bore their weight.

"Power down the engines and remove the reflective shielding."

"Captain, I must warn you, once the reflective shielding

is down, they will ascertain our limitations and target their weapons at the deficient areas of our hull."

Dana nodded. "I understand, ARI Three. Keep your finger on the trigger just in case."

The ARI turned around, a small frown on his face. "I am sorry, I do not understand your orders."

"She means to get ready to fire when she says so, Ari," Eartha explained.

"Oh," he said, turning back to the console. "Ready, Captain."

Dana looked between the two of them. If they weren't in such a dire situation, she'd find their routine comical. Instead, she opened the communications channel to speak with the Begarans before they got it into their heads to blow them up.

"Begarans, stand down! I am Captain Dana Pinet of the *Starship Hope*. I'm prepared to release our escape pods, unleashing your little virus on the nearest community, if you don't hold your fire. I have over two-hundred infected. If you don't meet our demands, not only will we stay here, I'll make sure my people infect your population before you can give the order to get rid of us."

There was a brief silence where Dana debated whether or not she should repeat her message.

The ARI broke into her debate. "We do not have the capability of launching the escape pods from the ground. If they choose to fire on us, I doubt our passengers and crew will even know to escape."

She grit her teeth. "Yes, I know."

"Captain Dana Pinet of the *Starship Hope*." The garbled voice over the comms made her name sound like something dirty he had to spit out. "You are not welcome here. Leave our planet and our space at once."

Dana watched three fighters take relative positions far enough away from the ship that she needed sensors to track them. She laughed out loud, which forced the ARI to turn around to see why. Eartha was looking at her with concern, but Dana wasn't infected. This was something else. The Begarans had no idea how far she was willing to go, and it tickled her.

"Are you all right, Captain?" the ARI asked as he moved to stand.

She waved him back down and shook her head. "I'm fine. I just think these aliens are more afraid of us than we are of them."

"Like bees," Eartha said.

Dana looked back at her; brows raised. "Like what?"

"Mr. Jennison told me about this animal they used to have on Blue Earth called bees. They would fertilize the flowers to help them grow. They have a horrible stinger, so a lot of people were afraid of them. But if they stung you, they died, so they were often more frightened of us than we could ever be of them."

Dana thought about the story of the bees. She'd heard of them, of course, but the thought never occurred to her to believe she was the bee in this scenario.

"Good point." Dana nodded to Eartha and returned to the comms. "No, we will not leave until we have the cure for this virus and our embryos. You have ten minutes to comply."

Dana had to wait five before she got an answer.

"We will give you a cure for the virus. However, we cannot return all the embryos."

Dana cut in before they could make an excuse. "No, I want them all, or else your people will have to deal with a bunch of aliens running around their world carrying this virus with them." Dana waited a beat before adding. "Did I mention we brought the Fashin Teku survivors with us? I'm sure they have their own issues with you as well."

"Captain, they have put something into our cargo bay," Ari announced. "It appears to be containers carrying the embryos however, there are a total of seven that appear to be missing."

Why seven? Dana swallowed the bile in her throat as she stared down at the readout and waited for the timer to run out. On it, she saw what must have been the formula to engineer the vaccine.

"ARI Three, can you come over here and review the vaccine? Tell me if we have what we need."

Ari moved to the console and looked down at the readout, then back at her.

"It is complete. We have everything we need to distribute the vaccine."

Dana nodded. "And we'll have to assume the embryos are safe without going down there."

"We have given you everything," said the muddled Begaran voice.

"What did you do with the missing embryos?" Dana demanded. "Did you use them for food?"

There was a brief silence before they made a sound like a chortle. They seemed more impatient to be rid of them than ever. But their answer was slow and deliberate as if speaking to a young child.

"No, they were not used as food. Our scientists discovered a genetic compatibility between your young our people. Seven have been added to our gene pool. They will be born as sons and daughters of Begara."

"You know nothing of our race or our physical needs," Dana argued. "They may not survive here."

"They must. We will ensure their births and integration into our society. Now leave, Captain Dana Pinet of the *Starship Hope,* and never return."

Dana slammed a hand down on the console, making Eartha jump.

"*Seven*? They took seven of our people, and they expect us to just leave them here and never look back?"

Dana pulled away from the console to pace the floor. When she could finally breathe again, she spoke.

"Let's get out of here. Start up the engines." Dana slammed herself back into her chair. "All hands prepare for take-off."

"Ready on your mark," Ari answered.

"Mark."

CHAPTER 15

The second law is this: should any hand rise against us, we shall one and all fight for our independence and peace from the tyranny of all other species.
-Taken from The Three Laws of the Begarans

Impatient once the virus had worked its way through the ARI's vaccine and back into her system, Dana paced the bridge, waiting for the ARI to complete the new vaccination instructions provided by the Begarans. They'd kept their word, and so had she.

Dana opened up the fasteners on her jacket again as soon as they were out of their space. She was about to lose it when she heard the communications signal from the med-lab.

"Tell me you've got that *sou* vaccine ready by now,

because I'm about to go down there and see if I can make a weapon out of your good arm and beat you with it!"

"Captain," the ARI replied calmly, ignoring her outburst, "the vaccine is ready for dispersal. Permission to release it using the ventilation system for general population?"

"You're sure this isn't going to kill us or something?" Dana asked, realizing she should have thought of that before.

"I've already tested the compound on the Fashin Teku and Peter Barnes. They are now cured of the virus, and thus far have shown no ill-effects."

"Okay. Disperse the vaccine, then escort Barnes to the bridge as soon as the dispersal is complete. He and I have some things to discuss."

"Yes, Captain."

The air filtration system hissed as the life support systems re-initialized, carrying the vaccine in an aerosol form throughout the ship. A cold mist covered everything. It made Dana cough. Eartha sneezed and giggled when the mist hit her face.

"What now?" Eartha asked as she turned in her seat toward Dana.

Dana's heart rate slowed and the boiling anger she fought moments ago dissipated with the mist. Her head cleared enough for her to think about what needed to be done, so she answered honestly.

"Now we have a lot of work to do cleaning up the ship," she told her. "We are in serious need of repairs, and though I could have insisted on it, we need another place to land to take care of many of them."

Eartha's shoulders fell and her mouth formed a small, disappointed pout. Dana hadn't meant to suppose that the work would be Eartha's responsibility. Talking out loud was just something Dana had grown accustomed to doing. She realized she would have to be more careful doing so around those who weren't crew members.

"You've done enough for one day," Dana told the girl. "Head back to your quarters and see how Esme and Eric are doing. I'm sure they're wondering where you are."

Eartha's face lit up and her lips formed a pleased smile. "Yes, Captain," she said, raising a fist to her heart in an amateur version of a salute before she ran forward and hugged Dana full on.

Astonished by the gesture, all she could do was hug the young girl back. Then, remembering her vid, she held out her pinky.

Eartha's eyes went as big as saucers as she repeated the words as her best friend had done. "Us for one and one for us!" She dashed off the bridge without another word.

Dana re-fastened her jacket as the mist settled on the back of her neck, giving her a chill.

"Computer, readjust temperature controls throughout the ship to standard."

"Temperature controls are currently offline."

Dana sighed as she sat down in her chair. She'd taken them off-line in order to divert energy to the shields. She would have to wait for the rest of the bridge crew to make their way back to their stations before things could be fixed.

To keep warm and busy, she put together a schedule of needed repairs for the heads of all departments. She needed to know how many of the crew and passengers were still alive after their intense exposure to so much truth. She'd been filled with enough anger to consider killing Maggie and Wade both. Doubtless hers weren't the only relationships onboard that wouldn't be back to normal for some time.

She thought of the Fashin Teku and how there had been so many of them floating out in space when they'd arrived. Dana shook off the horrifying thought and reminded herself that they had prepared her as best they could. She'd locked down the ship and secured the bridge when she knew things had gotten out of control. The haze had been hard to control even then, but she'd managed it.

The ARI was the first to arrive, but when he stepped on the bridge, he was alone. Peter Barnes was nowhere to be seen. She wanted to believe for a moment that the android had brought him directly to the brig.

"I apologize, Captain," he started. "Barnes slipped out of the med-lab while I was speaking with you. He was gone before I had a chance to apprehend him."

Dana waved a hand in the air. She'd expected as much. Peter wasn't a fool, and he'd been a master at hiding himself onboard thus far. She was sure, however, that Eartha had an idea where he was and just hadn't told her.

Maybe now that they'd grown closer, she could get it out of the young girl over another bowl of ice cream.

"It's fine. Thank you for all of your help. You did an excellent job keeping our mission in the forefront and keeping the crew alive. We wouldn't have made it without you, Ari Three."

The android looked pleasantly surprised. "You called me Ari Three, as Eartha does. Am I to ascertain that you and I are now friends?"

Dana snorted. "I wouldn't go that far." Then when she saw his expression was unchanged, she sat up straighter. "Finish your report."

"The vaccine has been dispersed through the entire ship," he continued. "There is no one onboard showing symptoms, including the Fashin Teku. Is there anything else I can do for you?"

Dana glanced at her office door behind him, where Maggie and Wade were no doubt free of the infection, but still behind separate force-fields.

"Yes, there is something," she said, pushing herself out of her chair.

Ari followed Dana into her office. Maggie was holding a stiff upper lip in one corner, almost turned to face the wall, clutching her robe closed at her neck. She was shivering against the cold. Wade was in his uniform again and seated at the conference room table with his head down, which he raised when they entered and winced with the movement. The headaches would subside, but the rest would take more than a night to set right.

Dana turned to Ari. "I need you to be Dr. Jabar one more time."

Dana put in the security code and released the force-field. She didn't get a chance to apologize to Maggie before she'd dashed out of the office, the door closing behind her. Wade stood up, his jaw working as he stared at the wall behind her instead of meeting Dana's eye.

"Captain," he said stiffly, holding his salute and waiting for her orders.

"Commander, you have the bridge. I've already started a list of repairs needed. Please see that the heads of each department receive their duty lists." She gave him a curt nod. "Dismissed."

When Wade walked past her without a word, she let out the breath she didn't realize she was holding. Around her, the office was a disaster where they had thrown her things to the floor in their feverish passion and rage.

The photos that had hung on the wall from her home on Zelenia were either askew or on the floor. Two picture frames lay broken, their prints hanging out. Her pristine desk was top-down, legs in the air, her monitor and keepsakes thrown in opposite directions. Her chair was turned over and near the opposite door. She could still hear Wade calling out to her, begging her to let him in.

"Captain?"

The ARI was still in the office with her. She'd forgotten all about him.

"Yes," she said, coming back to herself, straightening

her uniform, "please report to Dr. Walker for your own repairs before you assist the crew."

"Yes, Captain."

The ARI left the room, leaving Dana alone with her thoughts. As she righted the desk and chairs, Eartha's words from earlier returned to her. Someone else onboard had destroyed the cryopods. Was it someone working for the CAH, or someone acting alone? Eartha had said it was someone the size of Wade with dark hair. In her mind she scrolled through the crew manifest, looking for similarities between Wade and the rest.

"Captain to the bridge."

Dana placed the remainder of the broken items on her chair. She knew she had a job to do before she could even consider diving back into another CAH mystery. She had a ship full of people coming out of a fugue. They'd done serious damage to their own ship, and even worse to their close relationships on board.

Dana squared her shoulders and faced the doors to the bridge before taking in a deep breath.

CHAPTER 16

"Perfection is the unattainable standard by which all are being
evaluated.
I say to you, stop judging yourself and others by a law that you
cannot obey.
Find the place between virtue and vice.
Live in that enlightened middle and avoid passing judgement on
others.
In that light you will be made just, righteous, and good."
-Ancient Holy Writings Scroll 7D

B ack on the bridge again, Wade glanced her way
before his eyes quickly darted off again. Cliff and
Nancy both acknowledged her, but their shame-
faced looks said it all. The last time she'd seen them,
they'd been all over each other like dust on a gas giant.
From the scratches on Cliff's face and the bruises on

Nancy's knuckles, she didn't have to guess how things had gone between them. They'd all been at their absolute worst.

Her own awkward moment would be amplified when she had to face Maggie Brooker again. What was she going to say to the woman after what happened between them? Wade aside, she'd gone for the woman's throat, and would have killed her if she hadn't set up the force-field. No apology covered stealing a woman's fiancé and then attempting murder.

Dana sighed. She knew what needed to happen, and the sooner she made the announcement, the better.

"Commander, locate my chief of security."

"He's currently down in the brig," Wade replied. "It seems to be overrun at the moment. He's been trying to figure out what to do with all the offenders for the last thirty minutes."

Dana shook her head. If all the offenders were going to the brig, then there would be no one left to fly the ship.

"Ensign, open a ship-wide channel."

"Open," Cliff replied.

"This is your Captain," Dana began. "I'm going to ask that you put aside the events over the last few days that have resulted from the infection. Not one of us didn't do something we regret. However, considering we were one and all under the influence of an alien virus, I'm suspending all arrests and charges for criminal activity until after the ship is back in order—excluding that of Peter Barnes. If you have a specific grievance, please submit it in writing. We need all hands to assist in the cleanup. Crew members, report to your duty stations to assist in ship repairs. Passengers should begin cleaning all common areas before attending to their quarters. Senior officers, be prepared to report on the progress of your departments in one hour. Pinet out."

Lieutenant Commander Adrien Valente reached the bridge half an hour after the announcement. He looked as though he'd showered and changed his uniform before making his way to the bridge. His shaved head and brows were wrinkled into a scowl that transformed his face. Dana made the assumption there was something on his mind.

"Lieutenant Commander?" she asked.

"May I speak to you in private?"

Dana nodded, preparing herself to hear his objection to releasing the prisoners. As the chief of security, it was his job to see to the safety of the ship. No doubt he was dissatisfied with her proclamation and blanket pardon of all activities over the last couple of days. She readied herself for his complaint.

Dana walked into her office. It had been mostly set to rights, but she'd left some of the broken items on one of the chairs that sat in front of her desk. She ignored them. It was as good as it was going to get for now.

Valente still hadn't said a word and had declined the comfort of the other chair. Instead, he pulled back his shoulders and spoke to the wall behind her. She'd been expecting his challenge to come eye to eye, but braced herself anyway.

"Captain, I would like to submit my official resignation."

Dana blinked twice. Valente wasn't known for his sense of humor, and he remained as rigid as he'd been when he'd entered.

"At ease," she said with a wave of her hand. "Where is this coming from?"

His shoulders fell forward, but he didn't move. "I'm unfit to carry out the duties this position commands."

"Everyone was infected, Valente. No one was immune." *Except for Eartha*, but she didn't mention it, as it went against her argument at the moment.

"I'm not speaking of only the alien virus," he went on. "I wasn't able to do my job in any capacity. I haven't apprehended Barnes even now, and the two other adult Coalition members are now dead because I could not keep them under guard. I can't do this job, and I think you made a mistake in promoting me."

Dana moved to pick up one of her broken frames. She'd thought keeping the former Coalition members in the brig would keep them safe. It was clear now that it had only made them easier to find.

He stood erect, waiting for her to comment. She usually kept her desk clear, but she reached into a thin side drawer. Her hand landed on a small miniature figurine of Victor.

"Ah, there you are. I thought you might have gotten broken in all the commotion." Dana held up the figurine. "Do you know what this is?"

Valente stared at the statue and shrugged. "A dog."

"Yes. My dog, Victor. I got him when he was just a pup. He'd been abandoned or lost. I picked him up at the shelter. I thought I was doing him a favor. Then, one year, he got out. I lost him for two hours. I didn't know where he'd run off to, and combed the neighborhood and all our usual places, trying to track him down. Do you know where he was?"

"He returned to your home and was waiting for you?" Valente guessed.

"You'd think, right? A happy dog, getting fed every day, long runs on the weekend and all the chew toys you've ever heard of. But no, he wasn't home when I returned. I'd given up and had a little cry. It was my fault, of course. He was my dog, and I'd left the door open. I was still wiping my eyes when the doorbell rang. He'd found his way into a neighbor's yard but hadn't been able to get out. She brought him over, and he went to his water bowl and drank like he always did. I didn't punish him that night. Do you know why?"

"Because you were so grateful that he hadn't been hurt, or worse, killed?"

"No, because he didn't do anything wrong. He did what dogs do—play, run, eat, drink, and sleep." Dana sat down at her desk. She unfolded her hand out in front of her gesturing to the empty chair across from her. When he didn't move, she looked up at the baffled security chief. He took the offered chair this time and sat quiet in front of her. He hadn't gotten the point, but it was because she wasn't yet speaking his language. "I understand you're a Believer."

He nodded. "More than most."

"Humble, too," Dana snickered.

Valente broke into a half-smile. "It's only that a lot of people claim the Belief, but don't live by it. I do."

"And you take the Holy Writings very seriously?"

"I do."

"Then according to the Holy Writings, 'A person who gives his word is either a truthsayer, or a liar.' Which are you?"

He seemed taken aback by the question, but answered, "I speak the truth. At least I thought I did, until recently. I may have been holding back a few things."

"Perhaps, but according to the Holy Writings, there is a 'place between perfection and effort,' where most of us live. Would you say that is also true of you?"

His eyes widened. He hadn't expected her to quote the Book of Belief, or probably even know it. He nodded once.

"Then resignation denied. I need my security chief at his post, doing the best he can, as he swore to do when he put on his uniform."

Valente gawked at her, and then his mouth closed. He inclined his head toward her before standing and returning to the bridge.

Dana glanced around the room. She'd kept it in a minimalist style, and it suited her. She wondered if she'd done her best, considering the circumstances.

Dana heard her father's voice:

"You can't make a pitcher of lemonade if you've only got one lemon."

He used to tell her that whenever she lost at cards. It was his way of saying she didn't have the cards necessary to win. This mission, from beginning to end, had been a no-win situation, but she couldn't resign any more than Valente.

She glanced down at the figurine of Victor sitting on the desk and ran her finger over his head, whispering, "Good boy."

CHAPTER 17

Despite locking down the weapons lockers and sealing off the bridge, when all the reports came in, they'd lost seven people. The number included a nurse from the med-bay and the two adult members of the CAH cleared by the Justice Committee. To her amazement, the boy Luke and Barnes had both escaped the mob violence.

Dana read report after report of people stabbed or beaten near to death during the mob activity that swept the ship. Considering all the cases, it was a wonder there weren't more deaths. It helped that opening up hatches on board took more than standard clearance, so no one had accidentally been blown out an airlock.

Even so, Dr. Jabar had his hands full trying to keep that number from rising. There were far more injured than dead, and it had been a long night of critical cases. He'd also tried to submit his resignation, though it was half-hearted at best. He knew he was needed, but felt he'd failed them in clearing the Fashin Teku too soon. Dana assured him he couldn't have known how the virus would change and adapt before sending him back to work.

Dr. Jabar was still up to his elbows in surgeries. In his place, his brother Rido arrived to the conference room meeting she'd called with senior staff the next morning. His brown eyes could look through her in a way that made her squirm. He was the first to sit down, and took the seat to her right, normally reserved for Wade.

"You've not slept," he said, taking her hand.

Dana pulled back against it, but his warm grip didn't budge. "There's a lot to do."

"Yes, but not by you. Let someone else take on command so you can rest."

Dana didn't want to talk about her lack of sleep. She'd already sought out the comfort of her tin of anti-anxiety nanodots. She'd taken another when she'd gone back to her room to change out of her sweaty uniform and into a clean one. Now there were only three left. Only one person on the ship knew about the dots. She wasn't sure which she feared more; his freedom or his capture.

"We'll see if you're saying the same thing after this meeting. The reports I've received so far are not promising." Dana shook her head and turned her hand over in his. The warmth of it seep into her as she spoke. "How are people doing?"

It was Rido's turn to sigh as he looked away. As their onboard Healer, he was no doubt as busy as his brother. His background in psychotherapy was all they had to combat the aftermath of the emotions the virus had stirred up in everyone.

"Everyone who's willing to come to me is a wreck, which means the ones that don't are far worse." He lifted their joined hands to his lips, and that was the moment that Wade and the Rogans arrived.

Dana pulled her hand away, but not before Wade's eyes went from their hands to her face. He turned away, scowling, choosing a seat as far from them as possible where he could stare at the wall. *What did he expect?* she thought. It wasn't like he wasn't engaged less than seventy-two hours ago. She didn't have to justify having feelings for Rido. Though she wasn't sure what those feelings were, only that she liked his company more than most.

If Rido noticed Wade's reaction, he didn't comment on it.

Chancellor Jeremiah Evans and President Hector Muñoz arrived next, along with Lieutenant Commander Valente, who sat on her left. The table was almost full, leaving one seat between Rido and the Rogans. Despite her announcement to the contrary, the chancellor wanted to discuss the seven dead.

"What should we do about those involved in the murders? We can't turn a blind eye to this kind of thing," Chancellor Evans blustered, slamming a fist on the conference room table. He couldn't surprise or intimidate her with his dramatics anymore. Dana, like the others, was accustomed to his outbursts now.

Beside him, President Muñoz raised a hand. "There are

some who are having a harder time forgiving than others. Is there some way we can handle the matter as opposed to pushing it aside?"

Dana ran a palm over her face, and she saw Rido stiffen beside her. If she allowed everyone with a grievance to have their way, they'd be right back where they started.

"I don't have time to go through those individual's cases one by one," she told them. "I have a ship to run and too many things on my docket as it is."

President Muñoz raised his hand again. "May I make the suggestion that we set up a more permanent Judicial Committee so that those with severe circumstances that preceded or extend beyond the time of the virus can make a case, and a defense be made in front of a court of peers?"

It wasn't the worst plan she'd ever heard. If she'd been sleeping well, she might have thought of it herself. "Can I trust this is something that you and the chancellor will see to?"

Both men looked to the other, then back at her.

"Yes," they said in unison.

"Good. Well, that's some of the best news I've heard all day. Now to the bad news." Dana turned to her right and nodded to Rido.

"There are still five people in critical condition," Rido said. "Once we know if they'll survive, we should hold a memorial for those we've lost."

"Can you see to the services, and I will be sure that everyone attends?" Dana asked.

Rido nodded his assent.

Dana turned to the far end of the table. "Commander Wade, you've submitted a report on the damage sustained throughout the ship. Are there any critical areas that need our immediate attention?"

Wade shifted in his seat so he could see everyone without looking at her. She wasn't sure why he was still acting like he had a grudge against her. Was it because she hadn't leaped into his arms the moment he'd asked, or because he'd seen her with Rido and had come to some conclusion about them? Either way, it was unwarranted, and she was losing her patience.

"No critical areas were damaged. However, the Commons was raided. No one seemed to bother with the onboard aeroponics bay, but the food supply in the kitchen took a major hit. We need to go down to rations, or we won't make it far."

"See to it, Commander. I'm leaving that one up to you and Cook Stamford."

He nodded, his eyes on the table.

Dana moved on. "Where are we with engines?"

"Amazingly enough, there's been no significant damage to the propulsion systems," Eric began, then glanced at his wife. "But there is another problem."

Esme finished the thought before Dana could ask the question. "We're dangerously low on fuel."

Dana leaned forward, sure she misheard them. "We're low on fuel? What happened to our state-of-the-art bio-filtered fuel system that runs on waste?"

"We've touched down on more planets than expected," Eric replied with a small shrug.

"The engineers—well, *us*," Esme said, looking to her husband, "we didn't expect we'd be awake during the first leg of our journey, so refueling wasn't on the list of things to anticipate."

"The area of space we've been traveling through doesn't have much for the refined Thiutite-Compound-V that our ship uses for high speeds, take-offs, and landings," Eric finished. "What we have won't get us very far. We need to find another fuel source as soon as possible."

"Is this something that the Fashin Teku can help us with?" Dana asked.

Eric and Esme looked at each other as if communicating telepathically, and turned back to her to answer.

"Maybe," they said in unison.

"I'm going to hand them over to you. Maybe the five of you can come up with something helpful."

"Are we going to just forget that the Fashin Teku got us in this mess in the first place?" Chancellor Evans asked. "You can't be so naïve as to trust them again."

"They should answer for their crimes," Valente agreed, his voice a low grumble.

"We're not obligated to care for them, or even keep them on board," Wade agreed.

"We just don't have the resources." He still didn't meet her eye, but he was looking hard at Rido.

"No, we're not obligated," Rido said, "but neither are

we so primitive as to leave them floating in space with no rescue in sight."

Dana nodded in agreement. "The virus destroyed their ship, and despite their misdeeds, I believe they've paid for their mistakes. We have our stolen goods back, and we have them. The technical knowledge they possess and their experience in this area of space is priceless at the moment. They've promised to provide us with coordinates to a space station called the Nexus where we may even find food and fuel."

"But can we trust them?"

The question came from Valente, but all eyes focused on Dana. She'd be lying if she said she trusted them, but she planned to get as much help out of the three as she could.

"For now, they owe us their lives. That's to our advantage. When that advantage ends, we may want to find a place to drop them off."

"The sooner the better," Chancellor Evans muttered.

"I believe they'd rather help us than suffer confinement in the brig," Eric said. "They're not lying to us about the space station. The big question is will we run out of fuel before we get there."

"I'll have Lieutenant Westlake coordinate with you and the Fashin Teku on the quickest route to our destination. As it may be our only chance, we need to take it." Dana shifted in her seat, leaning forward. "Commander, I'll leave it to you to assign them a room and post a guard. They should not have the run of the ship."

"We need to prepare ourselves," Wade added. "Once we're at the space station, some passengers and crew may want to stay. That puts us right back where we started before we got the embryos back."

Dana hadn't considered anyone would want to leave the ship before they found a new world. She glanced at Wade, and when she saw his expression, wished she hadn't. Was he considering leaving?

She rolled her shoulders, dismissing her doubts. She couldn't let her uncertainty derail her mission. They needed a world where they could prosper and grow. A space station was nothing more than shore-leave.

There was, of course, the knowledge that there might also be two other ships that had made it off of Zelenia alive. As long as they were out there, Zelenians would live on. She had to believe they weren't the last of humankind. Someone at the space station might have run into their people already.

She gave a quick look to Chancellor Evans and President Munoz. There was a near imperceptible nod between them, as if they were thinking the same thing.

"No one on this ship will be forced to stay if they want to leave," Dana said.

The table was silent as they all considered the possibility.

"What about Barnes?" Wade asked. "We still don't know where he's hiding."

Dana hadn't been thinking of him, but it reminded her

of what Eartha had said earlier. Someone else had destroyed their cryopods, and she didn't have enough information to track down another hidden CAH member. Perhaps they'd be glad to get off, saving her the trouble of having to hunt them down.

"If he gets past our security," she said with a significant look at Valente, "then he's free to go. Along with anyone else who would rather we didn't find a new home."

"You say that as if you believe there are others," Wade replied.

"I do. I don't have definitive proof, but I know we don't have all the CAH members."

For the first time, Wade met her eye as if she'd spoken to him.

"Good riddance," President Muñoz said.

"They should still pay for their crimes," Chancellor Evans growled.

"Yes, well, perhaps they'll be happy on a space station full of aliens instead of with us," Dana concluded. "Either way, we will allow anyone who wants to leave to go. We no longer have the supplies to keep anyone who doesn't want to live among us in peace."

"I don't like the thought of someone with the knowledge of our security systems just roaming around the galaxy," said Chancellor Evans.

"Better than keeping him while he nurses a grudge against us," President Muñoz countered. "In the meantime, we're feeding and caring for him, and waiting for the next bomb. The captain is right. Let him go. He'll do more damage to us here than he'll ever do out there."

Dana nodded and gave Valente another look. She didn't want Barnes on board, and she thought she'd already made herself clear. However, if she had to spell it out to him, she would later. Barnes was getting a one-way ticket off the ship, and she didn't want anyone to stop him. Valente nodded.

President Muñoz raised a hand. "There may be an opportunity to establish some new diplomatic relations among the aliens we meet there. At worse, we could learn more about the area where we'll be visiting. At best, we might engage in some trade relations."

"Agreed," Dana said. "We should speak with the Fashin Teku about that before we send them packing. They are no doubt more familiar with the variety of species we'll be meeting there." She sat back in her chair and looked around the table. "If there's no other business, you're dismissed."

The group dispersed as if the table was on fire. It would take some time to deal with what had happened. No doubt their feelings and emotions were as raw and open as her own. Wade left the room without a word, and she had to steel herself against the disappointment.

Rido lingered as the others left, waiting until they were the only two remaining before he leaned down and whispered in her ear.

"You will get some sleep tonight, even if I have to see to it myself."

The whispered promise tickled her ear and warmed her neck. There was no one else left in the room to see his satisfied grin.

Thank the Merciful!

CHAPTER 18

Captain's Log: 4327.10.7

T his week, we tracked down the Fashin Teku who stole our embryos, and got them back from the Begarans they were sold to. We contracted a dangerous infection that forced us to recognize some truths about each other that we weren't willing to voice on our own. Eartha, our young stowaway, helped save the entire ship with two former CAH members and our ARI. We took on three home-less Fashin Teku pirates who will pay for their crimes and passage by being of service to the ship, and are currently leading us to the nearest space station called the Nexus.

Now that we have the coordinates, we'll go there and see if we can get more star maps and supplies, as ours have been low for too long. We are also in need of time off the ship. I've declared that no one will be forced to stay should they choose to make a home on the space station.

No matter what obstacles come our way, we'll continue to live by the values that make us who we are. We're the last Zelenians, and our search for a new home isn't over.

CAPTAIN'S PERSONAL LOG:

I'm in trouble. Feelings that I thought were long buried have resurfaced. Thanks to the truth virus, I've said and done things that I can't deny. My only opportunity to get out of this unscathed is if I lay down and die. That wouldn't be very convenient, but it would be much easier than looking my ex in the eye while working side-by-side with his ex-fiancé.

Things have gotten more complicated than I could have ever imagined. I used to love watching Maggie's updates about the ship and crew. Now I can't bear to look at her any more than she can at me.

The idea that there are other ships out there plague my waking hours as much as Wade plagues my dreams. I'm not sure what he'll say when he finds out what else I've kept from him. If another secret doesn't ruin everything, I'll be extremely surprised.

AFTER A NEVER-ENDING DAY OF APPROVING REPAIRS AND meetings with department heads, Dana was more than ready for a night alone in front of a vid. She'd already picked out one of her favorites, a father-daughter movie about letting go while holding on. It always made her cry, but she was in the mood for a tear-jerker. She donned her silky robe and fuzzy slippers and poured herself a cup of chamomile tea.

She climbed into her bed slippers and all. Dana's tablet served as a projector, displaying the vid on the blank wall opposite her bed. Once she situated herself on the pillows and was tucked in, ready to relax, the door chimed.

"Computer, who is it?"

"Rido Jabar."

Dana huffed in frustration. She didn't want to be rude, but she needed some solitude. Rido was a skilled conversationalist, and normally she'd love to have shared a drink with him. Tonight though, she wasn't in the mood for any mental gymnastics. She had a lot on her mind, and she didn't want to put on a pretense for anyone.

Instead of answering, she let the door go unanswered. Maybe he'd give up and go back to his own quarters.

A moment later he knocked on the door, then called out from the other side.

"I know you're in there. I'm not going anywhere until I see you."

The mortification of knowing that anyone passing by her door might hear his declaration had her leaping from her bed, cursing him all the way. When the door slid open, she saw he carried his equipment. On his face was an unbothered smile, as if she hadn't tried to ignore him a moment ago.

Dana blocked the door with her body. She imagined it

was a clear sign she didn't want company. "What can I do for you?"

He ignored it and pushed past her and into her quarters. "I'm here for your weekly healing. I know I missed our usual time, but I thought considering the circumstances . . ." He let his voice fade, along with her thoughts.

She huffed as he chose the same spot on the floor where he'd done their first healing. She hadn't committed to anything after the first time, let alone weekly sessions. He'd brought another candle and lit it, putting it down on the edge of the side table. He then knelt in front of the mat with his hands on his thighs, waiting.

"It's late, and I was just about to turn in," Dana said with a glance toward her room. She longed for her tea before it got cold, and the vid she had was already set up and ready to go.

Rido's eyes followed her to the bedroom. "Oh, are you entertaining?"

She didn't know if it bothered her more that he might think that, or that he didn't seem bothered by it. Either way, he didn't budge. She explained herself before his imagination ran rampant.

"No, just . . ." Dana sighed. "I want to be alone right now."

Rido nodded but remained immovable. "I see. How about I give a silent healing? No talking required. All the benefits without the mumbo jumbo."

Dana had to admit she'd been looser after his last visit.

It wasn't as if she didn't need the relaxation and sleep. And there wasn't any harm in having someone drop some oils on her and realign her bachi, was there? It was something her mother often enjoyed.

Thinking of her mother brought emotions to the surface she didn't want to face, and Dana had to look away. She didn't want to think about her mother, didn't want to dwell on the past, but the meeting in the conference room had gotten her thinking of all the people who might have found their way onto the other ships.

It was ridiculous to think her mother would be on one or have even been invited to board one of the other ships, but it didn't matter. The idea of seeing any of her friends or family members again was enough to put her on edge. When, if she saw them, what would she say? What had the other captains had to do to keep their people alive? Were they faring better or worse than her? Would they agree with the decisions she'd made so far, or be disappointed?

Dana kicked herself for caring so much about what others thought. No two captains thought alike or had faced the same circumstances, so why was she letting it bother her?

Maybe she needed healing after all.

"Fine," she said at length. "But just one hour."

Rido smiled, dragging his finger and thumb across his lips as if to zip them closed.

She was about to relax when he reached around her and removed the tie on her robe. She stiffened, but the robe didn't move. He left the robe in place, only folding it down to her shoulders. There, on the exposed skin, he used oiled hands to rub at the base of her neck and shoulders.

"Computer, play Rido Relaxation Pinet one."

His soft, warm hands kneaded her stiff muscles to the chosen music. A few plucked notes on guitars hummed through the air with the accompaniment of soft chimes, a deep flute, and a babbling brook in the background. Dana was transported to another plane. Her mind emptied and her body relaxed with each deliberate squeeze of her muscles. She floated above the ground like a bird soaring through, above, and below the music.

Rido moved around her body, pressing on various joints and muscles for a full hour before the music stopped. His hands released her, and the robe was readjusted to cover her again. He didn't say anything as he packed, and Dana didn't move from the mat on the floor. He got up and walked to the door. When she heard the door slide closed behind him, she let out a light sob that became a full-on cry.

She wasn't sure how long she lay there, only that when she'd finished crying and sat up, she felt lighter. The healing had lifted a weight she didn't even realize she'd been carrying. Rido had set out a glass of water for her and she drained it before filling it again and drinking half.

She folded Rido's mat and placed it near the door, determined to return it to him as soon as possible. Then she made a note of the date in her log and put a reminder in for the following week for her next appointment with Rido. This time, she wouldn't forget.

Dana went back to her bed and slid underneath the sheets. She didn't pull up the movie she'd been hoping to watch. Instead, she tapped on her video message from home. This time, when she finished watching it, she cried for her mother.

CHAPTER 19

Something woke her, and Dana's eyes flew to her digital display. The 3D numbers showed the current ship's time:

03:15

Her mind raced to fill in the gaps, to find what had dragged her out of a deep sleep. Rido's healing had done its job, and she strained to listen to any change in the ship's engines or movement. Everything seemed in order, but she hadn't been dreaming. Something had woken her.

The sound of a boot brushing against the edge of furniture had her reaching for her sidearm on the bedside table. Her belt was there, but her weapon was gone.

"I thought I'd relieve you of your weapon in case you tried to take my head off."

Barnes' words hit her like a bucket of ice-cold water, and she was wide awake.

"Computer, lights."

Three error beeps were her answer. She tried again, but the lights remained off. Her eyes were already adjusting to the dark. Barnes's pale face looked back at her from where he was seated in the chair she kept at the end of her bed.

"What are you doing here?" she demanded.

Barnes smiled indulgently, as if she'd asked him what his favorite dish might be. "To be honest, I'm not sure. I guess I wanted to make sure you were okay."

Dana's face grew hot as he glanced down at her open robe. She clutched it together at her neck with one hand as she felt under the pillow for her knife.

"I'm fine. Now leave," she said between her teeth.

"If you're looking for the knife, I already have it." Barnes lifted the knife from his lap, waving it at her. "That's probably what woke you."

"Computer, alert security to my quarters," Dana said, her full voice carrying enough to bounce back to her.

Three beeps signaled that there was an error in the command. She tried again, but it still didn't work.

"I disabled that function, too," Barnes informed her, "so we could chat without being rushed."

"Weapon or no, you've got one minute to state your business before I go for your throat and force you to shoot me."

Barnes put her weapon and knife on the floor beside him and raised his hands in the air. "Neither one of us wants that. I'm just here to talk."

"You could have come to my office, like a normal

human being. Creeping into my bedroom at night while I'm sleeping says something else entirely." Dana shifted in the sheets, so her feet were underneath her, ready to spring out of bed if needed.

Barnes squirmed in his seat. "I'm tired of hiding. I don't deserve the brig any more than the others did."

"You're a murderer," Dana hissed. "If you think I'm going to just let you roam the ship again, you must be intoxicated. You've been living in the ventilation tubes too long as it is."

Barnes waved a gloved hand in the air. Dana noticed that in addition to the hand coverings, he wore a tight-knit hat on his head which covered his bright hair. However, he hadn't shaved since his original arrest, and his full short beard was the same orange as the hair peeking out from under the cap.

"I'm not going back to the brig." Barnes stood up and approached the bed.

Dana leaned back against the bed frame. She could use it to propel herself at his face if it came to it. She wouldn't try going hand-to-hand with him in her nightgown unless it was the last resort.

"I want you to drop me off at the next habitable planet. Aliens or no, I'm willing to live anywhere other than this ship."

Dana listened to his plea while at the same time imagining him being sent off in an escape pod to the nearest planet. How quickly he'd forgotten the disaster of the prehensile planet. She had the space station in mind for him. A place where he could disappear in the crowd and never be seen or heard from again. It was almost too good for him.

"In case you hadn't noticed, we're looking for a place to live ourselves," she told him. "If we should find it while you're onboard, you'll be forced back into the brig indefinitely."

Barnes hung his head and sighed as if he were ready to give up. He sat down on the edge of her bed as if he had every right to be there. He was close. She could almost reach out and touch him, which meant his long arms were well within reach of her.

"Don't," she warned.

He lifted his hands again and stared back at her. In the dark, his blue eyes were black, only adding to his ominous proximity.

"I won't hurt you. I only want you to consider getting rid of me someplace on the way."

Dana already had a plan to be rid of him. She wondered if telling him about it now would be smart or foolish. She split the difference.

"Time's up, Barnes. Get out of my quarters, now." Dana reached the floor with one foot and then the other. "I've got far too many things to deal with. We're running out of fuel, not that you or any of the other CAH members would care."

"The CAH are dead. I would have helped them if I could, but the virus . . ." He shook his head. "I wasn't thinking straight."

"Yes, three in total now. That leaves three still onboard."

His head snapped up, and he met her eye. So he hadn't known there were other CAH members still alive. She'd been planning to press him, but it was obvious he had nothing. Had he known; he'd have tried to bargain with her.

"Yes, you, Luke, and one other," Dana said as she stepped back, keeping the bed between them. Her tablet was on the floor, where it had fallen in her scramble to get to her feet. She slipped it out from under the bed with her toe. "Any ideas who the last Coalition member might be? I'll make sure you get dropped off at the Nexus, the space station we're heading for."

He looked back at her doubtfully. "A space station? Out in the middle of nowhere?"

"Yes, and we're headed there now. If you give me a name, I'll give you a free pass off the ship and onto the station. It's the best deal you're going to get, so don't bother trying to renegotiate."

She could see him considering the offer. While he did so, she activated the tablet with her toe and signaled security with three more taps.

The light from the tablet was too bright to hide. As soon as Barnes realized what she'd done, he shot off the bed, stepping up onto the chair and opening the ventilation shaft above, where he climbed up inside. So *that* was how he'd gotten into her room.

He poked his head back out to speak to her.

"All right, you've got a deal. As soon as my feet are touching the space station, I'll tell you what I know. Though you're not likely to believe me."

He disappeared again, securing the ventilation grate back in place.

CHAPTER 20

A minute later, security was at her door, and Valente charged into the room. She pointed to the ventilation shaft, but knew it was too late. Barnes was already gone.

"He's used the ventilation shaft to get into my room, but that doesn't explain how he's disabling my voice commands." Dana snatched a uniform from the closet and held it over her arm. "I want to know how he's able to render my codes useless no matter what I do."

Valente sent two guards to follow the ventilation shaft, just in case, then turned to her. "I'll reset your passkey in the meantime. We'll figure it out, Captain."

She left Valente and his guards out in the main area of her cabin while she went to change in the bathroom. Inside, she stared at her reflection, at the bags under her eyes from two nights of interrupted sleep. She stripped out of her gown and put on her uniform. Her hands still shook as she fastened the jacket around her. She huffed in frustration.

"Get it together, Pinet."

She had three anti-anxiety nanodots left, but she wouldn't touch them again. They hadn't done anything but delay the inevitable. It didn't remove the reasons behind the anxiety, only the symptoms. Dana preferred Rido's method for dealing with it, though it required more time and wasn't available in nanodot form. She was also pretty sure that he wanted more from her than he was saying.

When she came out of her room, Wade was there with the others. He rushed over to her.

"What happened?"

Dana shrugged and ignored the fact that it was the most he'd spoken to her since they'd both been rid of the infection. "Barnes decided to pay me a midnight visit."

"Did he threaten you?"

"Actually, no. Other than coming in here while I was in my nightgown, he just wanted to talk."

His brow furrowed. "Talk?"

"He wants off the ship."

"Of course he does. So he came to your cabin to catch you unaware with your guard down just to tell you what you already knew?"

Dana shrugged. "He wanted me to drop him off at the nearest habitable planet, regardless of alien or plant life."

"What did you say?"

"I told him that if he wanted off the ship when we

arrived at the Nexus, he'd have to tell me who the other Coalition member is."

"Other Coalition member?"

She nodded, crossing her arms over her chest. "It seems there's at least one more. I want their name."

Wade took a step back in surprise. "Are you sure you can trust him?"

"No," Dana said with another one-shoulder shrug. "I wouldn't trust him to pick up my laundry. But regardless of that fact, he knows who the person is, and he's agreed to tell me once he's gotten free passage off of the ship and onto the space station."

Wade ran a hand through his hair. "But we can't believe a word he'd say."

"Perhaps not, but he helped Eartha, Luke, and Ari when the rest of us were under the influence of the pathogen. He could've left us all to die."

Wade shook his head. "He wasn't being selfless. He was looking out for himself."

Dana had considered that point too and nodded. "True, but according to Eartha, he did more than just save the ship. He saved them. There's a difference. He got into this room and disabled my command codes, which means he could have easily gone to the bridge and done the same thing. He chose to help them and keep them alive when they might have been torn apart."

Wade opened his mouth to say something but was cut off as Valente came over to give his report.

"We've been over the cabin, and we've secured all the

grates from this side, which means he can't get in the same way again. Your passkey is reset and ready for input whenever you're ready. I'll put two security officers outside your door for a few days just to make sure."

Dana didn't like the idea of diverting security to watch her door at night. She needed her people focused on getting the ship in order and hunting Barnes down. If he was in the brig, she wouldn't have to worry about him sneaking into her bedroom again.

"That won't be necessary," Dana said.

Wade was in the middle of objecting as Valente protested, "But Captain—"

Dana raised a hand. "I want your people doing their jobs. Find Barnes and send him back to the brig where he belongs. I'll sleep better after that than I would with two guards outside my door. Am I making myself clear?"

"Yes, Captain," Valente said with a curt nod, brown eyes still searching her face. "What about letting him off the ship and onto the space station?"

"That's still the plan, but I'd much rather escort him off than let him make a run for the doors. Understood?"

"Yes, Captain." Valente put a fist to his chest and signaled his team to leave.

Wade shook his head. "I don't like the idea of you facing him alone."

"I won't be alone," she said. Before he could ask her any more questions, she diverted his attention back to their duties. "It's oh-five hundred. I'm going to head to the bridge. Can you meet with the Rogans and the Fashin

Teku this morning? Find out where we are on our current fuel reserves and a trajectory to the space station."

"Um, yes, of course." He stared down at her; confusion etched in the furrow of his brows.

"Something wrong, Commander?"

"It's been bothering me. You knew. Before I told you about Maggie. You knew about Bill."

Dana felt the sharp pain of guilt stab her in the gut. Her face must have confirmed it, because he shook his head.

"Why didn't you tell me?"

She braced herself. "You know why. I tried to warn you and you practically took my head off. Nothing short of seeing that vid would have convinced you."

"So why didn't you share the vid with me instead of letting me get blind-sided in the middle of an epidemic?"

Dana lifted her shoulders and let them fall. She was so tired. Tired of keeping things from Wade. The last thing she wanted was to give him another reason to be upset with her. She had enough secrets.

"I knew you'd find out eventually, and it wasn't my place to say anything more than I did," she said, doing her best to keep her voice level. "I don't know what Barnes thought it would accomplish, but I went to Maggie myself. We spoke and urged her to tell you. I'm sorry you were hurt. I genuinely wanted you to be happy."

Wade's eyes fell to the floor for a long moment, and then slowly climbed back to her eyes.

"What about us?" he asked, so lowly she barely caught it.

"There is no us while you're mourning her," Dana told him, the words coming out harsher than she intended. She reached out a hand and placed it on his arm. "I'm not going anywhere, but I think keeping our relationship on a professional level right now is for the best."

He nodded, then turned to see himself out. Once he was gone, she reset the code for the second time.

The computer beeped in confirmation.

"Let's make it stick this time," she said aloud to the room. "Computer, send the following message to Rido Jabar at oh-eight hundred. Slept better than last night. Thank you, the healing helped. Wondering if you'd be interested in spending the night this evening. Come by around twenty-one hundred, if it's not inconvenient. End message."

"Message will be sent at oh-eight hundred RST."

Dana held out her hands and found them steady again. "Good."

CHAPTER 21

Friend /frend/ n.
A person closer than an acquaintance. Someone with whom you
share a strong interpersonal bond without familial or sexual
relations.

By midday, two days later, Dana was dragging. She'd spent the last two nights fighting two kinds of nightmares, followed by full days of reports and repairs. The hull had taken some hits that required maintenance that couldn't be done while in route. The ship was limping along, but it looked like they wouldn't be back to spec until they reached a docking location with real energy and tools.

Esme Rogan delivered the worst of the news later that day when she'd requested a meeting in Dana's office. She walked in the door with Ashwin Zeppel, and Dana understood why her chief engineer had requested the meeting off the bridge, as the former freighter captain and leader of the surviving Fashin Teku wasn't welcome there. Since their abrupt departure over two weeks ago with part of their cargo and the embryos, none of the Fashin Teku were allowed near the bridge. They weren't even allowed to roam the ship without an escort.

Ashwin had the decency to keep his beady eyes on the floor. His traditional tunic, his family crest embroidered on the front, a leather tool belt at his waist, hid some of the long blond hair that covered his body. She absently wondered if he'd been able to salvage his formal attire before the destruction of his ship.

"What?" Dana asked without preamble. Whatever it was, she already knew she wasn't going to like it.

"There's a problem," Esme began, "and I think it warrants your attention."

"If the Teku captain is misbehaving, they can drag him to the brig on your word."

Ashwin's eyes bolted to Esme's face, and she smiled, giving him a slight shake of her head. Her hand rested on her belly, though she had several more months before the baby would make an appearance. The unconscious gesture of concern was ever present, and Dana noted it.

"What's wrong?" Dana asked, her tone softer.

"As you know, the damage to the ship's engines was not extensive. In fact, with the help of Zeppel and his friends, we've been able to increase efficiency and improve our overall speed by twenty percent."

"That doesn't sound like bad news," Dana said, looking between them for whatever she was missing.

"It's not. The problem was when we checked our fuel reserves." Esme wrung her hands as she stood in front of her. "They're a lot lower than we thought."

"Please, Esme, sit down," Dana said, gesturing to the chair in front of her. Ashwin continued standing, as she had not invited him to sit. Dana was still assimilating some of the information she'd learned about his people. They had no written language for the COMP to translate. She and the others on board had to learn about them through Ashwin's Teku Tales during the Maggie's Minutes broadcast slot. It had been the president's wife, Maria's idea. Dana wanted to learn everything she could about the strange aliens who were now passengers on her ship.

Esme settled, but it did nothing to soften her words. "We don't have enough fuel to make it to the Nexus."

Dana felt the punch of the news in her stomach, and it took her breath away. Without the space station, she didn't know how long they could go on with the damage they'd sustained.

"Are you sure?" Dana asked, desperate for there to have been some miscalculation, some mistake.

"Yes, Captain, many sorries," Ashwin quickly added. "The ship's push is not long or fast. No two ways. We go to the Arch, no wait." He shrugged as if he had nothing else to offer.

"The Arch?" Dana echoed.

"He means a wormhole," Esme clarified.

"He knows where there's a wormhole?"

Ashwin nodded his furry head with vigor. "Yes, Captain. Very nice, and there every day, to get to the Nexus."

"So we have enough fuel to get to the wormhole?"

"Yes," he said.

"No," Esme said at the same time.

"Well, which is it?" Dana huffed.

Esme looked over at Ashwin as if she were ready to pummel him. Her heart-shaped face and frown seemed in direct contrast with each other. "We have enough fuel to get there, but not enough to make it to the other side. At this rate, we'll be gliding in on fumes."

Dana leaned her elbows against her desk. "Is there any way we can get more out of the engines?"

"If we cut down on everything non-essential—and I mean everything," Esme said with a bleak look, "we still won't have enough to do more than put the nose of our ship in and wait for a stiff breeze to push us in."

Ashwin waved his hands. "We go. We go to the Arch now, or we wait."

"Wait for what? Why would we wait?" Dana blurted out and her gaze passing between them.

Ashwin gave a sad shake of his head. "Wait for death."

Esme waved a hand in his direction as if to erase his words. "Eric and I think we might have a better chance if we don't take the more direct route to the wormhole.

Instead, we look for the Othiutium elements we need to make Thiutite-Compound-V. Ashwin isn't sure about the locations, but there may be planets in a more circuitous route with the component minerals we need." She frowned. "However, they lost their maps when their ship detonated, so we're going on estimates here."

"Why wait?" Ashwin asked, slapping his hair-covered hands against his sides.

"So we don't know the precise location of the fuel components or the wormhole?" Dana ran her hands over her face and looked between the two of them. Both Esme and Ashwin nodded.

"Every second is precious. We need to conserve energy now." Esme stood up. "On your orders."

"How extensive are the cuts going to be?"

"We need to cut our power usage down to minimal. That's minimal energy outputs throughout the ship. Anything that requires energy needs to have departmental approval, from showers to hand tools."

Dana didn't like the sound of that. "For how long?"

"Your ship so slow," Ashwin said, shaking his head, then snapping his mouth closed when he caught Esme's glare.

"Regardless of the direction we take," she continued, looking back at Dana, "we're going to need a bit of energy to convert the Othiutium or get through the wormhole. It's going to be a calculated risk either way."

Dana let out a long sigh. "Fine. I'll send out the orders."

Esme stood up, then paused. "The only other decision

left is navigation. Are we going for the wormhole, or the Othiutium?" Esme rubbed her belly as she waited for Dana to answer.

"Running out of fuel in the middle of nowhere and nothing is not an option," Dana reasoned. "We need to get to that wormhole, no matter what it takes." She sat taller in her chair with the weight of her decision. "Computer, set condition three throughout the ship. Divert all available energy to the engines."

The lights in the room went black. Only the yellow lights around the edges of the room and door were lit.

"Ashwin, come with me," Dana said. "I need you on the bridge."

Dana couldn't see his face light up in the dark, but he was quick on his feet and at her heels as she entered the bridge.

Wade spared a glance for the Fashin Teku as she entered, but then was looking at her again. "We're at condition three?"

"We need all the energy we can spare to get to a wormhole to reach the space station," she explained. "We'll barely make it with what we've got, so we need to preserve as much energy as we can now."

Wade nodded at Ashwin. "What's he doing here?"

"He's going to assist in navigation. We don't exactly have the wormhole coordinates, so we need him." Dana looked to Nancy, her pilot. "Lieutenant, please assist Zeppel in plotting a course for the wormhole. Maintain whatever optimal speed is necessary to get us there on the most direct route you've got."

"Yes, Captain," Nancy said, turning in her seat and directing Ashwin to join her.

Dana sat down in the command chair, and Wade joined her on her right.

"Commander, any word on Barnes?"

Wade shook his head. "No, he's disappeared again."

She waved a hand. She hadn't expected him to be caught yet anyway. He'd made it clear he could get to her, and that was enough to throw her off. She wouldn't give him the satisfaction of ruining her life though. He could sleep in the sewers, or wherever he was, as long as he didn't hurt any more of the crew or damage the ship.

"Putting us on condition three will take care of any trouble we might have had with Cook," Wade quipped dryly.

"Agreed. We'll be on SRs for the time being." Even in the dark, she saw Wade make a face. "What?"

"It's been a while since I've been on standards."

Dana raised a shoulder. "If you don't want your rations, I'm sure we'll find someone who will appreciate them."

"Captain, course laid in," Nancy called out, Ashwin beside her.

"Go ahead." Dana sat back in her chair. "Computer, at our current speed, how long to the programmed destination?"

"Two weeks, one day, and eight hours."

Wade leaned in over her seat and whispered, "Fifteen days in the dark? Passengers are going to go stir crazy."

His breath was warm on her cheek. In her light jacket, she shivered against the difference in the ship's temperature. The last time she'd noticed it, she'd been coming out of a fever. This time was different, and her proximity to Wade was forcing her to think about their time alone before Maggie showed up. She didn't like thinking about what they'd have done if she hadn't.

"I trust you'll be able to handle the passengers and crew, Commander." Dana stood up and Wade rose with her.

"If it's not too much trouble, I'd like to discuss a few things with you."

Dana held up a hand. "Of course, but now isn't a good time. Can it wait?"

Wade stopped short, as if she'd slapped him. He frowned but nodded. "Yeah, I guess it can wait."

"Good."

Dana retreated to her office and sealed the door. She waited a moment for her eyes to adjust to the room without the light of the consoles or the main viewer, then sat down in the dark and opened her tablet. The desk console used too much energy.

She saw the message indicator light flash as she picked it up, letting her know she had a new message.

It was from Rido: >>*I can't wait for my very first sleepover tonight. Is it too much to consider this evening a date? Let me know, as I may or may not be bringing pajamas.*<<

Dana snorted with laughter. She hadn't intended to be vague in her request. She'd just wanted someone in her room with her so she could sleep. Rido had gotten the wrong idea, and it was her own fault. She rubbed her hand over her forehead. *When am I going to learn to think?*

The door chimed and her heart thumped hard in her chest.

"Who is it?"

"Lieutenant Nancy Westlake," the COMP announced.

"Admit."

The door slid open and Nancy entered. Dana waved her in.

"Come on in, Lieutenant. What can I do for you?"

"I didn't come in here for me," Nancy admitted, looking sheepish. "I saw Wade working up the courage to come in here, and I thought I'd give you a heads-up since it seems you've been avoiding him."

Dana started to shake her head in denial, but Nancy raised one blonde eyebrow and crossed her arms over her chest.

"Fine," Dana said with a sigh. "I'm avoiding him. But I'm not the only one avoiding people. You and Cliff have barely said two words to each other since we came out from under that virus."

Nancy's cheeks blossomed into bright pink circles. "We got a few items out of our system, but . . . things are awkward now."

"I can see that." Dana tilted her head to one side and

stood up. She moved around the desk so they could both sit on the same side, facing each other.

Nancy sat down with a huff. "I don't know what happened. I thought if we were, you know, together, things would work themselves out."

Dana shook her head. "Things are rarely that simple." Those words applied only too well to them both. She tried to stay focused on Nancy's situation and not her own, as it wasn't exactly the same. Both Cliff and Nancy were free to explore their options.

"Why doesn't he want to move forward?" Dana asked.

Nancy let out a short laugh. "He does want to move forward. It's me that doesn't want to."

Dana sat back in her seat and waited. She'd thought it was Cliff who wasn't ready because he was so young. They all were. Coupling up this early in the voyage wasn't for everyone.

"I'm just not ready to settle down with the first guy who comes along. I told him that before the virus. But then…" Nancy trailed off, and she looked over at Dana, her eyes pleading for understanding.

Dana knew too well what it was like. Her heart wanted someone she couldn't keep.

"You obviously care for him," she said kindly. "He's just confused because he feels like he's getting mixed messages."

"That's exactly it." Nancy's head hung down for a moment, then sprang up. Dana could see the wheels in her head turning. "Want to go rock climbing?"

Dana looked down at her console, at the reports that were piling up, and shook her head.

"I need a good climb," Nancy pressed. "And since we can't use any of the virtual machines while we're in condition three, I think you need it as much as I do."

Dana looked at the door to the bridge. There wasn't anything left to do for the day, and they were on course. If something went wrong, she'd hear about it.

"Let's go."

CHAPTER 22

They were halfway up the wall when it dawned on Dana. She wasn't a skilled climber and doing this in the dark might be the biggest mistake of her life. She was tethered to Nancy, who was already a full body length ahead of her. Her climbing shorts and top were bright pink, and clung to her toned arms and legs. She called back down every once in a while to make sure Dana was still there.

"How are you doing? Need a little more rope?"

Dana shook her head. She needed to keep going. If she slipped, she didn't want the slack to bring them both crashing to the floor.

Nancy waited while Dana grabbed for another hand-hold. She was thankful the virtual googles were off limits in order to preserve energy, sure she didn't need the added feel of dangling off the edge of a real cliff. The VR experience allowed for the addition of weather elements for those who wanted the added challenge of heat, or even rainwater. The handholds could be rotated and eliminated to provide more variety, but Dana couldn't imagine making the climb any more difficult. Her leg shook as she lifted her left foot up to the next nodule and pushed herself upward, closer to Nancy.

"I can't believe you do this every day," she huffed.

"I don't. Sometimes I do the skiing program. Reminds me of home."

Dana had forgotten Nancy was from the southern polar region of Zelenia. She enjoyed the snow and cooler temperatures more than most. Despite sweat pooling in all the places her skin touched, Dana could still feel the chill in the air as she climbed. The fitted navy-blue shirt and shorts weren't designed to keep her warm, and the ship's temperature would continue at ten degrees cooler than optimal to conserve whatever extra energy they could. It was just another of the many sacrifices they'd made in order to reach their destination.

"It's not much further now," Nancy said, turning back to search for her next handhold. "So . . . you never told me why you're avoiding Wade. I thought he and Maggie broke up."

"They did."

"So that means he's free to go after anyone he wants." Nancy pulled herself up with an ease Dana envied. "You're surprised it's you?"

"I wouldn't say it's a complete surprise," Dana panted. "We have a history. He's comfortable with me, but I'm the captain. I can't get caught up with someone on my crew."

"Yeah, but this is different. You have feelings for him."

Dana grunted rather than disagree.

Nancy glanced down at her. "Don't deny it. I saw your face the night of the party, and later on in the Lounge."

Dana frowned back. "What about my face?"

"Look, let's just say if Maggie hadn't been there, the night might have been different."

Dana shook her head and huffed. The cure for the virus hadn't erased the intense feelings she had whenever the memory surfaced.

She reached for another nodule with her left toe, boosting herself up. "I don't have any designs on Wade, engaged or not. We're just friends. Besides, he and Maggie just broke up. Neither of them are dealing with it very well, and I'm not going to be his reason for avoiding her. We all have to find a way to live on this ship together regardless of our histories. I can't have their relationship interfering with ship's business."

"Maggie hasn't done a broadcast in over a week," Nancy reminded her.

"I know. As much as I wish it wasn't the case, she has an effect on morale, and until the two of them come to terms with what's happened, the rest of us are going to suffer. Wade is grasping for me because I'm the closest. I'm no one's rebound."

"Fair enough. But I wouldn't mind being his rebound."

Dana slipped and had to regain her footing before she fell.

"You all right?" Nancy asked, not bothering to hide her smirk.

"Fine," Dana said once her stomach had settled back into place, its contents thoroughly jumbled. "What do you mean? Are you interested in Wade?"

"I don't think there's a woman onboard who isn't interested in Wade." Nancy managed a shrug while still clinging to the wall. "He'd never look my way though, so you've got nothing to fear from me."

"Wait . . . is that the reason you can't settle on Cliff?"

"No, I just don't want to settle." Nancy sighed. "I'm young. There's a lot of galaxies left to see, and I don't want to be tied down to the first boy who gives me butterflies."

It seemed like a sound plan. There was only one flaw, and Dana was quick to point it out.

"Yeah, except you love each other. Everything is all fun and games until there are actual feelings involved. How long do you expect him to wait while you're off seeing the galaxy?"

Nancy was quiet for a moment, as if considering her words. She was at the top a moment later, and she sat on the ledge and waited for Dana to finish her slow ascent. When she reached the top, Nancy helped pull her up, and they pulled out their tubes of water and drank.

Nancy answered after Dana's breathing returned to normal. "I guess I don't know. We hit it off right away. I'm not denying it. But we're just . . ."

"Friends?" Dana smiled and shrugged. "That makes two of us." Dana stared down at the floor and noted from where they sat in the dark, they were practically invisible. "I invited Rido to sleep over tonight."

Nancy choked on her water, turning to look at her. "Wow. You do know how to pick 'em."

"It's not like that. After Barnes broke into my room last night, I realized I'm not going to get any sleep unless I know there's someone else in there with me." She looked down at her dangling shoes. "But I think he might have gotten the wrong idea about the whole thing."

"You asked him to spend the night and you think he might have the wrong idea?" Nancy let out a laugh loud enough that a couple working out on the mats below looked up at them through the dark.

"I wasn't exactly clear about why I wanted him to stay over. I was just trying to make sure he was available."

Nancy bumped her shoulder with her own. "But you do like him?"

Dana was sure she liked him. That was the easy part. It was the rest that got complicated.

"He's not a member of your crew," Nancy added. "There's nothing stopping you."

"No, I guess there isn't." Dana knew logically he was a good choice for her, but she wasn't ready to complicate her duty with a relationship.

Nancy tried to search her face. "Unless what's stopping you is Wade."

Dana was grateful for the dark. In her heart, she knew she found Wade as comfortable as he found her. He was the easy option, but not necessarily the smart one.

Rido, though . . . he had a molten desire that appealed to her. There always seemed to be something more under the surface, and she wanted to know him better. However, she couldn't imagine openly dating the ship's mind-shark.

"To be honest, I don't know."

"Rido's a great guy." Nancy rubbed both hands down the front of her thighs as if to get rid of the gathering sweat. "You should know, I made out with him once."

Dana turned, looking at Nancy with fresh eyes. "You did?"

Nancy waved a hand. "It was a while ago, early in the mission, when we thought we were going into cryo. We made out, but there was nothing else there, so neither of us pursued it. I didn't want you to hear it from someone else."

Dana nodded. It occurred to her at that moment that she had no idea how many women on board had been with Rido, and that bothered her. Nancy was young, blonde, and agreeable. However, many women fit that description, substituting hair and skin color.

Did she want to be just another woman he'd had a thing with? The acrid taste in her mouth at the thought forced her to admit the answer was no.

"It's fine. I'm glad you told me. Rido and I aren't serious, and I'm not sure we ever will be. For now, I enjoy his company, and I'm glad he agreed to spend the night so I can get some proper sleep." Dana kicked her feet in the open air. "You know, the next time we take this wall, you'll have to keep up with me."

Nancy laughed, and Dana joined in.

"So, how the *sou* do we get down?" Dana asked. In the dark, she couldn't find a ladder or rope.

"We climb down," Nancy said, sliding off the ledge and positioning herself back on the wall. "Ready?"

Dana's arms felt like limp noodles, and her legs were still tired from the climb. She shook her head.

"Merciful be kind," she muttered. "On second thought, remind me never to do this again."

CHAPTER 23

EARTHA

Peter hadn't revealed her secret, as he'd promised, but for some reason keeping him hidden felt wrong. He'd helped her, Luke, and Ari, but now things were returning to normal and the others were searching for him. Eartha knew she had to tell someone.

The problem was, then her secret would be out. It was hard enough when her own family gave her strange looks when she talked about the odd feelings she had.

She finished her homework early so she could meet Luke and Mr. Jennison in the Commons. They'd sent her a message that morning to let her know where they'd be. It had been over a week since she'd seen Mr. Jennison, and Luke's imprisonment had made it impossible for her to visit him until she'd planned his escape with Peter to save Ari.

She gathered up her pack and flung it over her shoulder as she headed for the door.

"Where are you headed off to, young lady?" Esme asked.

"The Commons. Mr. Jennison and Luke are going to be there."

"Not until you finish your homework."

"It's finished," she said, taking another step toward the door, but Esme called her back again.

"Just a minute." Esme placed her hands on her hips the way she must have thought mothers did. "You didn't ask for permission to go roaming the ship."

Eartha hated it when she did that. She was thirteen now. She shouldn't need to ask to go to the Commons to sit with an old man and a boy from school.

"May I go to the Commons?" she asked with a roll of her eyes.

"Where is this attitude coming from?"

Eartha waited with her arms crossed for Esme to realize how stupid this conversation was. "Is there something else?"

Esme frowned back at her. "Yes, you haven't cleaned your room in a week, and the smell is seeping into the rest of the cabin. Why don't you go in there and find out what the floor looks like?"

Eartha's eyebrows drew together. She couldn't be serious. "Now?"

"Yes, *now*. Mr. Jennison and Luke will be in the Commons again. Tonight, you have chores to do. I'm sure you've got enough laundry in there to last me a week. Why don't you gather it up and place it in the basket, and I'll get started on it for you."

Esme didn't budge, and Eartha knew when she was beaten. She went back to her room and threw her pack on the floor. She fell back on the array of clothes she'd pulled out when she'd been trying to decide on the jeans and floral shirt she was wearing. Her room smelled like death, but it wasn't all her fault. While the virus had infected her family, they'd been too concerned with themselves to notice she'd been eating in her room. She may have forgotten a plate or two somewhere.

She pulled her tablet out of her pack and called Luke. He answered, and she could see he was sitting with Mr. Jennison, the three virtual boards already lit up and the pieces in play. It seemed the game had already started.

"I can't go."

"What?" Luke's mouth turned down as if he were disappointed. Maybe she was imagining it.

"Esme's making me stay home and clean my room."

"Are you going to play, or talk to your friend all night?" Mr. Jennison said out of view.

Luke tucked a wave of his chin-length brown hair behind his right ear and gave her a killer smile. "That's too bad. I was sort of looking forward to seeing you."

Was she dreaming, or did he just say he'd wanted to see her?

She felt the heat under her arms as she took in his words. After the way he'd looked at Dana while under the influence of the virus, she'd thought she'd lost any chance at him. She was only thirteen, he was three years older, and he probably wasn't thinking of dating someone her age. When she was sixteen, though, he'd be nineteen, and by then maybe she'd have changed his mind.

Thankfully, there were few options on board. The other girls in school, though pretty, couldn't keep his attention. He'd said once that they shared the same brain. He didn't mind hanging out with her alone or with Mr. Jennison, and she wanted to spend every moment possible with him.

She looked up at the ventilation shaft she'd used to get out of her room the last time. Eric had made her promise not to go crawling around in them anymore, but that didn't mean she'd forgotten how to get around the ship through the tubes. She'd avoided the areas that her mother had marked off as dangerous, and she realized in that moment she was no longer a stowaway bound to the tubes. Eartha only needed to go as far as the next maintenance shaft. From there, she could climb out and walk to the Commons like everyone else.

"It won't take me long to clean up. Wait for me, I'll be there."

"If you hurry, you'll get to see Mr. Jennison wipe the floor with me." His deep laugh tickled her belly.

"I will."

She signed off and tucked the tablet back into her

pack. Eartha glanced around the room and then shrugged. She'd clean up later. Right now, she had a place to be, and friends to see. Becky would have been so proud to see her rebelling. It was exactly the kind of thing she'd have encouraged her to do. Her voice was as clear in her head as if she were in the room with her.

"Go ahead, girl! Go and get him."

"What if he doesn't like me the way I like him?" Eartha asked aloud.

"He so likes you. Why else would he ask you to meet him?"

"I'm going to be in so much trouble for this," Eartha said as she climbed up into the ventilation shaft.

Becky's voice took on a dreamy quality. *"Yeah, but it's going to be worth it when your first kiss is with Luke."*

Eartha smiled as she imagined it, then she spoke to the COMP.

"Computer, play Eartha's music list two."

Her music came out loud and angry. It was the music she used to shut out Esme when she didn't want to talk to her. She'd get the signal and leave her alone until the playlist stopped. It gave Eartha an hour before she had to be back maybe more.

There was a sharp pain in her stomach. She'd told herself a lie. She probably wouldn't make it back before she was caught.

"Besides, it's not like the Rogans are your real parents. You're a teenager now. They need to deal with it."

Becky's voice in her ear firmed her resolve. Eartha nodded to herself as she secured the grate behind her and headed for the Commons without another thought about her smelly room. She crawled through the shafts until she reached a corridor next to the one where their cabin was located.

Eartha had her hands on the grate when there was a sound behind her. She turned, wondering if someone was doing maintenance in the area. Eartha's mouth fell open at the sight of Peter Barnes.

Peter carried a small light the size of a pen that illuminated his face. He held a finger to his lips and motioned with his head for her to follow him. Eartha turned back to the grate. This was eating into her time with Luke, but she made the tight turn in the shaft and follow him. He was leading her toward the location where he slept, but this time, instead of leading her up, he stopped at the junction and pushed half his body inside the tube so he could face her. Eartha stopped and stared at him as he used the pen light to illuminate her face.

"Who have you told about where I live?" The whispered question was a growl.

Eartha's eyes stung from the bright light. "Stop it," she said, holding a hand up over her face. "I haven't told anyone."

"I promised I would keep your secret if you kept mine."

"I did," Eartha insisted. "What's the matter with you?"

Peter huffed, lowering the light at last. Eartha's eyes took a minute to adjust, the bright red dots in her vision dying as she focused on his face.

"Someone's been up in my space. Now I can't go back there. I had to leave half my stuff behind."

"That's not my fault," Eartha said, her voice a whine.

"It is, because you're the only one who knew about it." His face turned cruel. "I'm going to shout your little secret from the comms, just wait."

"That's not true. People saw you running around the ship. They know you're here somewhere."

The last thing she needed was for Esme and Eric to have another reason to get rid of her. With their baby coming, they were already overly concerned about everything, and if she was a threat to their baby, she'd be the first to go.

"That's what I get from trusting a loud-mouth kid," he muttered, turning to leave.

"I'm not the one who murdered someone," she shot back. "If they find you, it's your own fault. I didn't tell anyone."

"Be sure you don't. I'd hate to think what the rest of the ship would do with you if they figured out you were the one putting people to sleep with a thought." Though she couldn't see his face, Peter snorted. "Don't forget what happens to people who cross me. I wouldn't want anything to happen to your robot, or your little boyfriend from the brig."

Eartha's heart sank. The thought of losing either Ari or Luke because of Peter made her blood boil.

"Don't you dare hurt them."

"Don't give me a reason to, or the next time you won't get a warning."

Peter disappeared into the dark corridor, and Eartha had to turn around and make her way back.

She checked the time. At this rate, she was too far from the Commons. She'd only get fifteen minutes before she'd have to return to her room. If she crawled back now, she might make it before the music playlist ended.

She reached the ventilation shaft of her room in time. She could still hear the music blasting as she opened the grate and crawled out, but when she looked up, she saw Esme sitting at her desk chair in the corner, her arms and legs crossed.

"Computer, end playlist."

The blaring music stopped, and Esme stood up. Eartha could see even in the limited light she was red in the face. She shook her head, then stormed out without a word. That wasn't a good sign. If Esme was so mad, she couldn't even yell at her, things were bad. At best, she'd be grounded. At worst . . . she didn't want to think about the worst.

Eartha plopped down on the bed and reached underneath. Her hand landed on a plate with a piece of bread growing two layers of furry mold. *Gross.* Maybe it was time for her to clean her room.

CHAPTER 24

Dana chose her purple silk robe and pajamas for the night as she waited for Rido to arrive. The last thing she wanted to do was leave him alone in her room while she went into the bathroom to change.

Of course, wearing silk pajamas sent a certain message, and she realized she'd have to be quick and state her intentions before he got any ideas. Dana would make it duro-glass clear why she'd invited him over the minute he walked in.

The door chimed and Dana glanced at the clock. He was only a few minutes late. That pleased her. Too early and she'd have thought him eager, and what she had to say to him would be a letdown. She closed her robe and moved to the door. It opened, and instead of Rido standing in front of her, there was Wade. The smile on her face fell as she saw the frown on his.

"I need to talk to you," he said, giving her a quick once-over before meeting her eyes again. "You've been avoiding me all day."

"I haven't been avoiding you, I've been busy. Speaking of which," she looked over his shoulder, "this isn't really a good time."

"I don't think you want to have this conversation in the corridor," he said, allowing her to see the two crewmen passing by behind him.

"Fine," she said, moving to one side so he could come in. She glanced in the corridor again, looking for Rido. *Where is he?*

"I know things have been weird between us," Wade started as he passed into the room, "but I think it's time to clear the air."

"Wade, I—"

"No, just wait," he said, cutting her off and stepping closer—too close. "Let me get this out. I realize that the viral infection may have been the catalyst for my breakup with Maggie. It wasn't about you, or about the man she was seeing, it was about her and me. We didn't feel comfortable enough to tell each other the truth, and that means something." Wade ran a hand through his hair and paced the floor as he spoke.

"What you said under the virus wasn't you," Dana supplied when she saw him struggling.

"That's the problem. It was me. Maybe not with a grain of salt to make it palatable, but it *was* me. You and I . . . we've been doing this kind of dance ever since I got here.

I'm here to tell you I'm not ready to give up on starting up where we left off."

"We can't just pretend like the last few years didn't happen. You and Maggie need time to heal."

Wade shook his head, returning to stand in front of her again, forcing her to tilt her head back to avoid staring at his heaving chest. "I know what Maggie and I had was real, but not deep. We weren't willing to put our pasts out on the table and admit to them until the virus forced it on us. That's no way to start a marriage, and I don't want that kind of person for a life partner." He reached out and put his hands on either side of her crossed arms. "Dana, you're the one that makes me smile, the one I can talk to about anything. You're the one that gets me. You don't keep secrets from me."

"That's not true," she said quickly. "I'm the Captain. Some things I'm not at liberty to tell you."

He waved a hand in front of his face. "I know you did what you had to do. You were following orders. But if we were together, things would be different."

Dana thought of the other ships that had left Zelenia. When he learned the truth about that, would he still look at her with those stormy gray eyes filled with desire?

She didn't think so.

"Wade, wait—"

"I don't want to wait anymore," he said. "You and I belong together, and the sooner you realize it, the better. I'll admit I was mad at first when you didn't come rushing into my arms after my admittedly sappy, heartfelt declaration. That was the virus, too. You just didn't know how you were feeling. But at that moment, just before Maggie showed up, I saw it in your eyes. You want to be with me as much as I want to be with you."

The door chimed and Dana sighed, letting her head fall forward. Wade frowned.

"Are you expecting someone?"

"That's what I've been trying to tell you."

Dana pulled away from him and answered the door. It slid open on Rido as he waved a handful of flowers and a bottle of something that looked like an amber whiskey at her. "I stopped off to get a little something for our slumber party."

"You're late," Dana said, gesturing for him to come in.

Wade was still looking between them as he did, shock on his face. "He's spending the night?" he asked, his question rushing out in a hiss.

"Yes. Perhaps we could talk about this another time." Dana gestured pointedly to the door.

Rido looked from her to Wade. "I get the feeling I'm interrupting something important," he said, but he didn't move to the door. For that, Dana was grateful.

"No, the Commander was just leaving." She gave Wade another significant look.

Wade stood still a moment longer. Rido took his cue and made himself more comfortable on the couch, then turned to watch them like an entertainment vid. Then Wade straightened and walked out the door without turning back.

Dana sighed as the door slid closed behind him. She turned back to Rido, who watched her with interest, but said nothing.

"I'm sorry about that. It was just a misunderstanding."

Rido stood up and grabbed the bottle. "You look like you need a drink. Good thing I brought some. Where are your glasses?"

She gestured. "Middle shelf, there on the left of the sink."

He poured her a glass and handed it to her before grabbing an empty glass for himself. Dana sat down in the nearest chair and downed the contents without hesitation. It burned her throat, and she felt the heat of it racing for her stomach. He filled it again before he filled his own, and she took a sip before placing it on the table. He sat back down on the couch, staring at her over the rim of his glass.

"Did that misunderstanding put a damper on our evening?"

Dana glanced over at the table where he'd lain the flowers and pinched the bridge of her nose.

"About that . . ." she began. "This evening isn't what you think. After the break-in last night, I realized I needed someone here so I could get some sleep."

"Ah." Rido nodded. "I see. So not only are you using me to get rid of your ex, you only want me for my body." He laughed at himself.

Dana shook her head and rubbed at her forehead. "I'm sorry if I misled you. The last few nights have been horrible, as you know. I'm just so tired. If I don't start getting some sleep, it's going to affect my duties." She looked up at him. "Are you still willing to stay?"

Rido put his glass down and patted the couch next to him. Dana got up and moved to his side. He put an arm around her and pulled her in so close she could smell the woodsy scent of his soap and aftershave.

"I'll be here every night for as long as you need me."

Dana sighed against him.

———

ONE NIGHT BECAME SEVEN BEFORE DANA WAS GETTING enough sleep. Despite her protests, Rido insisted on sleeping on a mat at the foot of the bed. She tried to persuade him they could share the bed, but he wouldn't have it. He insisted she'd relax more without him in the bed to distract her, and he'd been right. She'd slept better than she had since Barnes' escape.

Deep down, Dana knew it wouldn't last, though she clung to the moments with Rido until they reached the eighth day of their journey toward the wormhole. That would be the last morning she woke up from a full night's sleep.

CHAPTER 25

Darkness is a shroud that drapes his cold limbs about me.
It grips my heart, squeezing out the last of its light.
Dimming my eyes, he fills up my nose and mouth, suffocating
me.
Soon there will be nothing left of the girl I once was.
Into the black nothingness, the fear of him envelopes me.
Now I am Darkness, hunting down the light to replace what I
lost.

Eight days of darkness took their toll on her people. Most of the passengers and crew kept to themselves, staying in their quarters. They avoided the long, unlit corridors and passageways of the ship.

Dana walked the halls with the distinct sensation she was being swallowed up by the darkness, though sitting on the bridge was far worse. The never-ending silence and emptiness made her twitchy. What had her father done in the early days when they hadn't had ships fitted with advanced propulsion drives and virtual technology? She couldn't imagine the tedium he must have endured.

Called to the bridge moments ago, Dana didn't have a choice but to make her way through the corridors and back up. Not that it made any difference, but she, like everyone she passed, kept one hand on the wall while walking. It helped her avoid running into someone coming from the opposite direction, and kept her from losing her sense of orientation. Without the normal over-head lighting, it was easy to get lost. Every corridor looked the same.

Dana reached the bridge and called out, keeping her eyes on the floor. She didn't want to stumble over the small stairs leading to her chair, where her chief engineers stood waiting. Wade stood up as she entered, but she avoided searching his face for any reaction to her presence. Nancy was at the helm, facing them.

"Report."

The Rogans stood side-by-side. Esme held one hand over her stomach, and Eric wrung his hands. Dana braced herself for the inevitable bad news.

"We've diverted all energy to necessary systems days ago, as per your request," Eric began.

"It's not enough," Esme continued. "If we don't reach the wormhole within the next two days, we won't have the propulsion necessary to enter."

Eric jumped in again. "The engines will slow to a stop before we reach it, and we'll be dead out here."

"Lieutenant Westlake," Dana asked, "how far are we from the wormhole?"

"According to the coordinates that Ashwin came up with, we're still four days out," Nancy reported.

"So what you're saying is we won't even have the energy to turn on the lights in the event someone with windows passes close enough to see us when we're dead in the water. We may need to implement a secondary protocol," Dana muttered to herself. That meant going entirely to portable lighting. No music, no cooked food, no showers, nothing that required energy on the ship. Every scrap would be diverted to the engines. They might even need to drop the temperature another few degrees. As it was, her fingertips were numb, even while wearing her jacket. The only one not constantly shivering was Nancy.

"We're already at condition three," Wade cautioned. "Any lower and our living situation becomes extreme. The passengers may not abide by the new regulation. We'll have to have security standing by to ensure the others are complying with it."

"Make it happen," Dana said, turning her head to where Lieutenant Commander Valente was standing.

Valente nodded back. "Yes, Captain."

He had covered his bald head in a knit cap and wore a large, pea-green coat with faux fur on the edges. She wondered where he'd found it, as he'd been from the warmer northern continent.

"Ensign Harden, drop the lights. Everyone go to palm-lights for the time being. Drop the temperature another five degrees and hold. Divert everything to the engines, and recommend people huddle up in groups to stay warm. It's going to be a long couple of days."

"Yes, Captain," they said in unison.

"Lieutenant Westlake, steady as she goes. Continue to monitor our speed."

Dana turned and bumped into Wade, who she hadn't realized was standing right behind her.

"Captain, a moment," he said with a nod toward her office. "Please."

Dana didn't want to talk about anything other than dealing with the ship's energy crisis. She had enough on her plate without having to worry about a lovesick commander with a broken heart. She needed to set him straight right away.

As soon as the doors to her office closed behind them, she spoke. "Commander, I need you focused on the mission at hand. There are too many lives at stake. We're risking everything on this, and I don't have time to deal with whatever this is," she said, waving a hand between them.

Wade squared his shoulders. "I didn't come here to discuss my personal feelings for you. However, if you insist, I can tell you about my sleepless nights, worrying about if you're okay and wishing we were together. I can remind you of how much I'm hating the way things are between us, and wondering when you're going to stop shutting me out—or I can tell you what I came to say, Captain."

Ending with 'Captain' had been a smart play on his part. It was just on the other side of insubordination for him to speak so freely, but she had been the one to start it, and she realized her mistake.

"I'm sorry, you're right. What's on your mind?"

The corner of his mouth twitched, and then he seemed to be ready to get down to business. "You need to know that the permanent Judicial Committee is bringing forth formal charges against you."

She couldn't have heard that right. "Against me?"

"Yes." Wade cleared his throat to cover his amusement. "It seems that although most of what happened during the infection was no one's fault, there are some demanding your head on a platter for what's happened to them so far."

Dana wanted to scream, and as she paced, she forgot the corner of her desk. Her thigh rammed into it, almost dropping her to the floor. "*By the Majestic!* What the *sou* do they expect me to do out here?"

"Are you all right?" Wade took her by the hand and led her over to the couch, where she could sit down.

Dana propped up her leg across the cushions, forcing him to remain standing as she lay back. "I'm the Captain of this ship. I don't answer to them. My duties are clear. If someone has a problem with it, they're free to take an escape pod and wait for someone else to save them."

Wade nodded. "Agreed, however, as we would like the rest of the crew and passengers to recognize the limited authority of the Committee, there may need to be some acceptance of their role by you."

"I am their authority," Dana snapped. "They're questioning mine. I won't let them pull me into some kind of judicial circus to appease some grieving passengers."

"They're not all passengers. Some of them are crew. Not all of them are related to the seven who were killed in the most recent events." Wade's head tilted down. She couldn't read his eyes in the dark, as neither of them had picked up a hand-light.

"Fine. Tell the Committee I'll answer the charges, but I won't be prosecuted in a court of my creation, especially when the final say about sentencing comes down to me."

"I think, in this case, it's better to be vocal than to be silent. I'll arrange it."

She felt him turn to leave, speaking up at the last second. "Wade, I'm sorry about how things ended between you and Maggie. It's not right, or fair."

He might have shrugged, but she couldn't tell from where she sat. His voice was near the door as he replied.

"I'm not sorry. There's been enough time wasted." His footsteps drew closer until he knelt in front of her, his face so close she could feel his breath on her cheek. "I know I shouldn't have demanded anything from you. You're right, it's too soon." His breath tickled her ear as he leaned in. "So if you tell me there's no chance that we'll be together, I'll never mention it again. I promise."

Dana's breath quickened as heat radiated out of her. She didn't trust herself to speak. She wondered if she would always have such powerful feelings for him. They were bound together. He was like the sun, and she couldn't control her orbit around him.

He took her silence for an answer.

"Good." When he stood again, the cool air rushed in and she shivered in the dark. "I'll inform the Committee of your decision and arrange a time for you to meet with them. May I be dismissed?"

"Um, yes," she stammered. She watched him walk back onto the bridge, the lighting of the consoles the only thing to illuminate the smile on his face.

Oh, no . . . what the sou am I getting herself into? Dana rubbed at her thigh with one hand. She'd forgotten all about the pain until a second ago. Now she sat alone in the dark, contemplating what she was going to do about Wade and the Judicial Committee.

CHAPTER 26

He wasn't wrong about them being out for her blood. The next day, Dana received a message from them insisting they meet. She wasn't going to be pushed into some kind of trial while she was on duty. She risked provoking them further by putting them off until the end of the day. There was too much to do, and conserving energy was Dana's first priority.

The Committee members had already heard statements from those complaining about her decisions as captain. Because it was her actions being called into question, Dana wasn't privy to the full statements, only the summary given her by the Committee.

They were gathered in the converted conference room. They had removed the table, leaving just enough chairs for President Muñoz and Chancellor Evans, who it seemed were serving as the remaining judges. No doubt, due to the nature of the Committee and its judges falling under her purview, they hadn't attempted to conscript a third.

She sat in front of the Committee and two judges. One overhead light was in use, and it irked her that its energy was being diverted to this room for something as trivial as this.

"Please state your name and rank for the record," Chancellor Evans said.

"Dana Pinet, Captain of *Starship Hope*."

"Thank you, Captain," President Muñoz said. "Just a reminder to all parties that this is not a trial, but a hearing. This is an opportunity for the Committee to get the Captain's side on matters before making their determination on whether it warrants a trial."

Dana tried not to roll her eyes. In the dimly lit room, they might see it for the contempt it was. Though she was finding it hard to conceal. A panel who didn't understand her duties on board or the daily decisions she made was not a committee of her peers.

"Captain," Evans continued, "the accusations put before you are the following: Failure to secure the ship in a time of war. Failure to comply with Zelenian standards of living. Failure to capture and detain a known murderer. Failure to maintain a professional decorum, as required by your rank. Failure to establish a means of justice for those who have been killed in the line of duty."

Dana's mouth fell open as she listened to the outrageous charges. Her blood was boiling before it was all done.

"How do you answer these charges?"

Dana spat out the words, not disgusted that she had to say them. "I won't answer them."

"Then let's take them one at a time," the Chancellor said. There was a distinct smile on his face, as if he were enjoying this.

"No, we're done here," Dana said, standing. The committee squirmed in their seats, murmuring to each other.

"The Committee will remain silent!" Chancellor Evans called out. He was in love with power. She'd made a mistake in letting this go to his head. "Captain, you will answer the charges, or face trial."

Dana had indulged them enough. "I won't stand trial for doing my job. I've worked tirelessly for this ship and its crew. This Committee can't be allowed to make a mockery of what I have to do every day just to keep this ship running. Yes, we've lost some of our people, and we've had to deal with problems we didn't see coming. It's unfortunate, but not unavoidable when on a journey like this one. I am fighting to give our species a chance at survival. If someone else thinks they can do better, have them take it up with those on the ground who gave their lives so we could be here—the same people who chose me for this position and entrusted me with your lives. This hearing is over. You are all dismissed, and don't forget to turn off the light."

Dana stormed out of the room. Wade was waiting for her when she reached her office. She would have tripped over his feet if he hadn't rushed to stand up.

"How did it go?"

"What a load of *soul!*" she seethed. "It took everything I had not to throw them all in the brig. Sometimes I wonder why I bother to get up in the mornings when I have to deal with such ridiculous demands."

"It looks like you came out of it all right."

Dana turned toward her desk, feeling her way with her hands to avoid ramming her other leg into a corner. She made it to her chair without injury and considered it another disaster averted.

"Where are we on energy conservation?" she asked, wanting to put the farce of a hearing behind her.

"We're doing well. Valente and his team are on top of the energy spikes. He pays a special visit to anyone who's over their allotment. It only took a few noteworthy crack-downs for people to get the idea."

"Are we within visual range of the wormhole yet?"

He shook his head. "Nothing on our sensors that we can confirm."

Dana slammed a palm down on her desk. "We should see something by now. This is absurd. I'm tempted to strap that Teku to the nose of our ship."

"Maybe his calculations are off. He didn't have the exact coordinates . . . he may be off by a substantial margin."

"We can't afford to be off by anything. We don't have enough energy to do much more than sit in front of that wormhole. If we try to go through it, we don't know if our inertia will carry us through, or if we'll be stuck someplace in the middle."

"It's not looking good. The Rogans are doing everything they can short of pulling out oars and rowing."

Dana laughed, and Wade moved to sit in the chair in front of her desk, splaying his hands out in front of him. He was reaching for her. It was a question, not a demand.

She put her hands out and linked fingers with him. Despite the cold in the room, his hands were warm. They were always warm. Her mother used to say 'warm hands, warm heart' as if it were some kind of insight. In Wade's case, she wouldn't be wrong.

"Remember the history books about Blue Earth?" Dana asked. "The old ships made of wood that had used large swaths of cloth to capture the wind? It could propel them in the direction they needed to go."

"I saw a glass ship in a bottle in the old Captain Lethbridge display in one of the museums back home. What made you think of it?"

"I was trying to think of what it must have been like for them. Depending on the waves of the sea and the air to propel them forward and back. We need to think of something to keep us moving or we won't make it to the other side."

Wade let out a laugh. "If only there was wind in space."

Dana thought for a moment. An idea was forming in the recesses of her mind. Not close enough to catch, but close enough that it almost—

Then it was gone. She shook her head.

"What?" Wade asked as she pulled her hands away from his.

"Nothing. I was just thinking. What's the first thing you want to do when we reach the space station?"

"Have a nice hot shower," he said immediately. "I smell like a meat locker."

Dana laughed. "You're not the only one. It's like I can smell when someone's angry or frustrated these days."

They fell into a companionable silence, sitting in the dark, trying not to breathe in too much of each other's unwashed bodies. It made Dana giggle.

"You can smell me, can't you?" Wade said.

Dana burst out laughing and couldn't stop. Her eyes teared up, falling down her face until she hiccuped and realized she wanted to cry as much as laugh. The hot trails cooled on her cheeks too fast, reminding her that the temp had been lowered again. She shivered. The dark enveloped her again, and the only way out was her connection to Wade.

"We might not make it," she said softly.

"I know."

She liked that he didn't try to make her feel better. Dana knew he would understand her next words, so she didn't filter them. "After everything we've been through, it's not fair."

"It doesn't negate what we've done though." Wade reached over the desk again and felt around in the dark for her. His hands inched down from her elbows to her wrists until he could pull her hands toward him, the rest of her following, his breath centimeters from her face. "This isn't some fairytale from Blue Earth. There's no wand-wielding old woman who's going to save us. We've got you."

"But I don't know what to do when we get there," she admitted. "We won't last long on this side of the wormhole without help."

He gave her hands a squeeze. "You'll think of something. You're just like your dad. He never gave up, even in the face of impossible odds."

His words jarred something loose. Her father's last act as the captain of the *Atlantis* had been to launch the escape pods and ram an asteroid off course using his own starship. She and Wade had survived, along with many others. They'd lost a mutual friend, Bonnie, and several others in the asteroid field, but most had made it down to the surface in the escape pods. She'd hadn't forgotten what it took to save them.

"You're right . . . I am like my father."

"That's right, so let's stop moping in the dark and go huddle on the bridge where we belong," Wade said.

Still holding his hand, she felt him stand, tugging her around the desk to join her. Dana got to her feet and joined him. She was about to pull away when he held fast. She couldn't see his face in the dark, but the heat coming off him was unmistakable. His natural scent didn't bother her. In fact, she liked the smell of him.

His hand was holding the side of her cold face as he tilted her head up. "I don't like regrets, and if I don't do this, I'll regret it for the rest of my life, even if it's just a few more days. Please, may I kiss you, Captain?"

Dana's throat worked, but she couldn't form the words. Her head bobbed once, and he pulled her close to him, Wade's other hand cupping the other side of her face as he pressed his mouth to hers.

There weren't any fireworks. Not like the first time. Nor was it like the feverish grabbing they'd done while infected with the alien virus. No, this was different. The warmth from his lips melted hers, and he drank her in like a man with an insatiable thirst. The heat of their joined mouths spread down her body and radiated from her stomach. Her toes ached as she stretched to push against him, her hands finding his chest and reaching into his open jacket. If he hadn't been holding her, she would have lost her balance, as she had no way of knowing which way was up. Wade was the only thing grounding her, and if he fell, she knew she'd fall right after him.

When he pulled back with a sigh, she leaned into him, her mouth working up to a protest. Then Dana heard the call she must have missed the first time.

"Captain to the bridge."

Dana's feet were planted on the floor again, and though they were both breathing heavily, neither wanted to let go. Dana turned away in the direction she thought was the adjoining door to the bridge, but wouldn't be sure until she reached it. She felt the warmth of his hand on her lower back until the doors opened. Dana said a quick thank you to the Merciful for her dark skin and the lack of light. No one would be able to see much of their faces even on the bridge.

"Captain on the bridge," Wade called out in case they hadn't heard the door or noticed the two figures entering.

"Captain, we've got something," Lieutenant Westlake said. Dana could hear the excitement in Nancy's voice, and didn't have to ask what it was that had shown up on sensors, but did anyway.

"On screen," she said, waiting for it. The small circle that appeared still looked frustratingly far away. "Magnify."

The image drew close, and Dana wanted to reach out and touch it. But the hole in space seemed to spin away from them.

"Is it moving away from us?"

"Not exactly," Ensign Cliff Harden answered. His teeth were chattering together, though she'd seen him wearing a black hat and thick black coat. "It seems to suck up the surrounding space in a gravity field. If we can get close enough, we might be able to ride it over to the other side."

"That's good news," Wade said, clapping his hands together and rubbing them.

"How far are we?" Dana asked.

"That's the bad news," Nancy said as she stared at the console. "Even if we propelled ourselves with what we've got left, we'd still be too far to get picked up by the gravity field and pulled inside."

"How long do we have?"

"We've got enough juice to get us about two hours away."

Dana ran a hand over her face. They'd be close enough to stare into the thing and *still* not get pulled in. It would be funny if it weren't so ridiculously sad.

"Ensign Harden, get me engineering," Dana said.

"I'm here, Captain," Esme said, her voice coming from the dark in the back of the room. Dana hadn't realized she was sitting back there. Someone must have gotten her a chair. "Eric is in the engine room, though I can answer any questions you might have for us."

"You know what I'm going to ask," Dana said.

"Yes." Esme's voice was filled with defeat. "We've tried everything. We're on backup life support. She doesn't have anything else to give."

"We need a tow truck," Wade said with a dry laugh.

"No, we don't. We can get everyone through that wormhole, and that's all that matters," Dana said. She had made her decision, and was resolved to follow through, even though she knew Wade would hate it.

She was glad she'd let him kiss her when they'd had the chance. The warmth of his lips had left their mark.

"Lieutenant, get us as close as you can." Dana felt around in the black until she found her chair and sat down. "Let me take care of the rest."

Wade joined her a moment later, first bumping into her knees and then finding his chair. "You've got a plan," he said.

He wouldn't be so excited about it when he heard what it was. "Yes, I do. Sit tight. I'm going to save our people, even the ungrateful ones."

CHAPTER 27

The wormhole loomed in front of the ship like a beacon of salvation, two hours and ten minutes away. Their ship had come to a complete halt just out of reach. There was barely enough life-support to last them two hours, let alone get them through. The Fashin Teku had promised that there was a space station directly on the other side, but it wouldn't matter. Their ship wouldn't make it.

"That's as far as we can go, Captain," Cliff said. "Should I put out a distress beacon?"

"No," Dana said woodenly. "There's no point. I doubt anyone on the other side would hear it. Anyone on this side would see us in distress before they saw the beacon."

The bridge crew was silent as she spoke, and didn't ask any questions as she continued.

"Cliff, put us on red alert. Send everyone to the escape pods. Put in the coordinates for the wormhole. I want everyone through within the next hour."

"Belay that order, Ensign," Wade said, standing up and turning her to face her. "You're not going to do this. When I said you were like your father, this isn't what I meant."

"I mean to see this through, unless you have a better idea," Dana squared her shoulders. "The faster everyone gets to the escape pods, the sooner someone can come back for me."

"No," Wade said firmly. "If we leave, we all leave."

"I won't abandon our ship, and the only chance we have at finding a new world, when you could get to the other side and bring back a tow truck."

He couldn't see her smile in the dark, not that it would have mattered. Wade wasn't going to give in so easily. She remembered her father on the bridge the day he'd made his ultimate sacrifice. This wasn't that dramatic. She could survive until they came back for her. However, it was clear the crew was going to need a push.

"Commander, stand down, or leave the bridge. The lives of the crew and passengers supersede anything else." She addressed the rest of the bridge. "Now, launch those escape pods and get my people to the other side. That's an order!"

The others were silent, no one moved as they waited to hear what Wade would say. She didn't like that they were so willing to disobey an order to save her. This wasn't how they'd been trained. They'd all grown too attached to her, and she needed to sever the tie right here and now if they were going to survive.

"Captain, what about you?" Nancy asked. Her voice was pleading.

"I'll be fine. I'm not leaving the ship or our embryos for some passerby to take. Go with the others and come back and get me."

"Wait," Esme cut in, "there is another idea. I hadn't thought of it until you mentioned the escape pods. They have their own propulsion. They could, as you say, make it to the wormhole. The question is whether or not they'll survive to see the other side. An escape pod is quite small, and the trip might damage the majority of them."

It seemed Esme rambled when her husband wasn't there to finish her sentences.

"Your point, Chief?" Dana asked.

"Oh, I was getting to it. The shuttles. We have four working shuttles, all with power and shielding."

"Four shuttles aren't going to hold all our people," Cliff said.

Dana shifted and sighed. "What does that get us, Chief?"

"A tow," Esme said. "Or, since we don't have a way to hook ourselves up to the shuttles, more like a push.

Dana crossed her arms over her chest as she took in the new information. Using the shuttles to push the starship seemed like a long shot. She didn't know enough of the physics to be sure it would work without damaging the ship or the shuttles themselves, as they would need pilots.

"Four shuttles, four pilots, and a long push into the wormhole . . ."

"Exactly!" Esme's voice was excited. "I'll have Eric run the calculations," she said without asking, and Dana heard Esme tapping out the digital question to her husband down in engineering. "Yes!"

"What did he say?"

"He says it's possible! If we position the shuttles at precise points along the stern, we'll be able to push the ship far enough to get pulled through. We might even have enough time to dock the shuttles so we can all go through together, decreasing the chances of losing any of the shuttles to the gravitational compression of the wormhole."

The bridge was quiet as Dana thought about this new option. She'd thought sending the escape pods through was foolproof, but this might work, too. It was safer than risking the smaller shuttles or pods not getting through or being torn apart inside the wormhole's gravity field. It was a far better plan than the one she'd come up with, though it had been the seed that led Esme to her conclusion.

At last, Dana nodded. "I like it. Let's make it happen. Nancy, Cliff, Wade, I want you piloting three of the shuttles. We'll need a fourth. Someone with training."

"I can pilot the fourth shuttle," Lieutenant Commander Valente said. She thought she'd heard the sound of him raising his hand in the dark, though she couldn't be sure.

"Of course. May the Majestic be with you."

The four filed off the bridge, leaving Esme and Dana alone.

"Are you sure this is going to work?" Dana asked her lowly.

"I'm rarely wrong in my calculations, and when I am, Eric is the one to check me. If he says we're a go, then this is going to work. We'll just have to time everything just right. If they don't all push simultaneously, they'll burn out their engines. If even one runs out of fuel before the others, we'll go in lopsided." She shook her head. "Either way, we won't have the propulsion we need to get close to the edge of the wormhole."

Of course it wouldn't be easy, but Dana didn't want to imagine what would happen if they failed.

No, if they failed, they always had her plan. The escape pods would have to go through on their own. According to Susan MacLaren, the woman who'd designed the *Hope*, the pods could sustain a lot more than a typical escape pod. They had their own shielding and, short of cryostasis, it would protect them for hours if they were somehow separated from the ship. Even so, Dana didn't want it to come to that. She trusted Esme and Eric to work it out, but it would have been nice to arrive under her own power.

Once the shuttles had cleared the bay, Esme relayed their positions.

Dana sat at the helm to have a better view of their trajectory. She imagined the determined faces of her people and decided that she'd rather have them all linked on comms than not know what was going on.

"It looks like the shuttles are in position, Captain," Esme relayed. "We're ready."

"Open a channel to the four shuttles. Sound off when ready," Dana said as she checked the console.

"Channel open, Shuttle One ready," Wade said. "See you on the other side."

"Shuttle Two ready," Cliff said.

"Shuttle Three ready, and the first round of drinks on you," Nancy said. Her energy was so palpable, Dana felt like she was in the cockpit with her.

"Shuttle Four ready, Captain," Valente said.

"Ready your shielding and prepare for initial contact," Dana told them. She waited for each of them to butt up against the ship's rear hull, and though they were shuttles, she felt the resistance to their presence.

"Taking stabilizers and controls offline. It's up to you four. Countdown to push begins now." Dana activated the computer countdown and listened as they chatted among themselves.

"Ten, nine, eight..."

"Commander, I think you owe me some credits from that game you lost over a week ago," Cliff said.

"Give it a rest, Ensign, I'm good for it," Wade shot back. "Besides, I'm inviting Valente. He'll take you for all the credits you've got."

"Five, four, three..."

"You three don't have a chance in an aurora storm," Valente quipped. "Now buckle up."

"Mark!" Dana shouted.

She listened as the four shuttles revved up their

engines, hearing the whine over the comms as they pushed against the ship at equal levels.

"Are we there yet?" Nancy said between her teeth.

"Keep her steady," Esme said. "We're moving, but it's going to take a little more for that initial push. Then you're going you'll be able to back off together. Chief, standby."

"Standing by, Chief," Eric said from the engine room. They didn't have much left, but what they had they'd need to get the shuttles back on board and get to the other side of the wormhole.

"Come on, sweetheart, just a little faster," Dana whispered to the console.

The ship bucked, and she felt their inertia pushing them forward.

"Stay on us, shuttle three," Esme said. "You're not maintaining consistent contact."

"Sorry, I'm trying not to kill myself out here," Cliff said with a groan.

"We're moving, Captain! Distance to the wormhole?" Esme shouted.

"Two hundred and seven DSLs." Dana banged a hand on the console. "We're not going to make it."

"Don't give up," Esme said. "We've got one more trick up our sleeve. Shuttles, keep it steady. We're already picking up momentum."

"It doesn't feel like anything's happening." Wade's voice was filled with frustration, but he didn't back down. Dana could see the steady incline of their speed.

"That's it!" she shouted.

"We're moving, just keep your shuttles in contact with the ship," Esme said.

"We're almost there," Dana said. "Just a bit more, and we're kissing the edge of that wormhole."

"Chief, how are we looking down there?" Esme asked Eric over the comm.

"We lost a little energy in launching the shuttles from the bay. It will take a little more when they return. I'll have to divert all energy from life-support into our engines for that last push." Dana could hear the resignation in his voice. "It won't be pretty, but we'll be on the other side. Let's hope there's someone over there to catch us."

"From your mouth to the Majestic's ear," Valente said.

CHAPTER 28

The ship crawled forward until they were right on top of the wormhole.

"My shuttle is running out of fuel. I won't make it much longer," Wade said.

"Mine, too," Nancy said.

"Keep pushing with all you've got," Dana told them.

"Prepare the launch bay for the return of the shuttles," Esme called out.

"Launch bay doors open," Dana said. "Should I call them back?"

"Not yet. A little more. We need the gravity field of the wormhole to pull us through," Esme said. "Chief, get ready to divert power on my mark."

Dana held her breath as she stared down at the console.

"Captain, recall the shuttles now," Esme said.

"All shuttles return to the nest on the double!"

"Aye, Captain," Wade confirmed. "Shuttles three and four, load up. Shuttle two on my wing."

Dana watched as Nancy and Cliff entered the launch bay. Then the ship lurched forward.

"What was that?" Dana demanded.

"It's got us! We're being pulled in," Esme called out.

"We don't have all the shuttles onboard," Dana said. Then she spoke directly to Wade and Valente. "Shuttles one and four, I said double-time or you'll be left in my space dust!"

"We're on it, Captain," Wade said between his teeth.

"Eric, divert power now," Esme directed. "We're going to need it for what's coming next."

"Diverting power now," he said.

The ship's power revved up while at the same time the computer issued a new warning:

"Complete life-support failure."

"We need those launch bay doors closed!" Esme said.

"Wade, Valente, are you in?" Dana asked, the barest hint of desperation in her voice.

There was a *thud* in the rear of the ship, then the screech of durometal on metal.

"We're in, Captain. Seal the doors," Wade said. He was out of breath, but he was alive.

Dana sealed the doors just as the gravity field pulled the ship through the wormhole. The ship keeled to one side, and they exited the wormhole, careening toward a space station without any control.

"Esme, hold on! Get me stabilizers, something to right the ship!" Dana called out.

"We don't have anything more," Esme said, a thread of panic in her words. "Life support is down, and what's left of our engines is going to freeze if we don't get help."

"We're about to crash into a space station!" Dana called out. They were probably hailing her, and the ship was getting no signals in or out. "They might think we're hostiles."

"I doubt it," Esme said, gritting her teeth and her hands flying over the control panel. "We look like a dead ship out of control."

"Our chances of survival are minimal if we hit that space station."

Esme slammed a fist on the console. "I've got nothing on comms, no helm control, no *air*."

Dana watched as the main viewer returned to a view of the space station. Four ships were headed in their direction. "We've got incoming."

"Are they using comms?" Esme asked.

"I have no idea and I wouldn't know if they were based on these dead instruments. All I've got are my eyes on the duroglass in front of us. I don't know if they're planning to shoot us down or shield us from the space station."

Dana sucked in a breath as two of the ships passed them. Then there was a loud *thunk* on the bulkhead. Then another, and another. The four ships had attached some kind of tether to them, slowing them down just in time to miss hitting the space station. Then the two out front repositioned themselves like a tow and pulled them into one of the space station's stalls. The two that were out of view must have been doing their best to keep them stabilized. Without inertial dampeners, though, the *Hope* hit the deck with a crash.

The glaring bright lights of the space station docking zone bathed the ship. From where she sat, Dana could make out someone on the main deck aggressively shaking four muscled arms at her.

She burst out laughing. They'd *made* it. They'd survived the wormhole, and they'd made it to civilization. She was still laughing when the bridge crew returned.

"Wow, look at this place," Wade breathed, leaning over one hand on the helm and staring out the window down at the deck.

"Yeah," Dana said her voice soft as she grinned at him, "we made it. Thanks to you."

He turned back to look at her, and she saw his eyes fall to her lips, as if remembering. It wasn't something either of them would forget anytime soon, but they had a ship full of people running out of air. They needed to get an influx of energy and fuel as soon as possible.

"I'm assuming the air on this space station is compatible, but let's double check that information before we open up the ventilation system."

Esme leaned over her console. "Eric says according to their limited instruments down there, we're good."

"Fine, open her up and let's get some of that space dock air in here. It's time to go to work," Dana said, sliding out of the chair and away from Wade. "Chance, Valente, you're with me. The rest of you, stay put."

Dana led the two men down to the launch bay, where she ran into Eric.

"Permission to come along, Captain," he said breathlessly. "There are a few things we're going to need right away, and I'm the only one who can explain it to them."

Dana glanced at Wade, who'd she'd invited for that same reason, and he nodded.

"Okay, Chief. You're with us."

They disembarked to the deck, and from underneath she could see where they'd damaged the both the underside of *the Hope,* as well as the space dock, which was buzzing with activity all around them. She could hear ships powering up and powering down all along the dock, and this was only where they were stationed. The round design of the place meant the entire circumference could accommodate more ships than they'd ever had on Zelenia at one time.

There was a steady flow of people coming and going around them. Dana couldn't be sure if they were passengers or crew from their styles of dress, and they came in such a variety of shapes, colors, and sizes the assortment overwhelmed her. She must have looked just as strange to them. She didn't know where to put her eyes until someone in the crowd spoke up.

"Who's in charge here?" The deep voice belonged to a being with four arms and a tool belt that clapped against his tree-trunk legs as he walked toward her. She absently wondered where he found the boots to cover his large feet.

"Me," she replied, stepping forward. "I'm Captain Dana Pinet, of the Starship *Hope*. Thank you for the landing assist, Mister . . .?"

"Fazil. Just Fazil. You did some damage coming in. I'll have to charge you for that in addition to any equipment repair." He raised his one heavy brow. "I'm assuming you're fueling up?"

"Yes," she said with a nod, trying not to stare at his mouth as he spoke. The words and the tone she heard in her ear didn't match the strange way his mouth moved over the rows of short teeth. The TMIs were working. She was glad that she'd met the Fashin Teku first. She couldn't imagine not understanding this fellow on arrival.

He continued to enter what must have been work orders into a thin tablet that fit the width of one large hand. "Species?"

"Human."

"Human?" He scratched his hand with one of his free hands. It was the only one that had three fingers. Dana didn't know if it was a genetic abnormality, accident, or design. He scrolled through his tablet as if looking for something. "First time through the Arch?" he asked, still scrolling.

That was the same name Ashwin had given the wormhole.

"Yes."

"Ah, yes. Hmm . . . human . . . Before we start work on

your transport, you're going to need your passenger, crew, and product manifest, as well as financial credit approval."

"Credit approval?" Dana looked to Wade, who shook his head. They hadn't been prepared for an entirely new economic system. She was already regretting not asking the Fashin Teku more questions before they'd arrived. "Do you deal in barter?"

"Barter? You mean in exchange?" The male's four arms seem to settle on his hips as he regarded her with suspicion. "We don't make exchanges with your kind."

Dana caught the surprised look on Wade's face, but she pulled out her tablet and held up the manifest list to the dockmaster. He scanned the information absently before holding his device to the edge of hers. In a blink, it copied over the information, and he continued to look over what she gave him.

As he was looking over the tablets, Eric spoke up. "You've met our kind before?"

Still frowning down at the information, he answered, "Of course, everybody who comes through that wormhole and winds up in this system comes to the Nexus." He handed the tablet back to Dana. "You'll need to report to the financial district. Maybe one of the banks will take a chance on you. Until then, your people will have to stay onboard. When we've got credit approval, we can hook you up to our energy ports and begin refueling. I'm assuming you take standard Triucium?"

Eric shook his head. "We're working with an Othiutium fuel injected system. Do you have access to refined Thiutite Complex-V, or something comparable?"

Fazil laughed. The sound rumbled from his belly, then guffawed out of his enormous mouth, making his over-sized lips flap against his teeth. "Othiumtium? How in the barstool did you get here in this bucket running on refined space rocks? It's no wonder you barely made it. You're going to need a refit to take any of the fuel options we have. I recommend the standard, as it lasts a lot longer than the toilet-waste you've been using and won't explode your ship on impact."

Dana was getting more frustrated with the process as they went along. She needed financial approval, and that required her meeting with bank officials. This wasn't going to go well. If they already had a bad reputation in this system, that meant at some point, a human had come through the gate. Someone from her world.

"Let's go back to the point of you knowing our kind. Since this is our first time here, how could you know our people?"

"Had a ship come through here." Fazil shrugged. "Looked a little like this one. Might have been made from the same stuff. They didn't have your fuel line issues, though."

Dana's mind was spinning, trying to figure out how they'd followed another ship here. Wade was looking at her with mirrored confusion. He didn't know about the other ships. He wouldn't know that another of their ships could have made it this far.

"Are they still here?" she asked hopefully.

"No, they've been gone more than a month now. They stuck around maybe a day or two at the most. Didn't pay in credits. They paid in Temilite X gems."

"Temilite X?"

Fazil pulled a small metal ball from his pocket and held it up. It reflected the lights in the hangar as he spun it between two large digits of his three fingered hand.

"Highest value metal this side of the Arch. It's indestructible and shiny. They had enough to cover repairs, fuel, and food."

"What were they doing here?" Wade asked, turning to Dana.

The dockmaster answered, believing the question was directed at him. "Not sure. Perhaps running for one of the Triad, like most folks who come this way. They picked up some crates and headed out toward the Zeon cluster—seven planets on the edge of this end of space. There's a trade route in that sector controlled by three warring factions that have the whole strip divided among them."

Dana wanted to hear more, but her people needed showers, comms, and food. The history of the area and the current disputes could wait.

"Point me in the direction of the financial district so we can get you started on refitting our fuel lines," she said.

Fazil lifted two arms, pointing down the dock. "Head down to the end of this dock and veer right. When you see all the flashing lights, you'll be standing in the financial district. Get a loan from any of them and come back with your numbers. We'll get you up and running again, Captain."

He snickered as he walked away. Fazil seemed sure she wouldn't get the credit. She'd have to prove the pessimistic dockmaster wrong.

Dana started for the end of the dock and turned back to Eric.

"You two stick around. Eric, I want you ready to hook us up to the station lines as soon as we're approved. Learn whatever you can about the refit before we begin. I'll want an estimate on how long all of this is going to take. Valente, make sure your team keeps every one of our people on our ship and anyone else off. That goes for the Fashin Teku as well."

Valente inclined his head toward Dana, then returned to the ship, leaving her alone with Wade. Dana swiveled back around and made her way in the direction Fazil had indicated. She didn't know what she would have to give up in order to get the credit they needed for fuel. The prickle on the back of her neck warned her it might not be as easy as getting a loan from a bank back on Zelenia.

CHAPTER 29

"Prepare to receive the official docking manual and space station rules upon arrival.

In addition to these, disengage all engines and secure your transport before disembarking. We will not be held responsible for lost or stolen items or individuals. The Port Authority may request to meet with you. If so, be prepared to show all relevant documentation, including your passenger and cargo manifests. All life-forms that require nitrogen rich air for breathing are permitted to bring personalized breathing devices as long as they don't interfere with the air quality of those around you. Should you require further assistance, please see the dockmaster on duty once your ship is secured."

-Outgoing Looped Message from the Nexus Space Station to All Ships Upon Arrival

Dana walked the length of the docks, trying not to gawk at the varying creatures and species as they passed. Like the ships that lined the port alongside the *Hope*, they came in so many sizes and shapes that she wondered how far they'd traveled to get here. She noted they weren't the only bipedal species. She saw creatures with just the two arms and legs, but then their faces might have an extra orifice, or their skin came in a color she'd only seen in the waxy colored pencils of her childhood.

"I can't believe it either, but if you look too hard, you might get us into trouble," Wade said in her ear.

Dana reined in her focus and tried to imagine how they'd find flashing lights among the glaring overhead beams of the hangar bay. The dock seemed to go on forever. They passed ship after ship until they spilled out into what must have been referred to as 'the Nexus'. The station's name likely came from its proximity to the wormhole. No doubt it was a junction port for any travelers wanting to shorten their space travel by using the Arch. In addition to the space dock, the Nexus was comprised of multiple rings rotating in opposite directions, rising higher above them than she could see.

"This place is slammed," Wade said as he placed a protective hand on her shoulder. They seemed to be caught up in the flow of foot traffic, and if Wade hadn't grabbed ahold of her, they might have been separated. Not trusting him to keep hold of her, she took his hand and held on tight as they weaved through the crowd. She was grateful the natural movement of the crowd seemed to take them to the right, so they didn't have to plow into anyone to get to where they needed to go.

Shops and vendors selling every manner of food, from exotic-looking fruits to bowls of sludge, were set up on the right side of the walkway, the spices and pungent aromas blending in on each other until Dana couldn't distinguish one from the other. Despite the strange look of it all, her stomach tightened with hunger. On her left, a dozen or so square boxes whizzed by them, moving along the vertical center between the rings. Dana struggled to get a good look as one small box settled at their ring and one individual with long white hair and purple skin exited. They seemed to be of the same configuration and speed, with markings visible on the outside, perhaps to distinguish one from another. Every so often one of them would drop down or rise up to their level. One or two passengers would exit onto their ring and join the throng walking to the right on the footpath.

"There," Wade called out, pulling her attention back to the right. He pointed to the flashing signs. The words were unfamiliar, but the symbols made it clear they dealt in all manner of currency—though nothing familiar to her.

Fazil hadn't been wrong about being unable to miss it. The financial district was a strip of buildings that took up where the food vendors left off the main loop. It took several tries for her and Wade to get off the main loop and off to the side where the banks sat. As soon as they were free, she noted Wade's eyes staring at the crowd in wonder.

"Come on, Commander," she urged. "If we're going to enjoy this place at all, we're going to need some credits."

"I know it sounds strange, but that food shack back there smelled amazing. It might be boiled cat or rat, though I think I'd have enjoyed it either way."

"I know. We've been living on rations for so long I think anything smells good, but we'd better find out if there's anything out here poisonous to us before we go sampling anything." Dana sighed. "I feel like I'm visiting the Western continent on Zelenia. Nothing makes sense, and it just makes me miss home."

Wade nodded and motioned with his head to the first financial building. "Let's try this one."

The first building had solid metal doors with intricate carvings on the outside. There were no handles on the door, so Wade attempted to push them open. Nothing happened. Then he put his fingers into the crack between the double doors and tried to pry them apart. Nothing.

"Maybe there's a way to call inside." Dana ran her hand along the edge of the door. A panel lit up as her hand passed over it. Something scanned her before she could take a step back.

"Terran, please wait for the next available associate." The COMP had a soothing female voice.

"Are we doing our business out here?" Wade made a slow turn in place, scanning the crowd as if he expected someone to veer off the footpath and rush toward them.

"Not that it matters. We don't have any credits yet."

The doors slid open and Dana threw a hesitant look at

Wade before she walked inside. Before Wade could get a foot in, the double doors slammed closed.

"One Terran customer at a time, please."

Dana didn't have a way to communicate with Wade from within the building. She imagined the message could be heard on either side. He'd have to wait for her.

She gazed around the entryway and noted there was no one around to greet her. It seemed to be automated. Perhaps they were watching her from some kind of closed-circuit camera system. She checked the corners and walls for motion sensors or cameras but found none. She respected a competent security system. It made her feel a little more comfortable about doing business here.

"Please follow the lighted signs to the next available Financial Freedom associate."

The center of the duroplasty floor lit up, and she followed the lights down the corridor into a lift. There were no buttons or voice commands needed, as the doors closed and proceeded to the floor she needed without a word. *The system must work on heat sensors or something,* she theorized.

The lift rose inside the tubing and a flashing light indicated each time they passed a level. She reached four before the doors opened. On the floor in front of her was another row of blue lights, leading to the left.

Dana waited a moment, wondering if the doors would close up on her at any moment, but they remained open. As soon as she proceeded into the hall, they closed behind her. She couldn't tell if the lift was still there, or if it had been whisked off to another level. The air circulation was cooler here, and there were more closed doors on either side of the corridor. When the colored line reached her destination, she proceeded to the door and lifted her hand to knock, but the door slid open on its own. The room inside was small and undecorated. It was the person on the other side of the console that took her breath away.

A woman with pale, flawless skin and brown wavy hair wore a pea green pencil skirt and matching blazer sat on the other side of the console. She stood as Dana came in and gestured to the chair, with one elegant hand. Her smile accented by a pink gloss welcomed her. Dana gaped at the woman wondering how in the world she'd come to be on this space station working for a bank.

"Welcome. Please, sit down." She gestured to the duro-plastic chair in front of her. "Is this your first time in the Nexus?" She took her own seat on the other side of the console.

"Yes, I—" Dana stopped as a compartment in the console opened in front of her and she saw a juice tube inside.

"I thought you might like something to drink. It's a sweet juice with the flavor of pomegranate with bubbles."

"Pomegranate?" It was a flavor she hadn't tasted since leaving Zelenia. She'd never thought to taste anything like it again. She reached into the compartment and pulled out the tube. Dana bit off the seal and took a tentative sip.

The juice bubbles exploded in her mouth and the sensation forced a smile out of her. She couldn't believe how quickly the memories of home flooded back. Summers with her parents, begging her father for another tube of juice on days when the suns were so hot, they'd been forced to sit out by the pool. He'd taught her to swim the year before, and she leaped into the pool so many times she'd been wrinkled like a raisin when they finally dragged her inside. Unshed tears burned her eyes at the memory.

The woman's head tilted to one side the way the ARI did when it was thinking. "I'm sorry if it is not to your liking. We have others."

"No, it's perfect, thank you," Dana said quickly, looking down at the tube. "My home was destroyed, and the memories are still raw."

"Oh no . . . let me check my database." Her attempt at sympathy was stiff and perfunctory. Then she seemed to glitch in front of her pieces of color disappearing and then reappearing.

"What are you?"

"I'm a VFA," when Dana shook her head she continued. "A virtual financial assistant. We like to take on the form of our customers to make them feel more comfortable."

"Who's controlling you? Are they in the room?" Dana glanced under the console and then at the four corners of the ceiling looking for cameras.

"The operator is located on another level of the building, however, here at Financial Freedom we prefer to do business in this manner."

"Sure," Dana grumbled. "If a species doesn't like what you have to say you don't want to have to replace your assistants."

Her head tilted to one side again as if thinking and then she folded her avatar hands in front of her on the console.

"It looks like Earth is still showing up in the Primus Centauri region. Are you sure?" Her tone had the hint of doubt.

"No, not Blue Earth. I'm from Zelenia. It's a long story. Humans were driven from Earth long before I was born."

"Ah, yes, the Purge … it's in the historical database for your species. That also explains the difference in language and accent." She shook her head. "Well, I'm sorry to inform you, humans from Zelenia are not on the approved credit list."

Dread dropped in Dana's stomach. "What? Why?"

"It is unfortunate, but it seems your people have come through the Nexus before, and to be honest, your credit history is poor. We cannot extend you any credit or local currency upfront."

"My people have no planet," Dana said incredulously. "We don't have enough food to survive much longer, or enough fuel to leave here and try someplace new."

The virtual assistant gave her its most sympathetic frown, its pink painted lips falling to one side, looking more like someone having a stroke. Then it stood up as a signal that it she should leave. Dana sat drinking until she'd finished the tube of juice. The assistant continued to stand with the smile pasted on its unnaturally perfect features. It folded its hands in front of her.

"There is another way to proceed. The Nexus is filled with possibilities. If you choose to work for one of the established businesses, they may supply you with the credits you need. If they're willing to co-sign for you, we can extend the credit based on their financial history." Again, it gave Dana the stroke face. "Otherwise, there isn't much more I can do."

"What about going to one of the other financial institutions?" Dana tried. "Will one of them be more likely to extend us credit?"

"It is possible, but not likely. All the institutions that lend credits have this information at their disposal, and Zelenians are not sanctioned for lending."

Dana stood up from the uncomfortable chair with a sigh. "Thanks."

The virtual assistant put her fist to her chest in salute. Dana couldn't stop herself from rolling her eyes to the ceiling. They'd gone through the trouble of creating a virtual assistant model to provide service to Terrans, only to send her on her way. It didn't mean she had to leave empty-handed. "Can I get another tube of the juice before I leave?"

SHE FOUND WADE PACING OUTSIDE THE BUILDING AND handed him the tube.

"What happened?" he asked as he tore into the tube of juice, groaning with pleasure as he drank it down.

"Well, for starters, Terrans have been here before, too," she explained. "They made a mess of things, and we're not on the approved credit lending list. All the financial buildings have access to some database, and our species is already blacklisted on it. We're not going to get credits from a bank. We're going to have to find another way."

Wade nodded grimly. "Let's head back to the ship. Maybe the Fashin Teku will have some ideas."

"Good point. It's time for them to come through for us.
"

CHAPTER 30

EARTHA

To her horror, Esme agreed to let her go to the Commons for her first look at the space station if, and only if, they went together. Eartha trudged along behind her, refusing to engage her adoptive mom in any kind of conversation. She was still grounded for sneaking out. She wouldn't set foot on the space station until the Rogans' were good and ready—which meant never.

Eartha had cleaned her room, dispelling the smell that had been growing under her bed. Though now that the chore was done, she officially had no life. While everyone around them talked excitedly about what they were going to do once they were allowed to leave the ship, Eartha could do nothing but watch.

She bolted away from Esme the moment they were through the doors of the Commons. Mr. Jennison and Luke had grabbed their usual table next to the window. Neither saw her coming, as they had their noses pressed to the duroglass. She squeezed in between them as they stared down out at the docks.

"Where have you been?" Luke asked, not taking his eyes off of the scene below them.

Creatures like she'd only ever imagined in books peppered the docks. Some walked on two legs while others were sliding on something that looked like a gel. Then there were those trying to avoid the goo on three or four legs. Eartha's mouth fell open and stayed that way until Mr. Jennison reached over and lifted her chin with a finger.

"Never thought I'd see the day." Mr. Jennison's voice sounded far away and dreamy.

"I wish we could get closer . . . then we could see more of their faces. Most of them don't ever look up," Luke said. "Eartha, what are you going to do when you leave the ship?"

"I'm not leaving the ship," Eartha grumbled. She looked over her shoulder and spotted Esme a few tables over.

"Still locked down, eh?" Mr. Jennison patted her on the shoulder. "Don't worry. Your family will take pity on your plight and let you out."

"How do you know that?"

"I know parents. They want off this ship just as bad as you do. They're not going to risk you going alone, so they'll drag you along, too. Just be patient."

Eartha bit her lower lip. She wanted to believe Mr. Jennison, but he hadn't seen Eric and Esme when they'd grounded her. No matter how much she pleaded, she hadn't been allowed to leave the cabin in days.

An announcement over the comms system got everyone's attention:

"Passengers and crew of the Starship Hope, this is Lieutenant Commander Valente speaking. We're not cleared for general population departure. Please keep in mind that we will consider your requests to leave the ship only after we've passed our docking inspection. Once we are cleared, please await further instructions before submitting another request. We appreciate your patience. Senior officers, report to your stations until further notice."

The crowd at the windows groaned and mumbled their complaints along with Luke.

"We need to get off this ship," Luke said, shaking his head as he sat back down in his chair opposite Mr. Jennison. "We still don't have enough food or water. The Commons stopped serving us weeks ago."

"Really? That's awful," Eartha said. "I thought nothing could be worse than sitting in the dark in the middle of space. Watching every species in the galaxy go about their daily lives without us is much worse."

Esme approached the table. Mr. Jennison rose and

knocked Luke in the head for not doing the same. He stood as well, but Eartha remained planted in her seat. Esme gave her a disapproving shake of her head.

"I need to go check on Eric," she said. "Can I trust you to stay with Mr. Jennison until I return?"

Eartha's heart leaped in her chest at the idea of being able to stay with her friends, but she tried to play it off.

"Sure, I guess I can wait around here." She shrugged. "It's not like there's anything else to do."

Esme sighed and turned to Mr. Jennison. "If it's not an imposition?"

"Not at all. I'll watch the little gutter snipe while you attend to ship's business. Maybe it will get me to the front of the departure list." He gave her a wink, and she touched his shoulder before turning to leave. "If you're late, I'll make sure she gets back to quarters," he called after her.

Eartha was stewing with anger as she watched Esme walk away. It wasn't like she could get into any trouble with the lights off and smelling like she had a body odor problem. She hadn't had an actual shower in over a week. The medi-wipes only did so much. She'd been in her room most of that time. Despite the large space, if she moved in a hurry, she caught a whiff of herself. Eartha slammed her arms down at her sides.

Mr. Jennison flicked her in the arm.

"Ouch!"

"Give her a break. She's doing the best she can," he said. "I think it's your turn to play, Eartha."

Luke slid to one side, making room for her. She didn't

want to move for fear he'd take one sniff and run for the door. Instead, he rotated in the opposite direction around the table, as if to avoid her. Maybe he'd already been too close. She'd have to pay more attention.

"Are you excited for the new baby?" Mr. Jennison asked as he moved his first piece on the 3D virtual board. Eartha caught the weird look that earned him from Luke, but he quickly corrected his features and waited for her answer.

"I am," she said, then took her time planting her piece on the second level of the three-tiered board.

"I'm surprised. Usually, the first-born child has a hard time with the change of a new family member."

Luke huffed as he rested his head on his fist and rolled his eyes.

He turned to Luke for confirmation. "It's not true?"

Luke lifted one shoulder but didn't speak.

Mr. Jennison shrugged. "From what I hear, it's a tough time."

"I'm not the first-born. They're not my real parents." Eartha waited for him to make his move.

Mr. Jennison took a long time before lifting one of his pieces to the second tier. Then he smiled as if he'd figured out something.

"Oh, so I guess you don't have a real family, so it doesn't matter?"

Luke stared at Mr. Jennison, a strange look on his face, and then looked back to Eartha. His eyes looked panicked, as if Mr. Jennison had said something about him. She tried to listen to the words he was saying and the message underneath them, but she didn't understand what he was getting at.

"No . . . I don't think so."

"I thought it was interesting . . . The other day when I was speaking to Eric, he said something about you I was surprised to hear. He said you weren't happy with them." The words hung in the air around them, cutting through the virtual board and straight to her heart. "I wonder where you'd prefer to be. I lost my entire family on Zelenia. In a sense, I'm an orphan as well, but I'm far too old to be adopted. Which is a shame, really, because why wouldn't anyone want to adopt a sweet old grandpa like me?" He chuckled, and then his face turned solemn. "Some people don't ever appreciate what they have until its gone. If I were you, I'd hold on to that sweet couple. You're not likely to find anyone else onboard who wants to adopt you."

"They want to adopt me?" Eartha asked, and wondered why she hadn't understood that before. If they officially adopted her, then she wasn't just staying with the Rogans, she'd belong to them. She wondered how long they'd been thinking of adopting her.

"Are you sure they haven't adopted you already?" he asked.

Eartha thought for a moment. Mr. Jennison took his turn. She was still wondering if she hadn't already been officially adopted and just didn't know it when he looked up at her expectantly.

"I'm sorry," she said, shaking her head and standing. "I can't finish the game. I have to go."

Eartha grabbed her pack and raced down to the engine room. If they had officially adopted her, she wanted to know about it, and the two people that had the answer were down there.

CHAPTER 31

Dana and Wade reached the docks, having taken the long way around the Nexus. The station's design produced traffic on all levels that moved faster than felt comfortable. In walking the Nexus, the one-way traffic was much slower. It required taking the entire loop around to get back to where they'd started.

The intense lights of the dock made it difficult to gauge what time the space station was on. She'd been given the time by the dockmaster when she'd received her manual and operations instructions. It was already afternoon ship's time, but according to the station, it was only ten hours into their fifty-hour day. When they reached the ship, they saw Valente using both arms to hold Maggie back as she tried to charge off.

"Captain! Captain!" she called out. Today her bright red hair was in contrast with a yellow sun-colored dress and heels. The matching handbag she waved in the air only added to her attention-getting attire. Passersby stared at her as if she were an animal trying to escape its cage.

Wade averted his eyes as if he'd rather be anywhere else. Dana could sympathize. The last thing she wanted was a dramatic three-act show from Maggie Brooker on the dock. The reporter had been too quiet over the last few days, but a ship without power wasn't fertile ground for news. She'd no doubt been freezing inside her quarters like the rest of them, but she'd pulled herself together and dressed in her finest, as if she were ready for a night on the town.

Dana reached Valente; whose guards blocked Maggie from leaving the ship with their bodies as she called out over their heads.

"She refused to return to the interior of the ship," he reported over Maggie's shouts. "I had to station the guards further up to keep her off the dock."

Dana nodded. "Thank you. Any other news?"

Valente shook his head. "None on my end but check in on the Rogans. They've been pacing up and down looking for you."

"Keep her up there, and I'll be back shortly." Dana turned to Wade. "Can you find out what she wants?"

"*Me*?"

Dana gave him a look that said she wasn't interested in any personal objections.

"Fine." He stomped up the ramp toward the doors where Maggie was standing, her arms crossed over her chest.

Her calls quieted as he approached, and Dana knew it was like throwing gasoline on a fire, but it was all she could do to avoid strangling the woman herself. They'd been cordial with each other so far, and that's where she wanted their relationship to stay. Dana wasn't going to throw herself into a tug-of-war over Wade. If Maggie was still holding on to any plans on getting back together, Dana wanted them to deal with it sooner rather than later.

Dana didn't have to wait long before Eric and Esme found her. The dockmaster, Fazil, ambled about on his two beefy legs. He called out instructions to the crew racing up and down the docks, his massive arms waving behind him.

"How did it go?" Eric asked when they'd reached her.

"Not well. It appears that we're on the no-loans list." She crossed her arms over her chest. "We're going to have to figure out another way to get our hands on some credits."

"We may have a lead on something," Esme said as Eric waved the dockmaster over.

"Fazil," Dana greeted him with a curt nod of her head.

"Captain," Fazil replied, scratching his chin. "You don't look like someone who's rolling in borrowed credits."

"It didn't go well, no."

"There may be another way to get what we need," Eric said with an excited look between her and Fazil.

"Yes, your people are quite ingenious," Fazil agreed. "I could use a couple of them around here to work on other ships."

Dana placed her hands on her hips. It seemed they could make an exchange after all. "When will my ship get repaired?"

"Give them to me for a day, and I'll give you a full day's worth attention."

"Captain, you should know one day on their space station is two days' ship's time," Esme said.

"Chiefs?" Dana gestured for them to step away from the dockmaster. She didn't want him to know how desperate they were, though he was probably savvy enough to figure it out. Half of the negotiation process was pretending like it was the last thing in the world you'd ever want, let alone need.

Dana glanced between them. "Are you willing to give yourselves over to this man for two days?"

Eric and Esme stared at each other, some silent communication passing from one to the other until they nodded to her in unison.

"Captain, we'll do whatever it takes to help the ship and crew," Eric said.

"Our people need this," Esme agreed.

"You're my two best engineers. We can't afford to lose you. I don't like the idea of both of you being off the ship and under his power."

"The more we learn about the other ships," Eric began.

"The more we'll have to bring back to our ship," Esme finished.

They had a point. They were in an intergalactic hub

and would have access to valuable information they wouldn't normally be able to gather. It would be wise for them to learn as much as they could.

"Fine," Dana agreed, albeit with a hint of reluctance. "I don't have to tell you to watch each other's backs."

"No, you don't. I won't let anything happen to my Esme." Eric glanced at her belly, and then back to her face. Esme's cheeks flushed, and they both nodded in agreement.

Dana turned back to the dockmaster and shrugged. "I may be open to an agreement. However, my people need off of this ship."

"I'll allow a third of your number off at a time."

"Half, and you have a deal."

Fazil stroked his chin with one of his upper arms and laughed. "I don't know your species, but you don't seem the type to leave your crew behind. I'll agree to allow no more than half the ship off at a time, and they must all travel in pairs. If something happens to one, I'm won't be responsible, but at least you'll hear about it. I've heard that individuals can disappear in the Nexus."

"Disappear?" Dana echoed, a flare of alarm rising in her.

He shrugged all four arms. "It's a big place. Come with me, Humans, we have work to do."

Dana turned around in time to see Wade making his way toward her. They met in the middle, far enough away from Valente and his people to speak in private.

"What does she want?" Dana didn't have to name Maggie for him to know whom she meant.

"She's got a few interviews on the station."

"Interviews?"

"She says she wants to get off, and that she'd like to relocate to the space station," Wade relayed. "She lined up the interviews as soon as she had a stable connection to the space station's system."

"How did she manage that?"

He gave her a significant look. There was very little Maggie couldn't do when she set her mind to it. A lot of her equipment ran on independent systems, and when properly motivated, she could pull off just about anything. Dana couldn't fault her for wanting a fresh start. A space station would have far more news content than their small ship.

"So, what's the problem?" she asked.

Wade gave her another look that said the answer should be obvious. Dana shook her head and shrugged.

"Are we just letting people leave now?" he said.

Dana sighed. It was obvious he and Maggie hadn't resolved their situation since their infection, but there might be a way to help them along.

"I'm not going to force people to stay," Dana said, glancing up at the passengers, their faces plastered to the duroglass windows, watching the docks. "We have the embryos, and that will have to be enough. I don't believe that the majority will want to live in this space station, but it should be their decision to make."

Dana walked away from him and toward where Maggie stood, tapping one toe impatiently, her arms crossed over her chest.

"Captain, I'm going to be late," she called out, a pout on her red painted lips. "Can we please come to some agreement?"

"Security, let her through."

Maggie's open-mouthed surprise was so comical Dana had to stifle a smile. She slid past the guards with her upturned nose in the air, brushing her hands down the front of her sundress with its flirty frilled sleeves and hem.

"What changed your mind?" Maggie asked when she was facing her.

"We've been given some leeway by the dockmaster for some of our people to venture off of the ship," Dana explained. "However, there are some caveats. Only half the manifest can be off the ship at any one time. There's going to have to be some organized visits and time limits so that others can experience what the space station has to offer. However, since none of us carry the standard currency, there isn't much to do other than gawk."

"I can be back by the end of the day, ship's time."

"I'm going to hold you to it, Miss Brooker, and the Commander will be with you in case you should run into any problems."

Wade's eyes went wide as he shook his head. "What?"

"No!" Maggie snapped. Her lower lip pouted, and she crossed her arms again and stomped one yellow heel against the dock platform.

They were both objecting in unison. It hurt Dana's heart to see them in agreement about anything, but this was necessary. If either of them wanted a future with someone else, they had to make peace with their shared past. Dana wondered if on the other side, Wade would still want to pursue her. If she decided to give him a second chance, she couldn't bear the shadow of his previous relationship hanging over them.

"Yes. The dockmaster instituted the rule. Our people don't go off on their own. Pairs of people at the least. I'd be happy to get you someone else, but it will probably take at least two hours to get the rest of the ship organized for departure, and there's no guarantee we'll be able to find someone willing to follow you around on your interviews."

Dana waited while Maggie worried her bottom lip between her teeth, glancing up at Wade. He stood at Maggie's side, glaring at Dana. Maggie shrugged.

"Fine, but we need to leave *now*." She started down the dock in the wrong direction.

Wade gave Dana a parting groan before rushing to catch up to her. "You're going the wrong way."

Dana left the two of them to their unresolved issues and boarded the ship.

Arranging departure times for over three-hundred individuals was a monumental task only made worse by the growing impatience to get off the cramped, confined, non-functioning ship.

It took far less than an hour to get the first wave of people recorded and off the ship. Some people were already returning once they realized they'd have to walk the full ring of the Nexus to see anything. Half-way around most had grown frustrated with all the goods they couldn't afford, as they had no credits to purchase anything.

"Captain, the last group is heading off the ship," Valente reported two hours later, standing in Dana's office. "My people are on a two-hour rotation. Permission to put myself in the last group?"

Dana hadn't realized that Lieutenant Commander Valente would be interested in touring any of the station himself.

"Permission granted," she told him. "Thank you for seeing to the organized departure of everyone personally."

"There's still the question of Barnes," he said, an eye on the ventilation shaft above her desk.

"He's most likely still onboard. If he gets by us and he's lost to this space station, I won't be sending out a search party for him," Dana said, attempting to sound bored.

She had considered he might be spying on her from within the duct system, but not in her office. That would mean he'd been there when she and Wade were kissing in the dark. She couldn't stomach the thought.

"I'll inform my people." Valente nodded and saw himself out, but when he turned to go, Rido was at the door.

"May I come in?" he asked.

"Of course," Dana said, waving him inside.

The station lighting poured in behind her through her office's windows, illuminating Rido's eager face. He reached her in two strides and gave her a hug and a light kiss on the lips, as if they were already a settled couple. Dana stiffened at the kiss, too warm and familiar. She wondered if he was beginning to have more serious feelings for her. He looked and smelled amazing, considering that they hadn't had actual running water in well over a week, and she took a step back, knowing she still had at least a week's worth of stench under her uniform.

"I was hoping you would consider taking a stroll with me around the Nexus," he suggested.

Dana threw up her hands. "Normally, I would, but there's still a lot I need to oversee here. The repairs we can do on our own need to be approved and monitored, and while half the ship's manifest is venturing onto the Nexus, the rest are lining up to leave when those return."

"I see," he said, sounding vaguely disappointed. "Well, perhaps another time."

Rido inclined his head and took a step forward. This time, Dana turned her head to the left, so his kiss fell on her cheek. She wasn't ready to make any major decisions about her love life one way or the other. Although Rido was a contender, he wasn't the only man stepping up to the plate. She wouldn't lead either of them on when she hadn't quite made up her mind about what to do.

Regardless, her duties at the moment were clear and pressing. Everything else would have to wait.

"Enjoy yourself," she told him when he'd stepped back.

There was a hint of confusion before the easy smile resettled on his face. "I will, thank you." He moved to leave, calling over his shoulder, "We have an appointment at the end of the week, don't forget."

Dana smiled. She hadn't forgotten. She looked forward to his healing sessions now and wondered how she'd sleep once she was sure Barnes was off the ship.

CHAPTER 32

Captain's Log: 4327.10.20

My crew and my people are safe for the moment on a space station they call the Nexus.

The ship would have crash-landed on the opposite side of the wormhole (which they call The Arch, an intergalactic off-ramp where species from all over gather and find respite in the food, wares, and trade available in the immense facility) if hadn't been for the station's emergency crew. They used something called 'tractoring' to drop us onto the dock.

There are five levels, or rings, within the Nexus, and each of them are filled with businesses that deal in credits, or 'shinies'. I've learned that 'shinies' are a kind of precious metal or rock.

We're not home, but for some, it's close enough. We're losing several passengers who would rather take their chances on the Nexus than continue to adventure through uncharted space looking for an unoccupied planet. I understand their reservations. With so many species here, it's clear that our journey could continue beyond our lifetime. Not everyone is as comfortable as I am living my days out on the Hope.

Perhaps among these thousands of species, we'll find one that looks like us, or has seen our kind nearby. It may be naïve to believe our journey is almost over. Despite the challenges we've experienced so far, we've already learned so much and come so far.

I've sacrificed too much to give up now. Our people have a home among the stars, and it may not be far.

CAPTAIN'S PERSONAL LOG SUPPLEMENTAL:

I'm tired. I'm tired of scraping, starving, and searching. I want a chance at a real life, and by the Majestic, I pray we're close.

CHAPTER 33

WADE

Maggie walked two paces ahead, making sure he got an excellent view of her flirting with every male species she could find, and a few not so easily identified. Was she trying to make him angry? She was still upset, but he wasn't sorry. He'd given her his heart, and she'd run over it with a hauling transport. That he'd once proposed to her left a sick feeling in his gut and a stale taste in his mouth.

They approached a structure with a large digital image displayed on its front. The ad had what looked like a male tentacled species and a pink female with a human like upper body, except for the horns jutting out of her head like a crown. They looked to be in a heated debate with a table between them.

"You want to work here?" Wade asked as they approached the double doors of the building.

"Any where's better than the *Hope*."

The way she said it made it clear she'd come to her decision. Wade shrugged to himself. He wasn't going to be the one to convince her to change her mind.

Maggie pulled back her shoulders and put on her reporter's cool and intensified expression just as the doors slid open. Unlike with Dana, Wade could follow in behind her. The building was much bigger on the inside than he'd expected. He caught himself staring up. At the other end of the narrow building's lobby rose a clear lift, gliding higher than his eyes could track.

A mechanical droid with a metallic skin-job greeted them from a slender podium. "Welcome. Maggie Brooker?"

"Yes," she said.

"You're late. I'll attempt to get you in as soon as possible."

The smile on Maggie's face faltered, but only for a moment before it was back in place. "I have several appointments today. If it's inconvenient, I can always reschedule."

"That would be unwise," the mechanical android said in a careful, robotic tone. "We are booked for the next two weeks. Please wait, and I'll send you up when it's time."

Maggie didn't let out a sigh even as she shifted from foot to foot. She did that when she was anxious. Wade glanced down at her feet again, noting he didn't recognize the shoes. Maggie had filled a closet with the shoes she'd brought along. These probably hadn't been worn in months, or they were new and giving her trouble. She'd never admit something like that to him, so Wade stood motionless near her, falling on his training. He focused his thoughts on Dana. It hadn't been a full day since he'd planted a kiss on her mouth in the dark of her office, and it had kept him thinking about her. He'd caught her looking at his mouth just before Maggie had come along and ruined everything yet again. Dana seemed to have the same trouble forgetting it.

It was foolish to keep thinking about her. She'd made it clear she wasn't ready for anything. Like her father, she was all about her duty, the mission. She wouldn't take time for herself until they'd found a new planet.

He knew he couldn't wait that long, whether it was a month from now, or a year. Wade was going to return to the ship and insist they talk about what had happened, and start making plans. She wasn't going to get rid of him so easily this time.

The android called Maggie's name and directed her to the lift for her meeting.

"Wait here," she said when he tried to follow her.

"I'm supposed to stay with you," Wade insisted, but with only half a heart. Neither of them wanted this and being alone together was pushing the limit on his patience.

Maggie stalked off without answering and took the lift to another level, leaving Wade to stand in the lobby.

"No chairs, huh?" Wade asked as he leaned against the wall of the corridor and waited.

He didn't expect an answer from the droid and wasn't given one.

MAGGIE WASN'T GONE LONG, AND WHEN SHE RETURNED, SHE shook off whatever had happened upstairs and walked out the doors, not bothering to wait for him to catch up. She made her way to another portion of the ring and found an external lift. The line waiting to reach the upper levels was substantial, but she queued up with the others and wedged herself between the various alien types as she made her way forward.

They stood in the lift line for almost twenty minutes before they were allowed into the next compartment. The crowd unceremoniously shoved the pair inside until not one more body could fit. When Wade's shoulders were pressed tight against Maggie and the wall, the entire contraption bolted upward. Despite the fifty odd bodies packed inside, it was fast and smooth. It stopped on each level and the entire process began again. Before long, Wade and Maggie were pressed up against the back wall. She leaned in to speak to him.

"Two more levels, and we need to make our way out of here."

"Why are there so many on one car?"

"Did you see the ones in the center of the Nexus?"

Wade nodded remembering the sleek boxes traveling up and down the nexus and dropping off individuals when he'd been walking with Dana. "Yes, they took one or two people at a time. We should have taken one of those."

"Those are for people with credits. This is what you get when you can't afford to pay."

While the next passengers shuffled toward the back, Wade and Maggie wedged themselves forward and up the middle. He held his ground until he caught Maggie's eye. She nodded, signaling they needed to get out before the next group came spilling in.

Wade stepped on something squishy, but none of the creatures seemed put out by his stomping on an appendage. When the doors opened, he aimed his body and shoulders for the opening. The crowd around him had doubled in size, and Maggie was nowhere in sight. He turned back to the lift, but the doors closed before he could see inside.

"Maggie!"

"Did you miss me?" The question came from behind him and he whirled around. Surprised to see her standing there, looking no worse for the experience. "We need to keep going."

AFTER THE FOURTH LOCATION, WADE WAS HUNGRY, TIRED, and bored. Maggie kept her smiles and her conversations for the interviews. Once she came out, she had near to nothing to say to Wade.

"Where are we going now?" Wade asked for the fifth time.

Maggie waved him off, as she had the other four times he'd asked, and pointed to a business with a large digital marquee. The picture looked like something from a Blue Earth vid. Like all the other buildings, he couldn't read the languages on the advertisements. The TMIs tucked behind their ears were helpful for speaking with the aliens, but they were useless for translating written language.

On the outside of the building, lights were flashing, and something that looked like a timer ticked on. There were all kinds lined up to go inside. Their eager faces said the place was a hit, whatever it was.

Maggie darted to the front of the line and gave her full name to the tall guard standing at the thin podium. He was a lanky male with grey skin and sharp teeth. He nodded and spoke into a micro headset inside his small ear.

"Yes, I have a Maggie Brooker," he gave Wade a once over and, giving him a slight roll of his eyes, added, "and guest to see you." He nodded before pressing the device in his ear. "Someone will be here in a moment to retrieve you. Please stand to the right."

Wade noticed more than a few individuals in the line

giving them curious looks. He wasn't sure if it was in admiration or something else, but it gave him the creeps.

"How long is this one going to take?" he asked.

Maggie refused to look at him, and instead reapplied her lip color. This was the fifth interview she'd dragged him to, and she still hadn't given him any more information.

A young grey female with the same sharp teeth greeted them. Her bright pink hair hung in clumped strands down her back. Wade felt himself losing his patience.

"Welcome to Fantasy Adventures! Right this way, please," she greeted them with a sharp tap of her teeth.

The assistant led them into a waiting area, then she sat down behind a console. Her hands worked over the machine, and she nodded, as if given auditory instructions that only she could hear.

"Magnus will be just a moment. Have a seat, please."

Wade spotted the soft chairs outside the office and plunked himself down in the closest one. He let a sigh escape his lips as he closed his eyes, crossing his arms over his chest. If his feet were aching in his boots, he could only imagine Maggie's feet must be ready to fall off. When they'd been together, he'd paid attention to things like her comfort. Not anymore. He hardened his heart against her further. She refused to talk to him about anything, so he kept his mouth closed and his thoughts to himself.

The modest waiting room was comprised of plain, grey colored walls that were bare except for the vid posters decorating them. The pictures depicting tragic events and either a star or an 'x'. Wade wondered if it was a kind of rating system. Perhaps Maggie would interview the vid stars. She'd hate that, and it made him smile. She considered it beneath her sensibilities to do that kind of fluff journalism, though she'd done enough of it on the ship.

He imagined how great it would feel when she left the ship and was no longer forced to look at her and remember how she'd cheated on him.

"Do you mind?" Maggie asked, staring down at his tapping foot. He hadn't even noticed he was doing it.

"Look, this is what you get when you leave me half-starved and aching from head to toe. I don't care if this is the last one or not, we're going back after this."

Maggie lowered her voice to a chill and glowered at him. "Keep it together. You'll be back with your precious captain soon enough."

Wade's teeth ground down on the words he wanted to say. The receptionist, pretending not to listen, had ceased working, seeming enthralled in their conversation.

"Sometimes you can be so incredibly self-centered and obtuse," Wade grumbled.

"Those are big words," Maggie shot back. "Be careful. You might hurt yourself."

"If I wasn't a gentleman, the only person I'd be hurting is you."

"I'm not afraid of you, you big—"

The secretary's high-pitched voice broke into their argument like a hot knife through butter. "Magnus will see you now."

"Wait here," Maggie said without a glance at Wade.

"It would be best if your companion accompanies you," the secretary added. "The exit is on the other side, and I'm expecting another client any moment."

Maggie shook her head lightly and grimaced. "Fine."

Wade stared at the secretary a moment longer. There was something in the lilt of her statement that rang false. He'd played a lot of cards over the last few months, and he knew when someone was bluffing. This one was lying through her thin, sharp teeth, though she refused to meet his gaze as they passed, returning to her console as if engrossed in her work.

"What kind of job are you applying for?" Wade asked.

Maggie ignored him and put on a bright smile as she pushed through into another office, greeting a man with his back turned to her. He sat behind an enormous desk, over a dozen large monitors flickering on the wall before him. His eyes never left the screens as Maggie crossed the room to stand in front of the desk.

The monitors looked like the space station's version of entertainment. There was some kind of sport playing on one screen, a family arguing in the living room of another. Each vid showed some manner of programming. One had two men running for their lives from something the camera couldn't see.

Wade was never much for watching screens. He found it boring to sit in place for an extended period of time, watching others in action. However, his eyes kept glancing at the monitors, as the man behind the desk couldn't seem to drag his attention away from them for even a second. Maggie commented on the actor's abilities, reminding him they'd entered the room.

"From what I can see, they're excellent actors. So real and engaging."

"I agree," he said, keeping his eyes on the screens as he spoke.

Wade watched the vids for any sign of humans. There weren't any that he'd seen, but there were all other manner of alien. Each of them delivered such a convincing performance, he wondered if they might get a copy to bring with them to watch on the *Hope*. He wasn't much for them, but the crew would be thrilled to get some new entertainment. That was assuming Dana had figured out a way to make some credits.

He dismissed his doubt. Of course she had. Dana could do anything she put her mind to, that's why she'd become a captain at so young an age.

The guy still hadn't turned around or truly acknowledged them. Ignoring the snub, Wade caught sight of a chair off to one side of the room and made his way over to it, sitting down out of the way. This was Maggie's thing. He didn't need to hold her hand, or even pretend he was there to support her.

Magnus spoke without turning to look at her. "You must be Maggie Brooker. I got your demo, and I'm intrigued by your story."

"Thank you." Maggie stood still in front of his desk, waiting for him to turn around.

The guest chairs where Wade had settled were against the far wall, farthest from the desk. She nodded to Wade as if to signal him to move a chair forward for her. He feigned confusion and ignored her request with a light shrug.

He envisioned the steam coming out of her ears at his response. Instead of waiting, she moved to the chair nearest the door and dragged it over to the desk. She planted herself down with her legs crossed, waiting for the interview to begin.

The screens blinked off, and there was a moment of confusion as the man sighed, then turned around to look at Maggie for the first time. He stood up and reached a hand out to her. Maggie leaned forward, extending her hand in the same way.

However, she'd done something wrong, because he smiled and then shook his head, turning her hand palm up so that their hands slid across each other. He wore a well-fitted cream suit with the brightest pink necktie he could find. It made his short pink locks seem faded in comparison.

"You're charming," he said. His teeth clacked together over the way he formed the words in his own language. "Who is your friend?"

Wade had been watching the man's eyes. They hadn't left Maggie. He must have caught Wade through his peripheral vision alone. Maggie must have found that interesting as well, but instead of turning to where Wade was slouching in the chair, she waved a hand in the air.

"He's my escort, nothing more."

"I don't think so, you had a closer relationship I believe," Magnus said still smiling over his teeth.

"Nothing serious," she countered.

If she thought she could just dismiss him in public, she had another thing coming. He stayed where he was but spoke loud enough for Magnus to hear.

"If a fiancé is nothing serious," Wade said.

"*Ex*-fiancé," Maggie corrected.

Magnus grinned, showing his teeth. "Well, aren't you two compelling?"

"We're no longer a couple, and it's a long and boring story, I assure you," she insisted.

"I doubt that," Magnus said, coming around the desk. He flashed his bright pink runners as he regarded Wade.

Wade met his eye and held it, even when Magnus continued to stare at him with an intensity that made him want to squirm. He continued to look him in the eye until Maggie redirected his attention back to her.

"If you're uncomfortable with him being here, I can send him out. To be honest, I'm fine with him leaving and waiting outside on the street."

"That won't be necessary." Magnus showed all of his sharp teeth in a wide smile. His short pink locks stood up in an elevated Mohawk fashion as he moved around his desk. His gray face intent as he searched a drawer for something. He picked up two black, rectangle-shaped boxes and carried one in each hand. "I've got an assignment for you."

Maggie squealed in excitement. "Really?"

"Now?" Wade asked.

"Yes. Both of you, come with me."

Wade groaned and didn't bother to hide it. The last thing he wanted was to be out on the rings of the Nexus all night. He'd already spent more time with Maggie than he'd wanted. Why Dana had forced him into this, he didn't know.

"You don't need me," he said, trying to weasel out of it. "You two go ahead."

Magnus held out a hand to the door leading out. "Please, sir, this way."

Magnus reached out to put an arm around his shoulder, but Wade jerked away.

"My name is Commander Chance. I have other duties to attend to, so if this is going to take some time, I'll leave you both to it."

Magnus held up his hands. "Please, Commander Chance, we're all very busy, but this won't take long. Follow me."

Wade had been expecting the door to lead to an exit, but instead they entered another small room. It was no bigger than a closet on Zelenia, with two large gray chairs in the reclined position. They were side by side and facing each other.

"Both of you, have a seat."

Maggie climbed into her seat and waited for whatever came next. Wade crossed his arms.

"I'm not getting into that thing."

"Wade, stop embarrassing me," Maggie hissed.

"Stop acting like you know what this is," Wade shot back, glaring at her.

"Commander, this is one of our virtual rooms," Magnus explained. "The idea is for Maggie to give us a live interview on an event happening right now. If we like what we see, we'll be sure to add you to our rotation, and you'll be reporting on the happenings around the space station within the week."

"What am I supposed to do while she's reporting?" Wade asked.

"You'll be the spectator. Just react to what you see happening so Maggie has someone real to play off of. Do you understand?"

Magnus waited for Wade to climb into the chair beside Maggie. They faced each other but refused to look at each other.

Magnus opened the two boxes and pulled out two pairs of clear contact lenses. He gave them each a pair to put on. Then Magnus moved to Wade's side and lifted a leather strap placing it on his right wrist, before moving to his left.

Wade's wrists came up hard against the leather-like restraints. They tightened as he struggled.

"What is this?"

"Just relax. These are for your protection. As long as you don't pull against them, they'll stay loose."

Maggie turned her head to Wade, voice low and angry. "I'm getting this job and getting off of the *Hope,* so just play along, and we'll be on our way."

Magnus finished his ankle cuffs and did the same for Maggie. She lay back as if she were having a day at the spa. Wade huffed in frustration.

"You two will be great together. I have a gut feeling about these things," Magnus said just before gliding out the door.

The virtual lenses activated, and it seemed they were in the middle of a transport accident in the Nexus. Maggie could see herself positioned near the scene, and an avatar of Wade stood off to one side with the other spectators.

Maggie smoothed out the virtual yellow dress and put on her reporter's face. She took in the scene and was ready to report within seconds. Wade crossed his arms over his chest and watched her deliver an impromptu report on what she thought was happening.

Despite not having any information or facts, she was doing a brilliant job of making up the report on the spot. Wade regarded the crowd around him, their faces glued on Maggie. She lit up like the sun as she turned to the nearest onlooker. It was a woman who looked a lot like the receptionist, perhaps a few years younger, her pink hair in small locks hanging to one side. She placed a hand over her mouth as if in shock over what had just happened.

"Did you see anything?" Maggie asked her. "What can you tell us?"

As the passerby leaned in, she nodded. "I saw the whole thing."

"Take us through it. Where were you headed when the accident occurred?"

Maggie had enchanted the crowd, and the woman was retelling the story with waving arms and wide eyes. Something inside Wade twisted. He was willing to bet she'd get the job. She was great at what she did. Things hadn't worked out between them, but he could admit she was amazing at getting to the heart of a story.

He fought the smile that threatened to quirk his mouth as he watched her work. When the virtual image in front of them stuttered, he thought it might be part of the program. The ground around them shook, and the image blurred again. A loud *boom* shook the space station.

Maggie let out a whoop and Wade swore as he realized there was something actually going on, and they were both strapped to the chairs in the small viewing room. The virtual lenses were dead, but they couldn't move as they were still strapped to the chairs. Wade struggled until he remembered they would loosen if he made smaller movements. He wiggled one wrist back and forth. Then Wade worked a wrist out of one cuff after what seemed like an eternity before freeing himself from the rest of the restraints.

He moved quickly to Maggie's side, removing the cuffs from her wrists.

"Why hasn't someone come in here to help us?" she asked.

"No doubt they're saving themselves, which is what we're going to do."

The space station rocked again before he reached the

binds of her feet, and he stumbled back. Maggie had her hands on her ankle restraints, quickly working them off.

"That felt close," she said.

Once free, she leaped out of the chair and grabbed hold of him to keep from falling at each quake of the building.

"My guess is they're bombs—worse than anything we had on the *Hope*," he said as he traced the walls with his hands. "We need to find a way out of this room."

He tried to activate the door leading back into Magnus's office. Nothing happened. Then he found the edge of another doorway with no handles or comm panel. He wasn't sure what was on the other side, but it seemed to be their only way out. He pressed against the door, waiting for some kind of trigger release, then when nothing happened, he searched again for a panel that would release the door.

Maggie banged on Magnus's office door, calling his name.

"He's not coming," Wade said, still searching the wall.

"What are you doing?"

"Trying to find the trigger to open this door. Look around, see if you see anything that might get this door open."

"We might be safer in here," Maggie said as she turned in a slow circle. The next shock wave shook the room, and part of the ceiling cracked and crumbled into her face.

Maggie sputtered and spat the dust that had landed in

her mouth. She shook her head to shake the remaining debris off.

"Nope, we need to move fast," Wade told her. "Stop standing around and help us get out of here."

"Don't tell me what to do!" Maggie yelled back. She huffed once, then scanned the room.

The door hissed open and Wade turned around to see Maggie with a huge smile on her face. She had one hand on her hip and the other one pointing to the door.

"Where was it?" he asked, vaguely annoyed.

She gave him a small, self-satisfied shrug. "On the arm of the chair."

"Come on." Wade grabbed her by the hand, pulling her out and back into the ring of the Nexus. People were trampling over each other to escape as a dull mechanical voice spoke over the comms system.

"Emergency evacuation procedures are in effect. All guests, please proceed to the nearest escape pods."

The two of them raced along with the crowd pressing in around them. They followed the overhead arrows in neon colors pointing to the escape pods. Wade saw a small green child with two black pigtails and webbed hands. She stood off to one side, wailing. Her large brown eyes took up half her face and continued to fill with tears. They overflowed, falling down both sides of her scaled cheeks as she cried out for her mother. With Maggie in tow, Wade moved to help the little girl, but before he reached her, the mother returned and snatched her up in a panicked spin.

Rapid gunfire could be heard over the panic of the

crowd, and Wade didn't slow down enough to see where it had come from. Wade pointed the mother in the right direction and followed her down a corridor with rows of escape pod chutes on either side. He could feel Maggie pressed against his back as bodies around them shoved forward, pushing their way toward the pod bays. The corridor was continually flooding with people, some scratching, clawing, or fighting their way to the nearest pods. Wade dragged Maggie as far as he dared when ahead he saw people leaping into pods with fewer people around to shove them forward.

"We've got to hurry. There aren't going to be enough pods for everyone," he said.

"How do you know that?" Maggie asked.

"Because I can count. Doesn't matter where I land, I always want to know my escape options."

He was pulling her along with determination when she dug in her heels. "There's two right here, come on."

Maggie climbed into the nearest one and waited for Wade to follow. Wade grabbed for the pod next to her, then stopped as he realized he was leaping into the dark with Maggie with no idea where Dana was, or if their ship was even functioning yet. He glanced back behind him at the crowd as if searching for her face hard enough would make her appear.

What if she's trapped on the station? His thoughts were still swirling around Dana when he caught sight of the mother and child he'd seen earlier. She ran for a pod opposite of them until a colossal beast knocked her aside and climbed into the pod without a glance back. It was the last one in that queue. He was still staring when she looked up at them, and then at the pod behind him.

"Take it." Wade opened the pod's hatch and ushered them in. "Hurry, you can both fit."

"Yeah, but we can't," Maggie said from the other pod.

The mother took a second to glance around her, as if struggling to believe it, before she put her child inside and climbed in after her. When the duroglass closed her in, she reached one webbed hand to the glass as if to say thank you. The pod's automatic piloting was initiated, and she flew through the tube and out of sight.

Another pod didn't snap into place. It had been the last one.

He glanced further down, but the pod bays were empty. The surging crowd continued to scan the places where the pods had been, looking for mechanical disfunction. He caught Maggie's glare. She was still seated in the pod she'd claimed, fuming. She had yet to trigger the autopilot function, staring back at him.

He was about to make a proposition when another burly creature caught up to them and tried to haul Maggie out of the pod. She screamed, calling out to him.

Wade reached for his weapon, forgetting it wasn't on his belt. The dockmaster had restated the station rules that no visitors were permitted to carry weapons while on the Nexus, so he used the only thing he had left. Wade tightened his fist and pummeled the furry beast in the face. It growled while Maggie screamed and kicked at him. The sooner she left, the sooner she'd be safe. There were no doubt more of these things, and he couldn't fight them all.

"Go!" he told her.

"I'm not leaving without you! Get in!"

The burly beast with four limbs and two rows of blunt teeth shoved Wade against the bulkhead. It knocked most of the breath out of him, but he caught it again in time to see more of the creatures coming.

Wade used the wall behind him to inch up off of the floor, and with all his strength, kicked against the beast. Its hold on his neck fell away, and it stumbled back into the bulkhead and slid to the floor. He was dizzy, but not out. Maggie was still waiting, and he shook his head.

"You never listen!"

"Come on!" she yelled.

Maggie had squeezed herself to one side, making room for him. Their limbs bumped up against each other as he slid inside. The apology on his lips died when the burly thing recovered, banging his meaty fists against the duroglass. The glass held until the thing's nails protruded, cutting at the capsule, leaving deep scratches. If he couldn't get in and save himself, the beast was determined to leave them stranded. Wade was seconds away from asking about the autopilot feature when they were pushed out into the black space around the Nexus.

"*By the Majestic*, what just happened?" He whispered the question to keep his eyes from filling with the emotion choking him.

Maggie didn't give an answer, and he hadn't expected one.

Wade cursed at the sight of the silent explosion behind them. Maggie whimpered, working herself up to cry. Wade lifted his head and saw the space station ripped into two halves. Dana was out there somewhere. He had to believe she'd made it out in time. Everything had happened so fast––the explosions, their escape. Dana was quick and smart. She was okay.

He gulped down the worry and fear. She *had* to be, because he couldn't live without her.

CHAPTER 34

Dana made a complete round of the ship before she returned to the docking bay. According to ship's time, it was in the wee hours of the morning on the following day. The station was just as animated and busy as it had been when they'd arrived almost twenty-four hours ago.

She found a steady flow of passengers still coming and going, and the Fashin Teku hurried to approach her. She knew what was coming this time, and her back stiffened. Their last conversation had gone as expected. They didn't have any credit with the banks either, and would be less than helpful in getting them any good will. Ashwin's bashful admittance that they may not be welcomed on the Nexus at all reminded her of their true nature. He and his people were scavengers, pirates. There were many species here that might feel a sense of hostility toward them. It was best not to broadcast their relationship with the Fashin Teku around the station.

Dana was grateful the Teku had gotten them this far. Despite the Chancellor's feelings, it wasn't necessary to hold them any longer. They'd done all they could to help them with the supplies and technical knowledge they possessed. She considered their debt paid, and nodded when they requested to speak with her.

"Captain, many thank yous. We will leave you now." Ashwin bowed low and waited for her answer.

She could see Tovar and Oli both stiffen when she waited a beat to respond. They'd taught her to be cautious, if nothing else, and so she softened her stance to put them at ease.

"I wish I could say it's been a pleasure, but I think you know the truth. We are not an unforgiving people, but take from us again, and we'll finish what we started. Are we clear?"

"Clear, very clear." Ashwin bobbed his head up and down, along with his companions, though their eyebrows were drawn together in confusion. They were unsure if they were allowed to leave as they glanced back and forth among themselves, and then back to her.

"Safe journeys, and may the Majestic be with you."

They looked from one another and back again at Dana before the three of them bowed. Ashwin took a step forward and lifted his hand to her. She took it and allowed him to lick her hand. She returned the lick on the back of his hairy hand, to his delight. The three of them squealed with pleasure before turning to go. They had been helpful at the end, but she was glad to see them going. To be so small, they'd been far more trouble than their worth.

She ran her tongue along the sleeve of her coat after they turned away. She'd have to brush her tongue to get rid of that taste.

The *Hope* would see some drastic changes with the Teku and Maggie choosing to leave. There were already a few others requesting to disembark. Those tired of living on the ship or those who had lost too much to want to stay. Ensign Shu's widow, Jun Tan, had already put in her request. Even with the baby coming, she preferred to leave the ship rather than continue their journey. She'd been clear in her message that she didn't want the stigma that came with staying onboard. Dana had opened up a return message to protest before she caught herself. She wasn't wrong. If the infection told her anything, it was that people had long memories, and Mrs. Tan had no future onboard the *Hope*.

Dana knew it wouldn't be the only request to leave, and she tried not to take their choice as a personal insult. They weren't abandoning her; they were making a life for themselves some place new.

Whenever Dana tried to visualize her future, she imagined a rustic home on a planet that reminded her of Zelenia. In her dreams, she was always alone. In her waking hours, she tried to imagine that life with Rido, and then Wade. She could imagine Rido as a loving husband, though she wondered if he knew his way around an ax or manual labor of any kind. She could see Wade building their house with his bare hands. When she imagined a life with him, she was always smiling and laughing. When it came time to discuss raising a family, though, she drew a blank.

She couldn't carry a child to full-term. It was as hard to form the thought in her mind as it was to imagine telling someone else—including a man who may want children. She could see both of them as loving fathers, but the children she raised wouldn't look like her. Her future children would be embryos carried by healthier women. Dana had spoken with a doctor when she'd first noticed a problem with her cycles. She hadn't taken it too seriously. With the innovations in nanotech and its medical uses, it seemed there was nothing they couldn't eventually fix.

She'd laughed when the doctor had explained she *couldn't* have children.

"I'm only sixteen. I don't want kids."

"You may someday, and I thought it best to tell you early. This way you and your parents can prepare yourselves for the future."

"What about external fertilization?"

The doctor had shaken his head. "I wouldn't recommend it. You couldn't carry the child to full-term, and embryos are expensive—not to mention the toll it would take on your mind and body."

Dana hadn't considered it a big deal, but her parents had been nervous and beside themselves. Her father had been smart enough to have the doctor erase all traces of their visit and the results from their system. He'd told her to never speak of it to anyone. She'd thought it overprotective paranoia, but looking back, it had saved her life. If the World Government had known she couldn't bear children, she wouldn't have been chosen as the *Hope's* Captain. Dana would have died on the planet with her mother and everyone else.

She'd lost track of how long she'd been in the bay watching the doors. One of the security team approached her on the way out, a young woman who was as tall as Wade with short, dark hair. There was no hiding her physique in her uniform. She looked capable of throwing Dana across the room without missing a beat.

"Are you waiting for someone, Captain?"

Instead of telling her she was waiting to see how things had gone with Wade and Maggie, she made up something that sounded more feasible.

"I wanted to check on our progress. Are we still at half-cap?"

"No, in fact, we're at about seventy percent capacity at the moment. People are beginning to understand that without credits, there isn't much else to do but hang out here and wait."

Dana nodded. It was as she'd expected. "Any sign of the Commander?"

She shook her head. "Would you like me to have a team search for him?"

Dana worried her lip. She'd expected them to return hours ago. Wade had looked so miserable when she'd sent him along. She'd thought him impatient to return to the ship, though Maggie could be sidetracked by a pair of shoes. In fact, she'd bet the reporter was out shopping for the next pair right now.

"No, it's not urgent. How long have you been on duty?"

"For the last four hours."

"Get some rest."

"Yes, Captain." She lifted a fist to her chest, and left Dana to her thoughts.

Valente had snuck up behind her during the exchange, and though she flinched, her training kept her from letting out a squeak. Instead, the stifled sound died in the back of her throat as she let out a quick breath.

"Sorry, Captain," he said. "I don't mean to disturb you, but we have a problem."

"What is it?"

"The Fashin Teku."

Dana groaned inwardly. "Did they take something from us?"

Valente straightened, as if she'd insulted him. "No. They were picked up by the local authorities. It seems they were right about not being welcome here. The Teku are requesting to return to the *Hope*."

Dana ran a hand down her face. "You've got to be kidding."

"No, and there's more. They've incurred a fine which will have to be paid before their release."

She stared at him for a moment, knowing Valente wasn't one to joke around. In fact, he had delivered the bad news like a punch to the ribcage, and she was still reeling from the blow.

"I suppose that means I need to go and get them?"

He nodded. "They've requested you by name."

She sighed. "All right. Where are they?"

"They're being held on detention level five."

"Of course they are. And we have no way of getting transport?"

"They did not give us a time," he explained. "My assumption is that they don't have a closing hour."

Dana shook her head and started off the ship before Valente called out to her.

"Captain, you need someone to go with you. Would you prefer me to assign someone to accompany you?"

Dana glanced around the bay and caught sight of ARI Three against one wall. If he wasn't busy, he could go with her, and if they ran into any trouble, he was weapon enough.

"ARI Three, you're with me," she said.

His eyes scanned her face before he moved to catch up to her. "Captain? I will assist you in any way I can."

"Just try to keep up."

The Nexus was already losing some of its luster her second time through. The smells were overwhelming, and the flashing lights were giving her a headache. She couldn't imagine living on a space station permanently.

"Ari, do you have a full schematic of the Nexus?" she asked as they joined the crowd rushing to the right around the loop.

"Yes, Captain. Where would you like to go?"

She caught a few irritated glances as she jostled for a position closer to Ari. Most of the crowd made room for him. It was one advantage of being head and shoulders above most. Dana's own height kept her at the elbows of the species around her. There were smaller varieties that came up to her waist, but she wasn't brave enough to ask if they were children. The last thing she wanted was to offend someone while she was doing her best to make potential friends. They needed help if they were going to survive on the Nexus.

"We need to get to the fifth level of this place and meet with the local authorities."

Ari tilted his head to one side, his gray-green eyes focused on her face as if in thought. "Yes, the IC, the Intergalactic Consortium. They are a conglomerate of businesses that oversee the protection and safety of the Nexus and most of this region."

"They sound friendly," Dana said, her tone dripping with sarcasm as she rubbed her hands together.

Ari was quiet for a moment. "I do not believe they will be friendly, from the commentary reports about their activity in this region. The four agencies that make up the IC are each feared in the regions of the galaxy they patrol. Their 'Agents', as they are called, are trained in private academies on several planets. One of the more prestigious of the training facilities being the Academy on Red Moon, which is several months away at our current travel speeds.

They are fascinating. It seems they travel in packs of six, and there are species among them who are capable of extraordinary abilities like telepathy, though there are few."

"Mindbenders, *yikes!*"

"They also carry non-lethal weapons that offer various degrees of pain and immobility," he added.

"But they're not deadly?"

"Accidents have been reported, but in general, no. There are several occasions in which species were killed. I have the details of three incidents. The other four are coded under sealed records going back several years. I do not have access to them at this time."

"Pause the history lesson on the IC so I can figure out what I'm going to say to them."

"Yes, Captain."

He was silent while Dana tried to wrap her mind around the idea of someone reading her thoughts. She'd have to be careful with them inside of the IC, just in case. If the Fashin Teku were known by the local authorities, it didn't bode well for Dana and her crew in turning around their already sullied reputation. They might consider them guilty by association.

She rehearsed their story in her head, preparing herself for questions she didn't want to answer. Perhaps once they heard her account, it would be enough to begin negotiating to take the aliens off their hands.

"Captain, the Fashin Teku stole the embryos and cargo from us."

"Yes, I remember," Dana said between clenched teeth. "Don't remind me."

"I was attempting to extrapolate why you are going to help them, since they are criminals."

Dana sighed. She'd already disputed this question in her head. She shouldn't feel responsible for helping them, but when they'd provided the tech needed to replicate the intergalactic translation modules, she'd forgiven them. Without the Teku, they wouldn't have had any way to communicate when they'd arrived at the ship dock. They'd helped them find the Arch and the Nexus. But the answer was simple.

"I know. But sometimes it's better to make friends than to keep enemies."

Ari was silent for another moment. "So, they are our friends?"

Dana huffed. "I thought I asked you to keep quiet so I could think."

They were making their way to the IC when a large marquee caught her attention. It reminded her of the old-fashioned outdoor vids her parents used to take her to when she was young. Her father had insisted on an evening in the park, and Dana had been so excited to be watching a vid on a large outdoor screen along with perfect strangers.

Her mother had dragged her feet at the idea of an evening picnic, but he'd won her over. By the time the vid started, they were all cuddled up together on a blanket and cushions, watching the classic along with everyone else.

"Are those indoor vids?" she asked as they passed, her thoughts still on her family and their night outdoors.

"Yes," Ari confirmed. "It is a popular pastime here on the Nexus called Fantasy Adventures. The people are not actors. They are thrown into a virtual scenario and have to figure their way out with only the skills they possess. Spectators enjoy their struggles as entertainment. There is a note that some gamble on the outcomes in order to earn credits."

Dana filed the information away in the back of her mind. She wasn't one for gambling, but Wade was pretty decent at cards. If all other avenues of work failed, maybe they could place a bet or two to ensure they got some credits to repair the ship.

"How do the IC view gambling here on the Nexus?"

Ari was quiet for a moment, then frowned. "I can find no answer to your query. Perhaps we should ask them."

Dana huffed. She was sure that if there was no official position, then pressing them for a position would result in a negative answer. That they hadn't said one way or the other meant it was probably frowned on, but they wouldn't push for laws against it. She remembered a few of her senior officers sitting at gambling tables themselves.

They reached the doors to the IC and, like all the other buildings she'd encountered, the doors slid open, allowing them to walk through. However, as soon as the doors closed, an alarm sounded. Immediately, a crew of six armed guards wearing helmets surrounded her and Ari.

What the sou have I done now?

CHAPTER 35

"Cast off the shackles of your mundane life and dive headfirst into a reality like no other. You'll be whisked away to a remote island paradise with a new lover. Become the detective in a thrilling murder mystery. Fight for survival with your closest friends, and many more. Earn credits for playing the game of a lifetime when your vid goes viral."
-Ad copy for Fantasy Adventures.

WADE

The pod built for one required ample creativity to fit the both of them inside. Wade only had time to slide in on top of Maggie before the pod was ejected. The two of them were hurdling through space before they realized their mistake. In order to work the controls, the passenger needed to see in order to navigate where they were going.

"I can see a planet just to the right," Wade said.

Maggie turned left.

"No, to the right."

"You mean your right," she growled, but adjusted the controls to veer left. "Is it too much for you to shift your knee? I'm going to wind up with bruises all over."

"I'm not doing it on purpose. Maybe we should change positions."

"No, I've got it."

"It still looks like you're not on a straight trajectory."

Maggie huffed, blowing strands of her red hair out of her face and making another adjustment of the shuttle's position. "We wouldn't have even had this problem if you'd gotten into the other pod like you were supposed to instead of standing there watching the station fall apart."

Wade tried to shift his head so he could look at her face. "Wait, you're upset that I gave up my pod to a mother and child?"

Maggie huffed again. "That's not what I meant, and you know it."

The pod's speed was going to be a problem. He wondered if it was equipped for automatic reentry. If not, Maggie was going to get a crash test in piloting.

"I don't think I can land this thing," Maggie said, echoing his thoughts.

"You shouldn't have to. It seems they set the speed. All

you need to do is steer. But if it looks like we're going in too hot, I'll initiate manual control. That's going to require us to trade places. Do you think you can handle that?"

Wade knew the jab would get under her skin, but he didn't have time to think up the niceties it would require to get her to do what he needed.

Maggie scoffed. "Have you been waiting all day for that one?"

"Just focus on where we're headed so we don't land on a cliff or in the middle of an ocean."

"I would love to, but your colossal head is in the way. I can't see anything."

Maggie squirmed under him, but she didn't understand she was rubbing up against him in a way that made him stiffen rather than relax.

"Stop wiggling around."

"Oh," Maggie said, realizing what she was doing. "Sorry."

"My head isn't any bigger than normal," he grumbled after an awkward moment of silence.

"You do sort of have a big head." She laughed. "Your mom and I talked about it once."

"You did?"

"I think she was warning me that having children with you would require a medical facility stocked with plenty of pain-relieving nanos."

He huffed out a small laugh. "Leave it to my mom to scare off a girlfriend with birthing stories."

"She's from the old-school. I sort of liked it. I think

under it all, she implied that being with you would take some work." Maggie's voice dropped and her lips tightened. "That was all before I knew she preferred your ex."

Wade winced. He'd tried to forget most of the things he'd screamed at her from behind the force field Dana had erected. That was one thing he wished he could take back. It was a personal dig, and had been unnecessary. His mother's last message had been to tell him to find Dana and make things right with her. She'd always believed Dana was the one for him, and she'd been right all along. Maggie, though, didn't need to hear it yelled at her during an infected rage.

They both fell silent. He wondered if she replayed their time infected in her mind as much as he did. Did she regret anything she'd said? What would have happened if her lover had been onboard? What if he'd refused to go? Would she have ever told him the truth?

Wade already knew the answers, and that was the problem with being exposed to a truth speaking virus. It had taken all their secrets off the table, which included the fact that he wasn't over Dana.

When they reached the planet's atmosphere, the pod jostled them back and forth.

"Ow, watch it!" Maggie snapped after they'd bumped heads.

"I'm doing the best I can. But..." His voice trailed as he saw her face change from annoyance to barely hidden panic. He tried to turn his head to see what was going on. "What's wrong?"

"The controls . . . they're not responding."

"The autopilot feature must have turned itself on. Don't fight it."

"It shouldn't be this turbulent," Maggie said, letting out another startled yelp.

Wade wanted to agree, but he also didn't want to freak her out. It wouldn't help either of them for her to be any more panicked than she was.

"Switch," he said. At the same time, he was already rolling her on top of him.

It was an awkward, slow, and painful roll, as Wade had to alternate thrusting his hips up and shoulders over to get around the gears and chair grips. By the time he was in position, the pod was getting warm as they picked up speed.

"Hold on, we're going down too fast."

Maggie was already whimpering, her head on his shoulder and her eyes squeezed tight.

The pod wasn't on manual anything, and if he hadn't taken control of the thing, they'd have plowed into the side of a mountain. They crashed down hard in a wooded area, and after slamming into the fifth tree, he blacked out.

THE STRANGE SILENCE WOKE HIM. IT WAS AS IF SOMEONE HAD turned off the ship's engines and lights. Wade could sense that his eyes were open, but he couldn't see.

What time is it?

He reached for the tablet on the bedside table. His hand met cold metal, but no lamp. His extended reach pulled him from his bed, and he rolled over, but his bed wasn't the soft, ship-issued comfort it should have been. There was too much pressure on his leg, and it hurt like it was broken.

"COMP, raise lights to half." The command was a hoarse croak, one notch above a whisper.

His mind fought reality. What had he been drinking last night? He'd been dreaming of Dana. They'd been relaxing on the couch in her quarters. Had that really happened?

No.

He hadn't been drinking because nothing on the ship worked. His hand reached for her, but the floor felt cold, like ground. The dark had gone from a welcome cloak to cold and stark.

Wait . . .

They'd made it to the space station. The lights along the dock were so bright through his viewport he should be able to see his hand in front of his face but couldn't. He'd been walking through the space station with Dana—

No, not with Dana . . . with Maggie.

Dana had assigned him to take her. Dana thought she was doing them a favor, but it had only made things worse. There'd been trouble on the space station before the whole thing fell apart.

They'd landed without the autopilot system. He did a quick assessment of his body. Something was wrong with his leg. It didn't move when he demanded a response from it. The rest of his body seemed intact and responding. The scrapes he could see would need tending, but later. Maggie had been on top of him—

Where is she?

"Maggie?" His voice was another dry croak.

He tried again, a little louder than before, but still no response. The pod had been engineered to hold one body lying flat, perhaps to accommodate larger species. Their combined weight might have confused the sensors, forcing them down faster than planned. Though he and Maggie couldn't have outweighed those larger, beast-sized aliens.

The pod lay in broken pieces a few feet from him. His hand had been touching a smaller piece of the side. Wade could see the other half of the pod several feet away, the seat still attached, but Maggie wasn't in it.

On his left was a kind of tree. He wasn't much for biology studies, but he ran his hand along the base of the tree. The bark felt familiar, but the leaves hanging from its branches were larger than the small leaves on the trees of Zelenia. It reminded him of Planet 2396. He gulped down the sudden flash of fear. This wasn't the same planet. If the wildlife here were prehensile, they'd have gobbled him up while he was unconscious.

A glimmer of light in the distance drew a bright orange line across the sky. The sun was coming up, which would help matters, as he shivered against the cold and he wouldn't be able to find Maggie without it. The tree that was shading him now had rays of light slipping through its purple-tinged green leaves.

Wade cleared his throat, attempting more volume and distance. "Maggie!"

She didn't answer, which meant one of two things: she'd gone for help, or she was unconscious. He hoped it was the former as he looked around for something he could use to ease the pain radiating from his leg. He elbow crawled to the other half of the pod that the seat was still attached to. With every tug of his body, his leg resisted, screaming in pain. He broke into a sweat and grit his teeth. After every draining effort, he imagined Maggie would pop out of the bushes with an arm full of wood or something. In the vids, he'd seen people survive crashes worse than this.

A distant howl caught his attention. If there were predators in the woods or nearby, his situation just got a lot worse. The bleeding on his arms and body might smell tempting to something out there looking for exotic new flavors. With one good leg, he wouldn't get far running from anything faster than a tortoise.

He kept crawling, lifting his broken leg by the pants with every move until he made it to the bottom half of the empty pod. As he suspected, there wasn't much left. The safety belt hung from the tattered chair. He tried to activate the pod's control panel. If he could get a message out, perhaps someone would find them and pick them up. A proper med facility wouldn't be a bad idea, considering his injuries, but the entire pod was dead. Nothing worked, not even what looked like an emergency beacon. They'd have to signal the old-fashioned way. Their ancestors on Blue Earth had once been a fire and smoke communicating people. He was proud of himself for knowing that.

He had to rest his trembling arms a moment before he dug under the seat, hoping for a med-kit. Wade's hand clasped onto a small box, and when he popped it open, there were four injectors inside on a small tray. He stared at the injectors. The light green liquid in them didn't look like anything he'd ever seen before. This was the problem with alien tech. Without someone around to explain it, he had to guess at what everything might be. They could anything from an adrenaline like stimulant to a weapon designed to kill someone close range. The likelihood that any of it would be compatible with his human DNA, however, was nil, as they'd seen no other Terrans on the space station. Wade placed the injectors to one side.

Once he found Maggie, they'd figure out if they were usable. For now, Wade stared down at his broken leg. He'd needed to set and wrap it before he did anything else. It continued to dangle behind him, pulling on tendons and already ripped muscle. The belts would do for binding. He used a piece of broken duroglass to cut off the safety belt. Sweat broke out on his brow as he worked, cursing the thing for not being of use earlier. He'd grown too accustomed to the automatic belt system onboard the *Hope*.

Wade shook his head, then regretted it, as it made him dizzy. He couldn't think about that now. Once his head cleared again, he kept working.

The longer he was alone, the more he worried about where Maggie had gone. He didn't relish the idea of searching for her, but the alternative of not knowing was worse. She couldn't be far, as the pod's trajectory had come through the trees. He could see broken limbs and branches all around them, white inner bark poking out. The ground behind the pod was dark with fresh earth churned up by their violent landing. The pod might have thrown Maggie like it had him, and in effect was lying either somewhere ahead, or behind him.

He scanned the broken tree limbs around him and caught sight of one larger specimen to his left, large enough to make a decent splint. The arduous task of cutting the large branch into two equal pieces and placing them on each side of his leg made the nausea he'd been fighting grab him by the throat. He stalled, waiting for it to pass.

The planet's one sun was getting warmer as it rose. Wade suspected whatever was howling in the early morning hours was nocturnal, giving him the day to find a safer spot.

Then he stared at his leg. The limb hung at an unnatural angle. He'd have to set it in order to relieve the pain and for it to properly heal. The Space Fleet Academy had trained him to be ready for field emergencies, but he'd never imagined dealing with a broken leg by himself. He'd always assumed another member of the crew would be around to lend a hand.

He wiggled around on the ground and worked the belt

around the tree. Wade fastened the end together low on his ankle, the movement blackening the light on the edges of his vision. When he gathered his breath again, he fastened the other belt to the rest of the pod behind him. The length was just enough for him to wrap around his arm and wrist. He'd have to pull his own leg straight, then use his utility belt to splint it until he could collect the safety belts again. He wasn't sure he wouldn't pass out in doing so but tried to prepare for every likely scenario.

Wade glanced down at his leg one more time and said a prayer to the Majestic. He wasn't a Believer, but he imagined the Merciful wouldn't leave him, considering the situation. Then he remembered he might swallow his own tongue in the setting process. Wade reached for a small twig, then changed it out for a thicker one. He took a chance that this planet, with its purple leaved trees and breathable air, wouldn't have toxic bark. He put the piece in his mouth and placed his good foot on an edge of the pod as a brace. When it was secure, Wade took three quick breaths. Then, using all the weight from his upper body and both arms, he pulled his leg straight in one fast movement.

The black reclaimed him with his next breath.

CHAPTER 36

Dana tensed up, backing into the android, waiting to see what the offense had been.

"You've committed a four-oh-five violation." The voice came from a male, his voice distorted but deep. They were all covered head to toe in white uniforms, helmets hiding their faces. "In compliance with the Intergalactic Consortium, you are hereby commanded to hand over your android in accordance with section two, paragraph eight."

Dana repeated the charge number but didn't know what it meant. She turned to Ari. If he could look anxious, he would have, but at the moment he seemed confused, as if they'd accused him of being a pet. She turned back to the guards.

"My name is Captain Dana Pinet, of the Starship *Hope*. We arrived at the start of this standard day. If you would be so kind as to explain the problem to me, I'm sure we can come to some solution."

"You'll meet with Major Adams," the deep male voice said. "The android will come with us."

"I can't allow you to take a member of my crew," Dana said, keeping her voice calm even as her mind raced for an answer to her duplicated problem.

"The law states that are no weapons resembling a person allowed to be used on the Nexus."

Dana's mouth fell open. After a moment of gathering herself, she asked, "Ari?"

"Yes, Captain?"

"Can you scan the documents given to us this morning and confirm what this guard is telling us?"

"Yes, Captain. The law states: 'According to the Intergalactic Consortium, there are no weapons on the Nexus in order to ensure the safety of our citizens and guests. We strictly forbid artificial intelligence designed to pass for a member of your species and conducting business on your behalf. All artificial life-forms should be without clothing and/or skin easy to identify it among the species present.'"

Dana ran a damp hand over her face and placed both hands on her hips. "Why didn't you tell me this before we left the ship?"

"I am not bearing the full likeness of your species, as my hand and leg are obviously mechanical." He lifted the left pant leg to prove it before he continued. "I am conducting no business, nor providing service to members of the Nexus."

His explanation was flawless. She was glad he'd lost

the skin off of his left hand, as it made it quite clear she wasn't breaking the rules on purpose or trying to hide him.

The leader of the group lowered his weapon and stepped forward. "I regret your misinterpretation of our laws." Dana could hear the sneer in the leader's voice, even under the helmet. "However, your android is not permitted inside of the IC, nor to accompany you again on the Nexus. We will hold it until you depart. From here, we will escort you and the droid back to your ship."

Dana tried not to let her annoyance show. It was bad enough she had to be accompanied at all on the Nexus, and now they were going to march her through the rings like a criminal. If the locals saw her with the IC, it wouldn't help her make any friends. Ari might not be a person, but he was invaluable to her crew, and the last of his kind. She couldn't afford for anything to happen to him, either.

"If I come back here and my ARI is in any way damaged or changed, you'll have to answer to me." Dana glanced around and noted two white chairs designed for discomfort. "Ari, have a seat until I return."

"Yes, Captain." Ari dutifully sat, and the unit of guards backed away from him. Their leader kept his attention on Dana, and with one gesture toward a glass door, signaled her to follow one of his guards.

Like the entryway, it was stark white and as sterile as a hospital on Zelenia. The brightness and the click of her boots on the white tile made her eager to be on her way and back to the warmth of color the Nexus offered. They turned down a second corridor before the guard took up their position on the opposite side of the door. Dana would have to walk through the doors on her own. She didn't know what to expect. The guards all had helmets to cover their faces and uniforms covering every inch of them to the fingertips.

Dana passed by the statuesque guard and through the door. She gaped as she stared at the man behind the desk inside. He wore a white military uniform with his rank and medals below one shoulder, and as he stood up, she could see he was human.

All of his limbs and skin identified him as a Zelenian.

"Captain," he greeted, "it seems your passengers are making a mess of things on the Nexus today."

"Major Adams?" Dana asked, using the title and sketching a formal salute. Her mind was racing with questions she wasn't sure it was appropriate to ask.

His eyes were a sharp steely blue, but his grin lifted half his mouth. "Yes . . . I see the resemblance. You are human then?"

"Yes, from a planet on the other side of the Arch called Zelenia," Dana said in a rush. "But we're originally from Blue Earth."

"Ah, yes, Earth. Your people must have made quite the journey after the Great Purge."

Dana nodded as her knees wobbled. He must have noticed, because he gestured to the chair in front of his desk.

"Please, sit down," he said.

Dana fell into the chair, not able to take her eyes off him. He sat back down, folding his hands over his desk.

"Where are you from?" she asked, still shellshocked to see another human face.

The Major gave her a long-suffering smile. "My people never lived on Earth. We are from Red Moon. At current speeds, it's more than a month out from this space station. Those Agents you met out there are all from Red Moon. My superiors have assigned us to this temporary outpost in order to help the locals with repeat offenders, giving the place some trouble. I know it's not you, as you've just arrived, however, I'm wondering how you managed to stumble upon the notorious Fashin Teku crims?"

"If they're not welcome here, like the android, I can bring them back with me," Dana offered. "They've been a handful, but I have use for the three Teku until we can find a suitable location for them to be reunited with their own people."

Dana knew she hadn't answered his question, and wondered if he'd noticed.

"Three, you say?" he echoed questioningly. "But there are four of them in my hold."

Dana wondered who they'd picked up, and immediately dismissed the notion of taking on another. Their friend was on their own. Her non-existent credits couldn't help them. Either way, she didn't say anything more to the Major. He didn't need to know she had yet to meet the fourth.

The Major nodded, as if considering her proposal. He

said nothing for a full minute. If he was trying to make her squirm, it wouldn't work. Her father used to use the same tactics on her as a child, and she knew this game of silence well.

"Yes, I believe we understand each other," he said at last. "You seem to be a magnet for trouble, so I'm going to make this easy for you, Captain. Return to your ship with your android, and once you have made your repairs, leave this station. Don't return."

Dana was about to protest, looking around and drawing up short. She hadn't realized her escort had slipped into the room behind her, who stiffened and shook their head. She didn't have time to process what was happening between them before the major spoke again.

"No, you won't get the Fashin Teku out of holding without a considerable amount of credits, so they'll have to stay."

Dana's head whipped around again to the Agent, truly taking them in for the first time. His stealth was shocking. He was lean with narrow shoulders and a firm stance. He hadn't said a word behind the helmet, but was obviously having a dialogue with the Major. Was he communicating telepathically? Was that really possible?

"I can't just let them go free. There are bonds to be paid," he continued as he stood up.

"How much is the bond on each of them?" she asked as she stood mirroring his movement.

"A thousand credits each. Four thousand total."

Dana blinked. She didn't have one credit. Getting additional credits on top of what she needed for her ship felt impossible.

"Okay," Dana said.

"Okay?" He laughed. "Just like that? Without a credit to your name, a busted-up ship, and a sleep deprived crew? You're willing to pay for four criminals who wronged you in the first place?"

Dana listened as he gave her all the reasons she should just leave the IC and never look back, but there was one reason she couldn't.

"When you saw me, you didn't seem surprised to find I was from Blue Earth. You've met others? Like us, I mean?"

"Yes," Adams said. "There aren't many this far out, but many of the humans who fled the Great Purge were scattered throughout the galaxy. Red Moon isn't a place where your people travelled. Our ways are quite different from yours. I don't think your people would like living under our laws. My ancestors were unwilling to submit to the aliens on the chance they'd let us keep the blue planet. It was a risky endeavor from the start." He smiled pityingly. "I'm happy my ancestors were a bit more logical—no offense."

Dana wasn't offended because half of what he was saying didn't make sense. There were other humans from Earth. They'd made it. They wouldn't be extinct.

Her mind was filled with the possibilities. This could change everything for them going forward. But the Major had said his people had never lived on Earth. *How is that possible?*

"How many humans are alive in this part of the galaxy?"

The Major smiled. "More than I know. This outpost is one of the few exceptions. The Nexus draws aliens in from the Arch, so we never know what we're going to run into here. But if you're looking for more humans, there are star charts available with routes that will take you to locations like Red Moon. The quadrant is filled with planets full of humans."

Ari had mentioned that one of the schools that trained the Agents was located on Red Moon. She tried to imagine planets filled with humans and struggled to wrap her mind around it. Dana wasn't sure, but as she processed what Major Adams was saying, she had the distinct feeling there were wisps or tendrils probing her thoughts. She didn't glance to her right, where the Agent was standing, but she knew the feeling had to be coming from them.

"I guess that explains why you don't understand my actions. We thought we were the last of our kind. The idea that I'm willing to help those who've aided us on our journey to find a new world shouldn't surprise you." Dana felt her mouth spread into a smile. "We are a product of those who escaped the Purge and founded a new home, one that's now gone."

"You're willing to forgive them because they gave you some technology, helped make repairs on your ship, and showed you how to get here?"

Dana waited. She knew the Agent was deep in her thoughts. She didn't have to verbalize them.

"But I prefer when you do," Major Adams said aloud.

"I prefer you tell your pet not to go digging around in my thoughts without my permission, but it seems neither of us is getting what we want."

Dana let the thought project out in front of her, and the Major lifted one elegant eyebrow. "Despite that, I'm willing to forgive your rudeness, if you forgive mine, as you've done more good than harm today." He nodded to the Agent. "Agent Sorel, stand down."

She watched as the Agent removed the helmet revealing the face of her mental attacker. A woman with honey brown skin and sharp brown eyes. Though her head was as bald as a baby, she was also human. Agent Sorel didn't meet Dana's eye, but her stance relaxed as she stood holding her helmet.

The Major's intimidation tactics had been more annoying than frightening. Her father would never stoop to such ploys in order to get information. He'd had far too much honor.

"Your father sounds like an interesting man. You have three days to make your repairs and be on your way. Try to stay out of trouble while you're here, Captain. We'll be keeping a close eye on you."

"I'll do my best. In the meantime, I'd like to see the prisoners."

"No," he said, his tone firm.

Dana stiffened. It had been a while since she'd been so quickly dismissed, and it rankled. "It wasn't a question."

The Major's eyes flashed to her, as if he was trying to

decide how best to bury her remains. It seemed he wasn't used to being questioned.

Dana relaxed her shoulders and softened her voice. "Please, I would like to see the Teku. I'm not going to hand over credits for their release until I see them and how they're being treated."

Major Adams' jaw worked a moment, and he gave Agent Sorel a nod. She replaced her helmet once hiding her face without a word.

"Fine. If I see you again Captain Pinet, it will be too soon."

The door opened behind Dana, and the Agent ushered her out of the Ambassador's office.

Dana followed without another word. The Major was a piece of work. She was about to complain about being thrown out when they didn't turn down the corridor back toward the lobby. She was going to see the Fashin Teku.

The holding cells were like everything else in the IC. Stark, white, clean. The three Fashin Teku were in separate cells, all small enough to accommodate them.

Tovar nodded as Dana walked past their cell to where Ashwin was calling out to her. On the other side of his cell, Oli stood. The force-field structure surrounding and separating them made it easy to hear and see them, though she imagined if you touched it, you'd get a severe shock on either side.

"Captain," Ashwin greeted her gratefully, "many thank yous."

"I'm sorry, Ashwin, but I'm not here to get you out yet. There are fees to be paid, and I don't have the credits."

"Oh, Captain Dana, do not leave us here as rot," Ashwin moaned, as if ready to cry. She'd never seen him quite so frightened. From behind him peeped a small head covered in the same blond hair.

"Who's that?"

"My son. From the first wife. Please, help him."

Dana caught a flash of his blue eyes before his little head ducked back behind his father.

"What's he doing here? How is it that he's on the station?"

"My son, he was a..." Ashwin looked to the others looking for the phrasing.

"A captive." Tovar volunteered.

"Yes, a captive," Ashwin agreed then continued with more excitement. "He is the reason we come. I paid for my son, but we owe much to many. Too many to pay in all. Many sorries," he pleaded.

"Saying sorry doesn't it make it less of a problem for me." Dana sighed with the weight of the situation then ran a hand over her face. She couldn't leave the Teku and the boy behind. "I've met with Major Adams. I just wanted to make sure you were all right."

"We are well," Tovar said from her cell.

Oli was silent, but watched with his big brown eyes glued to her face.

Ashwin looked to the guard, and then back to Dana's face. "Captain, they are like you."

"Similar but different," she replied. "They are not my people from either Zelenia or Blue Earth."

"They are here," he said.

"Who are?"

"Your peoples."

Dana shook her head. "There are some humans here, but they are from a different world than ours."

"*Zelenia* people," Ashwin insisted. "From the destroyed world. I was making an arrangement to meet with someone who has seen them. Then the IC captured us." Ashwin made to spit on the floor before turning back to her.

Dana's heart was in her throat. Her people, here, on this very space station. She licked her lips and chose her words carefully, knowing the Agents were listening to everything she said. "How can I find the person you were going to meet?"

Ashwin pulled at the hair on his chin in thought. "He will not like meeting with you. Too much like IC," he said, waving a hand at her face.

"Captain, your time's up. I will escort you out now," Agent Sorel interrupted. She'd used her voice this time and it had a raspy quality that grated on Dana's nerves. It was too similar to Maggie's, like she'd inhaled a bunch of smoke from a fire. The guard joined her, flanking Dana before she even thought of moving. They had their weapons at the ready should she attempt to resist.

"Give me a name and tell me how to contact them," Dana yelled to Ashwin as she turned and started walking.

"Rohath. Find Rohath. He's seen your people."

IN THE LOBBY, ARI THREE STOOD WHEN HE SAW DANA returning with the Agent.

"You were unable to obtain their release?" he asked.

Dana shook her head. "No, not unless we have four thousand credits."

Ari's shoulders seemed to sink. "That is unfortunate."

"Yes, and it turns out that Ashwin has a child with him." She pressed the heels of her palms against her eyes, overwhelmed with everything piling up around her. "I can't leave them . . . but never mind that. We've got an escort back to the ship. While we're on our way, run a scan for a Rohath. Apparently, he's met our people before. He may have some information about how we can find them."

Dana ignored the curious stares as they proceeded through the Nexus back to their ship. The group of six had thinned to just four, but Agents flanked them front and back. She knew the leader was just in front of her, so she followed, wondering if she could get him to talk.

"The Nexus must be an interesting place to live."

The leader's head tilted to one side. His steady cadence never faltered as he answered, "I wouldn't know. I don't live here."

"Oh, you must be from Red Moon too. How far is the Nexus from your home world?"

"Far," he said.

"Captain?" Ari said lowly.

Dana dropped back beside him. "Did you find Rohath?" Her heart leaped at the thought of running into anyone who might know where they could find her people. Perhaps they'd even be able to help her get the credits they needed. Her mind was racing with the possibilities.

"No, but there is something else you should see."

Dana followed Ari's eyes as he glanced up at a moving advertisement for the indoor vid movies. She couldn't understand the words scrolling across the screen, but she recognized the two lead actors. Wade and Maggie were racing through what looked like the Nexus. Her heart sank when she saw the way he was clutching her hand. Maggie was racing to keep up, and the expressions on their faces wasn't an act.

"Hey, wait."

"No, stopping," the lead Agent said. We have other places to be, Captain."

"Those are my people up there. What is that?"

The Agent glanced up, then back to her. "It's a virtual reality entertainment center. The people that get into those things are usually desperate for attention."

"I know them," Dana insisted, seeing the real fear on their faces. "They're not acting."

"We don't have time for a vid. Disregard what you're seeing. It's not real. You'll have to come back for them once your android is stowed onboard your ship."

They moved Dana along before she could see where Wade and Maggie ended up.

The guards were pushing them along to what looked like a private lift. Once inside, they descended two levels before they stopped. They seemed to be communicating with someone over their comms. Dana could only hear the responses from the Agents.

"Are you sure?" the Agent on her left asked.

"We've got Agents trapped on the docking bay," the leader answered. "These two will have to return to level five."

"We'll never make it," said Agent Sorel.

"Shorthanded and stuck with babysitting duty." She heard the sneer behind the helmet as their leader regarded Dana and Ari. "We don't have enough agents to do everything."

"What the *sou* is happening?" Dana asked. "Stop talking around me like I'm not here."

He sucked in a breath then he nodded still speaking into his comms, "Yes, sir." The doors opened, and the leader and four others got off the lift before he held up a hand to Dana.

"It's not safe for you to return to your ship this way. Agent Sorel, bring them back up to level five."

"But—" she protested.

"Just do it, Agent."

Something invisible passed between before the Agent nodded. Dana watched him reenter the lift with them and lead them back up to the holding area.

"Captain, it is possible to reach Rohath," Ari whispered. "At least, I think I may have discovered a way to access the public database." He waved his hand in the air again as he must have seen Eartha do.

"Not now," Dana said under her breath.

Agent Sorel glanced over her shoulder at them, but when they reached the fifth level, she stopped. She was listening to a comm or something that Dana couldn't hear. She held open the lift door, but she hadn't moved.

"Check in at the front desk. They'll make sure you're safe."

"Safe?" Dana asked as she stumbled out of the doors behind Ari.

The doors closed and the Agent disappeared before she heard the answer in her mind.

"The situation has grown worse at the docks. I'm needed immediately to help with containment. Proceed directly to the front desk and the IC will make sure you're safe. Don't and you'll risk additional fines for breaking statute four-oh-four."

Dana processed what she heard in her head and when Ari stood staring at her, knew she'd been the only one to get those last-minute instructions. They were on their own, without an Agent escort and no one to check whether or not they made it to their ship. She couldn't have planned it any better if she'd orchestrated the whole thing.

"Tell me everything about that Fantasy Adventures thing, now," Dana said, waiting for Ari to realize she wasn't walking toward the detention center.

He turned back and returned to her while he relayed everything he could get from the system.

"It is a virtual reality game that convinces the gamers they are actually in a real situation."

Dana remembered the fear on their faces. "Are they safe?"

"The reality is controlled by the innovators. They strap the participants to chairs so they can in no way harm themselves."

"Has anyone ever died in the game?" she insisted.

"There are two documented cases in the thousands that have played. One was an alien with a special heart condition. The other was an elder in her species. The entertainment company issued an official apology, and they paid some kind of restitution to the offended species."

Dana bit her lower lip as she glanced at the digital marquee. Wade and Maggie were running as the Nexus crumbled around them. While the Agents raced off to deal with another emergency on the Nexus at the docks, she could get the information she needed. Though, what good was the information if she lost Wade? No, she had to be sure.

"Let's go," she said, making her decision and marching off in the direction of the marquee.

"But the IC will arrest and detain us if they discover I am not on our ship."

"We can't get to the ship, so either you come with me, or you wait here for them to detain you."

Ari thought for a moment. "If Eartha were here, she would insist I stay with you."

"The kid is right. Let's go."

EPILOGUE

WADE

The second time Wade opened his eyes, he was looking up at a bright sun. It was double the size of either of the two suns on Zelenia. He spit out the stick he'd used to keep from swallowing his tongue and lay there a moment, drinking in the sounds around him. There were birds that sang on this planet, and he wondered how he'd forgotten how much he'd enjoyed the sound.

He unwrapped his wrists and hands from the safety belt and pulled it toward him. Wade needed to wrap his leg between the two branches he'd gathered. He was tying together one belt when a scream pierced the air.

"Maggie!" He'd gained a little of his voice back.

"Wade! Help me!"

It *was* Maggie, and she wasn't far.

"I'm coming! Hold on!"

Double-time, he wrapped both belts around his leg and tried to stand. The pain was enough to make his head spin. He turned back to the shuttle pod and remembered the vials of liquid injectors he'd found. He didn't have time to wait around testing them. If it was anything other than a painkiller, he'd find out soon enough. He cleared his throat, calling out again.

"Maggie, where are you?"

"Wade, I thought you were gone!" The relief in her voice matched the relief he felt. "Well, don't leave me hanging here. Come and help me!"

She seemed impatient. No doubt she'd been yelling for some time from the rasp in her voice.

"I can't. My leg is broken. I need some painkiller before I come after you. Are you stuck under something?"

"No, not really." Maggie sounded strange.

He looked up and around him wondering if she was caught under a boulder. Wade frowned to himself when he didn't see her. "Where are you?"

"I'm hanging off the edge of a cliff. I landed on a large piece of tree root, but I'm not sure how long I can hold on," Maggie said. "Are we alone?"

Wade's head spun with the thought of doing anything more than rolling over. He was pretty sure he was going to pick up an infection on top of everything else. His leg felt too warm. This wasn't the time to be optimistic.

"Yes."

"Please, get help!"

Wade could picture her hanging over the side of a cliff, and it scared him when he realized he might be her only possibility of survival. The smell of the salt water reached him, and he knew that was the unfamiliar smell. Being land-locked on Zelenia, he wasn't as comfortable with the water as others.

"Help! Somebody help us!" Maggie continued to scream from over the cliff.

A shuffling in the trees behind him reminded Wade that despite there not being any others from the space station nearby, something was on the ground, and it might be hungry. Maggie needed a distraction.

"I don't think there's anyone else around. Can you see the cliff's edge?" Wade asked.

There was a moment of silence.

"Yes."

"How many meters down are you?" He'd need to keep her talking while he prepared the injection. It might help. It might knock him out. It might kill him. There was no way of knowing.

"What? How would I know? I'm no good with spacial math."

Wade took in the area and spotted another large broken limb he could use as a cane. He slid down to the ground. If he was going to pass out, he didn't want to make things worse by giving himself a concussion. There might be some rigging left over on the underside of the pod, but it was a long shot. Either way, he'd have to get to the ground to check.

"Compare it to something you know. The length of a corridor, the space inside your cabin," he called out. The injector trembled in his hand.

"Okay . . . I guess it's about the length of my cabin floor from the door to the bed."

"That's good." Holding the injector to his good leg, he said another quick prayer to the Merciful.

"What are you doing?" Maggie asked.

"I'm about to kill myself, or cure myself. The pod came with something that might be their idea of a med-kit. I'm not sure what they put in these injectors, but if it can help me get to you, I'm going to need to use it. I can't put any weight on my leg yet. It looks like it might get infected if I don't do something about it. Try not to focus on where you are, but where you want to be, because I'm going to need a minute."

His response was met with silence. He put the injector to his leg and pressed down.

"Wait!"

"Too late," Wade said as his eyes fluttered closed.

"Wade!"

Her screams broke through the haze. She was going hoarse again. How long had she been calling him?

"I'm still here," he called out, though his head spun.

"I can't hang here forever!"

"I know . . . but I think it worked." While he was on the

ground, he reached around the back of the pod. It was still sealed up tight, and he had to use the utility knife from his belt to pry it open. It took several minutes. Their chute was still inside. That explained the violent crash into the woods. The chute was the only thing large enough to reach Maggie so he could pull her up. He did the mental calculations and figured it would be a little short, but they'd have to make it work.

Wade attempted to stand for the third time. He used the branch-made-cane and his good leg and was successful. His bad leg remained straight, and his head cleared. Whatever had been in the injector had taken away the sharp pain in his leg and it felt cooler. The effects might only be temporary, but they should be enough to get to Maggie.

Wade grabbed the other belt he'd tied to his foot and used it to secure his left leg even tighter. It seemed to help, and he used his newly found energy to keep moving. He gathered up the chute in his right hand and leaned heavily on the staff in his left.

"Mags?" He realized a second after he'd called her, he hadn't used the nickname since their breakup.

"Yes?"

"Just checking."

"Are you going to pull me up by yourself?" Her voice was fading from overuse.

"Unless you have a better idea. Save your strength. You're going to need it to get up here."

That earned him some silence. It would take him a bit to get to the cliff, but he saw in an instant the path she'd taken from the pod. She must have slid right off the edge, though he wondered why she hadn't called out to him before. If she'd been unconscious on the edge of the cliff, waking up might have been what had pushed her over.

He scanned the trees for any movement. The howling had long since stopped, replaced by the chittering of smaller animals and birdsong. He didn't lay eyes on anything larger than a squirrel. A smallish creature with brown fur and large eyes skittered up and around the trees away from him. Wade put it in the non-threatening category and trudged on.

"Maggie?"

"Are you still coming?"

Wade rolled his eyes. "I've got what I need, but I need you to keep talking so I can follow your voice. Can you see any trees above you?"

"No, not really. There's a short bush with yellow leaves. Wait . . . yes, there's a small tree there with purple and green leaves right next to it."

She was on his left. He made his way over the uneven ground, using the crutch to compensate for his broken leg. He had to avoid more pod debris as he went, following the path where Maggie had been bounced out of the pod and right over the cliff through the yellow bushes just ahead. When he reached the drop-off, he realized he should have been looking for something to secure the parachute to on the way. Instead, he looked over the edge to see where Maggie had landed.

From his vantage point the ocean water was a dark blue the perfect contrast to the pale blue sky. Six hundred meters down the waves crashed against the reddish rocks below. Maggie clung to a tree root that jut out from the rock face four meters down. His foot slipped, dropping gravel and dirt over the side.

"Watch it!" she snapped up at him.

Her yellow dress was mud-stained and tattered, but she had a solid grip on the tree root. She wasn't going anywhere and from her annoyance she wasn't entirely defeated.

"Sorry," he said backing away from the edge and stepping to his left so she could turn her head to see him. "I have to secure the parachute, but I wanted to see how far down it needed to reach."

"Well, don't worry about me. Take your time! I'm not exhausted or anything."

Wade grit his teeth as he limped over to pick up the ropes of the chute. Stranded on an unknown planet with his ex and a broken leg. It was going to be a long day.

To Be Continued...

DID YOU LOVE IT?

If you liked this book in whole or in part I hope you'll let other people know by leaving a review. The fastest way to get another book from any author, including me, is to review and share the last one. Thank you!

ALSO BY T.S VALMOND

Starship Hope Series:

Ensign (Prequel)

Exodus

Marauders

Viral

Nexus

Arrival

Verity Chronicles Series

Exile

Divided

On the Run

To be notified about the latest releases, promotions, and giveaways, make sure you're a VIP Reader. Learn more at https://TSValmond.com

ACKNOWLEDGMENTS

Dear reader, I want to thank you for continuing this crazy ride with me and the *Starship Hope* crew. If you're having a hard time keeping up with the surprises in *Viral*, that makes two of us at least.

These characters have a life of their own and to be honest, some days I have no idea what's coming. Today, I was working on the next book in the series and wrote a line with no clue what was about to happen and surprised myself.

One of the interesting things about this gig is the amazing people I get to work with and meet. A fellow author recommended my editor, and he's worth his weight and gold, but he's nice to me. Thanks to Jack Llartin, as usual, for your editing touch.

G & Trea, thanks for being my first and last readers. Your feedback is invaluable and often given late at night, but it's always appreciated.

I wanted to add a special word of thanks to the amazing crew in Becca Syme's Office. You know who you are: the early morning weekday and the weekend evening folks who make my writing times a lot less lonely.

To my darling Matthew, your cover designs are gorgeous and I'm blessed to have you in my life. I can't wait to see what this year brings us.

ABOUT THE AUTHOR

Hi, I'm **T.S. Valmond** the science fiction and fantasy author currently residing in Canada with my husband and dog in an undisclosed location. One can never be too careful when exposing the secrets of powerful governments, worlds, and illegal aliens.

(Yes, they're watching.)

I was into science fiction and fantasy long before Browncoats, Trekkies, and Jedi were cool. Like my readers, I long for the days when Reality TV didn't mean anything and entertainment was entertaining.

When I'm not writing I'm–

Nope. I'm always writing.

TSValmond.com/links